EVENT HORIZON

Dean Crawford

© 2019 Dean Crawford

Published: May 2019

Publisher: Fictum Ltd

The right of Dean Crawford to be identified as author of this Work has been asserted by him in accordance with sections 77 and 78 of the Copyright, Designs and Patents Act 1988.

All rights reserved.

www.deancrawfordbooks.com

I

Bikini Atoll, Marshall Islands,

South Pacific

1954

'Boy, am I ever ready for this!'

Ensign Ernie Walker glanced across at an officer who was standing on the aircraft carrier's foredeck, and wondered if the idiot had ever seen a shot fired during his service. Lieutenant Vance Foster was parading up and down with his binoculars in his hands, scanning the horizon for some sign of the event.

'How the hell did that jerk ever earn his stripes?' someone muttered from the ranks behind Ernie, to a hushed ripple of chuckles.

The dawn was just spreading across the eastern horizon, a majestic sweep of molten metal spilling across the surface of the ocean as the USS *Bairoko* steamed its way south east across the azure Pacific. The immense ocean was silent around them but for the churning of *Bairoko's* boilers and the thick belch of black smoke tumbling from her stacks to stain the perfect blue sky behind them. A *Commencement-Bay* class escort carrier and one of the newest in the fleet, she had been commissioned just a little too late to see service in the Second World War, much like the officer now prancing about on the foredeck.

'You fellas just wait,' Lieutenant Foster enthused. 'This is gonna be something you'll dangle your grandkids on your knees and tell 'em about when you're all ninety.'

The voice that replied came not from the enlisted men but from the captain, his voice booming across the carrier's wide decks from the towering bridge behind them.

'If you don't get into cover, Foster, you won't make twenty-nine!'

Foster's excited face collapsed and flushed red as the enlisted men burst into unveiled laughter. Foster cursed and growled at them but Ernie couldn't make out much of what he said as the officer stalked toward the shields erected on the carrier's foredeck.

'What the hell are we doin' here, Ernie?' asked Ensign Henry Coleman, a nineteen-year-old out of Maryland and Ernie's bunk mate.

'Who the hell knows,' Ernie replied, 'some kind of test, so they're saying, but nobody really seems to know what it's all about. Probably turn out to be nothing at all, another "hurry up and wait".'

Coleman nodded, but Ernie could sense the fear in the young boy's expression. That wasn't surprising, given that the aircraft carrier's immense deck was arrayed with blast shields behind which the men crouched. Each of them had been handed a set of goggles which were smoked out, the glass almost black. The carrier had been steaming on its course throughout the night, repositioning after the captain apparently received orders direct from Washington the previous evening.

'Well,' said another Ensign by the name of Cooper, 'something's goin' off and I don't like the feel of it. You know the last time they handed these goggles out?'

When nobody answered, Cooper made an explosive gesture with his hands.

'When they were testing the H-bombs that we dropped on the Japanese,' he said, 'so that the people watching didn't go blind.'

A few of the men exchanged glances, some nervous, some apparently bemused. Ernie wasn't sure what to make of that, but then he and the other men looked around as the endless rumble of the carrier's boilers faded away. He felt the carrier's bow, ever rising and falling as it cut through the waves, cease motion as the huge ship slowed and turned, the bow ponderously sweeping to port until it pointed toward the west, where the sky was only lightly touched by the coming dawn.

Loudspeakers blared across the decks, shattering the sudden silence.

'Now hear this! Now hear this! All seamen to don their protective goggles!'

Ernie and the other men all pulled on their goggles. Ernie couldn't see his hand in front of his face, although he could hear the mildly irritated utterances of his fellow sailors as they sat like lemons in the darkness.

'Join up, they said,' someone quipped, 'it's a man's life, they said.'

Ernie waited, he and Henry Coleman keeping each other balanced as they crouched in their little worlds of darkness.

'How far away are we from the atoll?' Ernie asked. 'We only got the orders last night.'

'Not far,' someone replied, 'eight hours at ten knots, we're well within the blast radius. They should have…'

'All hands!' the captain boomed through a loud hailer. *'Stand up, but remain in cover!'*

Ernie and two hundred other seamen all stood, staring out toward the west where the horizon was still enshrouded in darkness. From somewhere to Ernie's left, he heard a man utter the sailor's hymn.

'For what we are about to receive, may the Lord make us truly thankful…'

There was a moment's silence, the only sound the lapping of the waves against the carrier's vast hull far below them. Ernie saw movement, and was able to make out Lieutenant Foster removing his goggles and pinning his binoculars to his eyes.

'Sir!' a seaman urged. 'They said we should…'

'Silence!' Foster snapped, the binoculars fixed to his face. 'I'm not missing this for all the world, it's too important to…'

Suddenly the horizon to the west lit up as though a sun had burst into life right there and then, which, Ernie realized a moment later, it had. Through the goggles he saw the horizon sweeping from left to right before them, black as night, saw threads and ribbons of high-altitude cloud scattered across the immense skies, and behind it all a fearsome flare of nuclear light so bright that even behind the goggles he squinted and threw his hands up to protect his face as he closed his eyes.

To his horror and surprise, he could still see his hands through his closed eyes. The fearsome light flashed through them as though it was a physical thing. He saw Lieutenant Foster standing with the binoculars to his face, saw the officer's skeleton within his body as though suddenly everything in the world had become transparent. The carrier's deck glowed with an unearthly vibrance as though alive, and Ernie could see the bones of his own fingers and forearm, every tiny vein and artery pulsing an eerie red as the blast flash seared every atom in the sky around them in utter silence.

The brief but infernal flare faded slowly away, and then Ernie heard the screaming. He yanked off his goggles, and in an instant his guts turned to slime within him.

Lieutenant Foster's binoculars dropped to the deck, his eyes nothing but scorched black holes trailing smoke as he sank to his knees, his mouth agape and a keening scream echoing out across the ocean. Beyond the lieutenant, the sky was ablaze with a light like nothing Ernie had ever seen. A roiling ball of nuclear fire several miles across was rising into the dawn sky, lightning bolts raging across its surface as it split the skies, rushing ever upward to tower over the aircraft carrier.

The ocean was still silent, but then Ernie saw the shockwave rushing toward them across the ocean, so fast that there were only seconds to react.

'Get down!'

The men dropped, but Lieutenant Foster's kneeling, screaming figure was hit by the blast to fly directly over the heads of his men. He crashed down onto the deck behind them and tumbled end over end, broken limbs flailing as he rolled off the side of the ship toward the waves far below.

Ernie crouched down as a howling wind seethed past them, his ears popping with the change in pressure, whorls of vapor curling over the blast shields. He heard men screaming in terror, saw some cradling broken limbs, crying out for their mothers, and then the heat blast crashed across the carrier. The huge ship reared up as though it were a leaf on a storm-tossed sea as tongues of flame seemed to ignite the very air around them.

Ernie heard his own scream as what felt like brands of fire scorched every fibre of his body. He risked a glance to one side and saw balls of glowing fire plunging down all around them into the ocean, and his stomach flipped as he realised that he must be witnessing the end of the world, the atmosphere of the planet burning in the nuclear fire that mankind had created. In a flash he thought of his children, his wife, his parents, of all the things that he had left behind to serve a country that had now betrayed him and sent him to die out here, half a world from home, burned alive by the horror that was the world's largest nuclear detonation.

Ernie whirled and ran for the side of the ship. The gales hurled him across the foredeck and he fell, tumbling, glimpsed fellow Ensigns flailing to remove their burning clothes, smoke spilling from their hair, unseeing eyes wide with pain and fear.

Ernie staggered through the hellish scene and saw the sanctuary of the waves before him as he grabbed a flotation ring and hurled himself over the side.

Time seemed to slow around him as he fell. He saw the huge aircraft carrier before him, her gray cliff-like hull aglow with a strangle blue light, the sky above her black and orange with flame and fire. As he plunged toward the waves, he could see other men tumbling over the side, trailing flames, and then Ernie hit the water and the terrible heat was replaced by a bitter cold and the impact slammed him into the lonely embrace of unconsciousness.

***

II

Present day

'I don't care, just get it done, okay?'

Xavier Colt sneered to himself but reluctantly turned and began pulling off his shirt and deck shoes. A deal was a deal and all, but he hated swimming and had no desire to get back into the water after what had happened to poor Jim Arenson just the week before.

The *Atoll Angel* lay becalmed on the rolling waves beneath a burning blue sky, her engine silent after her prop had become fouled as she was plying her way north east across the Pacific. A surveillance trawler hired by some godamned doo-goodie environmental group to track plastic waste in the south Pacific, her crew of eight was now accompanied by a group of scientists and hippies intent on ruining Xavier's day.

'You got the blade?'

The skipper, Barnie "Trouble" Trent, a thickly muscled man with forearms like hams and a permanent scowl beneath his beard, shoved a wicked looking barbed knife at Xavier.

'We don't got enough oxygen for you to be playing around too long down there, and I don't want to spend more money sending some other sap to pull your sorry ass out of the water. Make it quick and clean.'

Xavier threw the skipper a mocking salute. Barnie turned to grab Xavier's collar but the sailor let himself fall backwards over the bulwark with a smile on his face, just out of the skipper's reach. Hitting the water hurt like all hell but it was worth it to see Barnie's scowl deepen.

The warm Pacific water rushed over Xavier as he righted himself and came up for air. He broke the surface, the knife in his hand, and composed himself as he made his way astern to where the trawler's hull and rudder assembly bobbed on the mirror-smooth Pacific.

The *Atoll Angel* was not a large boat, just ninety-feet from bow to stern and a hundred tons displacement. She spent most of her time running errands and cargo for the island chains, sometimes for the local government folks who wanted the luxuries of life shipped out to remote communities scratching an existence out here. Once, by special permission, they had ventured into the no-man's-land of Bikini Atoll, a few miles north of their position, to measure radiation levels for the government back in DC.

'Down there!'

Barnie was pointing with one thick arm to the ship's screw, a few feet under the surface at the stern. Xavier put the blade between his teeth and took a few deep breaths, some of their passengers watching impatiently now. Xavier didn't miss the irony that their quarry, discarded plastic, was now hindering their tree-hugging mission.

Xavier took a last deep breath and then dove down.

The water was clear, the Pacific's sun-washed surface waters devoid of algae and other life forms that obscured coastal seas. Sometimes plankton blooms could get out of hand out here, but most often the water was clear and blue. That hadn't helped Arenson though, after he'd gone over the side to retrieve a piece of equipment dropped by one of their land-lubber passengers, and got himself stung half to death by a passing school of lethal jellyfish.

Xavier glanced around for any sign of life, stinging or otherwise, but saw nothing. He swam to the screw and immediately saw that it was fouled by a bright red and white streamer of plastic. Xavier did not recognise the object, but given that out here there were estimated to be millions of tons of plastic debris, that wasn't surprising.

Xavier edged a little closer, pulled the knife from his teeth, reached out and sliced neatly through the plastic. It parted, not sufficiently tough to resist the razor-sharp blade, and Xavier unthreaded it from the screw with relative ease. His lungs were close to bursting but personal pride forced him to finish the job in one go, just to irk the captain a little more.

Xavier pulled the plastic free from the screw and kicked for the surface just above, letting loose a stream of shimmering bubbles from between his lips as he rose up and burst out onto the surface.

'No problemo!' he called out as he held the plastic aloft with a bright smile.

The crew were all at the bulwarks, but none were looking at him.

'Gee, don't all go thanking me at once.'

Skipper Trent was staring out over the ocean past Xavier, the scowl gone from his features and his voice quiet as he replied.

'Xav', get out there, right now.'

Xavier turned his head and was shocked to see a man floating on the ocean amid a slick of oil and debris.

'What the hell?' Xavier uttered. The ocean had been devoid of life only moments ago. 'Where did he come from?'

Barnie Trent shook his head slowly. 'There was a flash, and there he was.'

Xavier stared at the man floating on the water, and saw him lethargically move his arm, trying to reach out.

'Now, Xavier! Barnie boomed.

Xavier didn't hesitate a moment longer. He hurled the plastic up onto the trawler's deck as he struck out for the man floating nearby.

*

Captain Barnie Trent walked down from the bridge of his vessel and headed aft.

The *Angel* was a small ship, all that he could afford to run after he'd left the Navy. Trent wasn't a man who was happy anywhere but on the open ocean, that being the motivation for him to move out here to the island chains where there wasn't a whole lot else *but* ocean.

He made his way to a bunk that had been set aside as a medical room. As luck would have it, one of the scientists aboard was also a paramedic, so the mysterious man they'd brought aboard the ship was in good hands. Mysterious for many reasons, not least of all because he had been afloat on the ocean while wearing Navy khakis that showed evidence of recent burning. Trent had immediately put in a call to the local coastguard to report a possible lost vessel, only to be told that there were no known missing vessels at that time.

The sailor was sitting up in the bunk, the biologist alongside him.

'He said anything yet?'

Trent tried to tone down his usual gruff tones, but it sounded more like an accusation than anything else. The biologist, a woman named Sarah who looked barely old enough to be out of college, shot him a cold blue-eyed glare.

'He's been through hell, so no, he hasn't said much yet.'

The sailor was maybe seventy years old, Trent reckoned, but that was where any certainties ended. His scorched uniform was clearly U. S. Navy, but the cut and the fabric were nothing that Trent recalled ever wearing, and the man was way too old to be in the service. The sailor's skin was covered with abrasions and there were chunks of his hair missing. He sat in silence, staring at the bed sheets, mumbling incoherently.

'He must have ingested too much sea water,' Trent said, 'sent himself mad.'

'He's not dehydrated,' Sarah replied without looking at Trent. 'He's not malnourished, and he's not showing signs of prolonged exposure. Nothing makes any sense.'

Trent would have argued, but he'd seen the brilliant flash of light just like everybody else. He's seen the ocean twist in turmoil, waves crashing on an otherwise calm sea, a slick of debris spreading as if from nowhere and then the waves calming to reveal a man floating on the water. He'd popped into existence as if from thin air, and now Trent was watching him and wondering whether he ought to call the Navy and report the sailor in. Just like everybody else, he had read the man's name tag on his breast pocket.

Ens. E. Walker.

'You got any idea what happened to him?' Trent asked. 'The burns, I mean?'

Sarah shook her head as she sat back and looked the man over once again. 'Could have gone overboard in a fire, but it's the hair loss and the bleeding gums that gets me. He looks like he's suffering from radiation sickness.'

That turned Trent's blood cold. If this guy had floated out here from the atolls, then who the hell knew what he'd come into contact with?

'Is that contagious?'

Sarah looked at Trent as though he were some kind of child. 'No, it's not contagious, captain. But we should get this guy into proper care as soon as we can. I don't have the medical supplies to treat him properly.'

Trent nodded. Whatever the guy had been through he looked like hell, and Trent could sure do without the Navy probing around his ship. There were a few supplies in the holds that Customs would ask questions about, difficult questions that he did not want to answer.

'We'll put in tomorrow morning,' he said. 'I want this guy off the ship and into whatever hospital they've got, with instructions to call the Navy. Let them take the heat for whatever this guy's been into.'

Trent was about to leave when the sailor spoke softly. 'Where's the ship?'

Sarah reached out and touched the sailor's hand, eager to establish a dialogue. 'Which ship?'

Walker swallowed, his eyes glazed and unfocussed.

'USS Bairoko, CVE One One Five.'

Sarah glanced at Trent. Trent did not move. He stood in the doorway and stared at the man before him, uncertain of whether he had heard him correctly.

'Bairoko,' he echoed. 'That's your ship?'

The man nodded, his head wobbling on his neck as though the muscles were no longer able to support the weight. 'Ensign Ernest Walker, seven-five-three-zero-eight-one.'

Trent blinked. The United States Navy had not issued service numbers since the seventies. The more he was hearing, the less he liked it. From behind Trent, one of the *Angel's* crew hurried up with a laptop computer in his hand and held it out to the captain.

'Satellite link with Majuro,' he offered. 'They have a berth ready for us for the morning.'

Trent nodded, but as he did so he heard a gasp from Walker and the sailor leaped off the bed and pointed with one wobbling arm at the laptop computer, his eyes wide.

'What's that?'

'It's a computer,' the sailor beside Trent said. 'Why?'

Trent pushed his crewman aside, and as he did so Walker gasped again and reached out with one hand to grab the captain's arm. Trent saw Walker staring in wonder and fear at the digital watch on Trent's wrist. The sailor seemed incapable of speech, eyes still wide with wonder. Then, slowly, the wonder turned to horror. Walker backed away from the captain, pointing at the watch.

'Is that the date?' he whispered, as though afraid to speak at all.

Trent remained still as he replied. 'Yes, it's the date.'

'It can't be,' Walker uttered. 'It's 1954. *Tell me it's 1954!*'

Trent held his breath for a moment before he replied.

'It's not 1954.'

Walker began shaking his head, quivering as though a live current were snaking through his body. The sailor's legs shuddered and he almost fell, Sarah lunging to one side to catch him and steer him onto the bunk.

'What the hell is going on?' Sarah asked as she stood and tried to support Walker.

The sailor allowed himself to be laid back down on the bunk. Trent gestured for the biologist to follow him out into the corridor outside. Sarah pulled the berth door closed to conceal their conversation from the man inside.

'*USS Bairoko* was decommissioned somewhere in the late fifties,' Trent explained. 'The Navy hasn't issued service numbers for decades.'

Sarah scoffed. 'He's probably confused, maybe suffering from some form of amnesia. He needs rest and treatment.'

'I want him off my ship,' Trent snapped. 'And I don't want a word of this breathed to anybody, okay?'

Sarah sighed. 'Captain, this is the modern world, okay? I know what you're thinking, but that guy didn't just get blasted here from the 1950's.'

'He sure as hell appeared in front of us all in a puff of godamned smoke,' Trent countered. 'Or didn't you see that happen?'

Sarah held the captain's gaze but he could see that she had no answer for him. Trent kept his voice low.

'When the navy gets word of this, they'll come down here like a force of nature and we'll be caught up in it. If this guy's who he thinks he is, I don't want anything to do with it. They'll seize my ship, all of your equipment, question us all at length, you name it. You think you'll finish your little expedition out here on time and inside budget without a vessel?'

Sarah bit her lip for a furtive moment, then nodded.

'Okay, captain, it's up to you, but I want it recorded in your log that I'm in protest about this course of action.'

'As you wish.'

Trent turned and headed for the bridge. Truth be told, he didn't give a damned about the good doctor's protest. Right now, he just wanted Walker off the *Angel* and out of Trent's mind, preferably for good.

***

III

Nevada National Security Site,

Yucca Flats (65 miles north-west of Las Vegas)

'Move, now!'

The voice was urgent, yet it registered as barely a whisper in the darkness as the section of troops moved silently out into the barren desert. The sky above was emblazoned with countless stars sparkling in the ice-cold darkness of the universe, but none of the soldiers moving through the wilderness were focused on anything but their mission.

None of the men wore disruptive pattern material, and none of their uniforms bore any insignia. They were dressed all in black, wore light armor and carried assault rifles at port-arms. They had no vehicles, for they had long ago learned that a vehicle was a liability on missions of this kind – they always stopped working once the first sighting was made.

General Scott Mackenzie kept pace with his men despite being a decade older than most of them. Such was the requirement of this unusual and yet fascinating posting, one that had taken over his life it seemed since he had been posted from his unit in the U.S. Army to Langley, Virginia. He cast an eye over his men, barely visible in the darkness, and allowed himself a small smile of personal pride in how well they now performed after just one year of specialist training. Professional, proud, silent and discreet – nobody on earth knew that they were out here, and nobody ever would. Which was just as well, because if what they were up to were ever made public, there was no way the United States government would ever be able to explain it.

The desert stretched for miles in every direction, barren, silent, devoid it seemed of life. Although tour buses brought curious civilians out here from time to time to visit the ruins of old nuclear test sites from the previous century, the excursions were in actual fact carefully managed public-relations missions. Visitors were allowed no cameras, no cell phones, binoculars or anything else that could conceivably convey information about the site. There was otherwise no human habitation out here and the skies above the area were strictly controlled. No aircraft ever overflew this region, and if it did, it would end up as a smoking hole in the ground.

Where they were now moving through the desert was a mere twelve miles south west of the more famous Groom Lake airbase, often referred to as *Area 51*. There was no name for the site, and despite being home to a mile-long runway there was no designator for the field, nothing to mark it out on any map. When journalists had finally realized it was there and started filing Freedom of Information requests, the National Nuclear Security Administration blocked the applications. After some time, it was finally revealed to the public that the airfield was used by the Defense Department and Homeland Security as a test facility for sensor development and work with unmanned aerial vehicles.

Mackenzie smiled as he moved through the night with his men. The explanation was the truth, plain and simple, and yet it hid the real truth behind shadows and mirrors, because the UAVs the explanation referred to did not belong to mankind.

The men reached the edge of a ridge, climbing up before coming to a halt in a line. Mackenzie joined them and looked out over a wasteland that, if it was possible, was more barren than the rest of the desert.

Stretching out before them was over ten miles of desert that was bordered on all sides by rugged mountain ranges, and that desert was pock-marked with vast craters, as though the area had been bombarded by meteorites from another world. They culminated at the north of the range with the Sedan Crater, the result of the displacement of an incredible twelve million tons of earth, the largest man-made crater in the United States. The cavity had been excavated by the Sedan nuclear test of 1962, a 104-kiloton thermonuclear device.

The men surveyed the ridge, and one of them checked their position on a hand-held GPS device and then switched if off.

'Here,' he whispered, a microphone attached to his throat amplifying his voice to normal volume to Mackenzie's ear. 'Synchronize watches.'

Mackenzie checked his watch, and as the team leader gave a command, they zeroed the chronometers and then set silently to work. One by one, the men produced folding tripods which they set up on the ridge of the crater before mounting cameras atop them. Other soldiers produced laptop computers and wired them into portable servers. Others still set up radio links with satellites orbiting far above, ready to relay data.

Mackenzie watched the men work for a moment, and then he turned his head up to the stars. They glistened like jewels afloat in a dark ocean, too many to count, soft white patches among them denoted the position of entire galaxies, each containing hundreds of billions more stars, all with the potential for life in their systems. It seemed that the universe was far too large for life not to be elsewhere within it, but even the quarry they sought had not come from so far away. The knowledge was almost melancholy, the understanding that though the universe might be filled with life, that life could never visit another world and remain in its own frame of time. To travel to the stars was possible, but one could never return again to one's own planet and timeframe – hundreds and perhaps thousands of years would have passed: perhaps that was why nobody had visited the Earth from other planets?

'We're set,' a voice broke Mackenzie out of his reverie, and he noted that his men had set up their equipment faster than ever before. 'Two minutes and counting.'

Mackenzie nodded.

'Let's get to it, ensure all cameras are on and all links are live. Let's see what we can learn this time.'

The men manned their cameras, like soldiers on machine gun posts, but this time aiming not to kill but to learn. The desert around them returned to absolute silence as they waited, always now with a sense of anticipation, for every man on the ridge knew what was coming. They had seen them before.

Unidentified Aerial Phenomena.

That was the official name given to the objects that appeared like phantoms in the skies, but until now they had been something of an oddity to Mackenzie, the kind of thing other people talked about in hushed whispers, the kind of thing people kept quiet about for fear of being ridiculed. Now, they were his life and his job, for he had learned that they were anything but a figment of the imagination, anything but a modern myth. They were here, they were here all the time, and Mackenzie had learned how to predict when and where they would appear.

'One minute.'

Big data had been the key, and the mind of a teenage computer hacker named Kyle Trent, who had had nothing better to do with his time than copy a successful crime-prediction algorithm known as PredPol, short for Predictive Policing, and use it on UFO sightings. Nobody could have predicted the result, a way to accurately predict the location and time of a UFO appearance based on data from all those that had been recorded before. With a hit rate exceeding eighty per cent, Mackenzie had located and apprehended the youth before turning his skills into something the CIA could use to gather data on this strangest of phenomena, but the answers the research had provided were so profound and disturbing that he didn't like to think about them much even now.

'Thirty seconds.'

The night air seemed charged despite the silence, as though awaiting something as yet unseen in the darkness. Mackenzie craned his neck back and looked up into the velvety blackness, as ever hoping to glimpse some sight of the object's appearance, seeking some clue as to how and when it might appear. Never had he been successful in spotting the object before it spotted them.

'Ten, nine, eight…'

Mackenzie looked back down and braced himself as the countdown was whispered by the troop lieutenant. Sometimes, nothing happened, the algorithms mistaken in their predictions. Other times, something appeared a few miles away, too far for them to gather useful data. But every now and again, something appeared right in front of them and revealed a universe that he could never have imagined existed, things so bizarre, so disturbing, that he was both fascinated and repulsed in equal measure.

'…three, two, one, now.'

Silence reigned.

Nobody moved, every man poised for action yet unable to move. Moments later, the lieutenant sighed and shook his head.

'It's a bust, guys, there's nothing comin…'

Mackenzie felt the hairs on the back of his neck suddenly rise up, tingling sensations racing down his forearms as though insects were scuttling back and forth beneath his skin. Suddenly he could smell an electrical charge on the air, which seemed to hum with unseen energy. Mackenzie's chest reverberated with a low frequency vibration that shuddered through his bones as he scanned the desert flats and the arrayed camera screens, but saw nothing registering on them other than the desolate wastes.

'What the hell?'

The men were looking all around them, the hair rising up off their scalps as though hauled ever upward by intense static fields, and then Mackenzie craned his head back again and his guts turned to slime within him.

Above the plateau, the stars had vanished, a perfect disc of absolute blackness blocking them out. Mackenzie opened his mouth to talk but no sound would come out, sudden and inexplicable fear of the unknown momentarily constricting his throat.

'Danger close,' he croaked, 'overhead.'

Ten heads jerked up and suddenly everybody was in motion at once as Mackenzie moved into a crouched position, one hand on the butt of his service firearm in its holster as he tried to see any detail in the black disc above them. He could both hear and feel an intense humming noise coming from the object, which was stationary and otherwise silent.

The lieutenant rolled onto his back and aimed a laser-rangefinder up at the object, and a moment later he whispered something above the humming.

'Two thousand feet.'

Mackenzie gasped despite himself. The object filled half the damned sky. At that height, it would be four times the length of a football field and have a mass many times that of a Boeing 747 airliner, yet there it was, hovering in relative silence in the night sky and closer than any object they'd seen yet.

'Get everything on it,' Mackenzie snapped, recovering from his stunned torpor. 'IR cameras, spectroscopic lenses, UV filters and…'

A brilliant white light burst into life like a new born star right above them, and Mackenzie ducked his head away to protect his night vision as his men hurried to tilt their sensors up to capture the object. Mackenzie fumbled in his pocket for a pair of sunglasses that he carried at night for just this eventuality, and he slipped them over his eyes before turning his gaze back up to the object.

The brilliant flare of light was dimmed, but it still concealed the rest of the craft in the darkness above it. He could make out very faint reflections in the lower surface of the craft, but nothing of detail and nothing that he recognized as man-made or anything remotely familiar to him.

'I've got it,' came a call from one of the men, who was directing a camera up at the craft. 'It's solid, panelled, definitely something that's been constructed.'

Mackenzie felt excitement quicken his pulse. This was one of the ones that they could analyse. He didn't even like to think much about the other ones they occasionally saw, objects of color and light that seemed to have no defined edges, that blurred the lines between reality and something else both alien and frightening to them all.

'Spectroscope?'

The soldier manning the device called back softly.

'Gathering now, but we've already got palladium and titanium.'

The spectroscope fired a beam of light at the object, and the returning reflection was split into a spectrum, the form of which betrayed the elements from which the craft was constructed. Once again, the presence of recognizable elements gave Mackenzie confidence that this was a craft whose attributes they could measure, and perhaps someday understand.

'Keep going,' he urged. 'Optical?'

'Nothing, sir, they're blocking our sensor with the light.'

The brilliant halo above them made the object visible for tens of miles, thus betraying its presence, but it also concealed its form from observation, an interesting characteristic that Mackenzie, as a military man, knew could only have a singular purpose: to prevent prying eyes from seeing what was just beyond the flare. Thus, it must know that it was being observed.

'Laser scanner!' he snapped.

Instantly, two soldiers manning a wide-field lens activated their device and bathed the object in high-intensity radar energy, essentially lighting it up as though by an intensely powerful air traffic control radar, in order to scan its surface in minute detail.

Instantly, the air around them changed and Mackenzie saw the object shoot upward by two thousand feet in an instant as its brilliant light went out. There was no movement of the air, nothing to betray the tremendous aerodynamic forces that must surely have been at work around the object. All that changed was that the static charge around them abated and the humming noise faded away.

The object hovered in the night sky for a moment, and then it suddenly zipped at impossible speed across the sky and vanished, so fast that he could not for certain tell which way it had actually gone.

'It's gone,' one of the troopers said.

'Negative, it's over the test area.'

Mackenzie turned and saw the object now four miles away, near the Sedan crater.

'Get the cameras back on it.'

The team swung into action, cameras all swivelling on their tripods to lock back onto the object as Mackenzie watched and realized that he was breathing fast, his heart hammering in his chest at the shock of the close encounter. He watched as the cameras scanned the object, saw the classic disc-shaped image in the centre of every display, a shallow dome on top of it. Then, he saw movement from below.

'We got a beam.'

Mackenzie tore off his sunglasses and looked directly out into the darkness. From the bottom of the object he saw a thin red beam of light emerge slowly and begin extending down to the ground, breaking every law of physics known to man. There was no known way to contain and control a directed beam of light, and yet here he was watching it with his own eyes.

The beam reached the ground in the center of the nuclear facility, then swept left and right, occasionally flickering as it seemed to search the site for something. They watched in silence as it made its way back and forth, and then the beam was slowly retracted into the craft.

The object hovered for a moment, and then it simply vanished from site.

'It's gone again.'

'No,' Mackenzie said as he glanced at a screen. 'It's still there.'

On the IR monitor he could see the heat signature of the craft still hovering over the site, the optical camera showing absolutely nothing. Then, the IR camera flickered and the object vanished entirely as though it was never there.

'Mark the time,' Mackenzie said.

The men all checked their watches, and then Mackenzie grabbed a radio and called in. 'Iron Eagle to Crow, time check.'

A moment later a reply came back. *'Zero one, fifteen and eighteen seconds, mark.'*

Mackenzie checked his watch. Zero one, thirteen, twelve seconds.

'Roger, check, time displacement of two minutes and six seconds.'

'Copy.'

Mackenzie set the radio down and leaned back on his haunches. During the encounter, he and his team had lost two minutes of their lives, because the impossible had occurred: the flow of time, for them, had been altered.

***

IV

Indian Hills, Nevada

Ethan Warner liked the peace and the quiet.

Indian Hills was a small community a few miles east of Lake Tahoe, nestled alongside the Carson River. The California border was a few miles to the west, with Reno further to the north, putting Indian Hills in an enviable position as a gateway to the Pacific and to some of the most popular getaways in the country.

The blue sky was untarnished by clouds as Ethan headed out for his morning run. In Nevada, running was something people only did in the cool of dawn or if they were fleeing from certain death, although Indian Hills and the surrounding area were a little more bearable. Temperatures were scorching most all year round, although snow was possible in the winter months if things got really cold. Now, it was perfect as Ethan headed out.

It had been a year since he had returned to the United States along with his partner, Nicola Lopez, after all that had happened during their previous investigation, working ostensibly for the CIA. What had shocked Ethan most of all since then was how little they had been able to discover about what had happened to them, how perfectly sealed the CIA had become in the wake of the revelations. The intelligence community had learned a great deal since the days before the war on terror, and now that was working against both himself and Lopez.

Truth was, they were nowhere nearer solving what had happened to them now than when they had first returned. Just about the only thing that was better these days was that they had several million dollars to their names, invested in banks and other deposits around the world, so their days of hunting bail runners amid the dangerous streets of Chicago's East side were long behind them. Unfortunately, their lazy and idyllic existence amid the island chains of the Indian Ocean were now also all but a memory, no thanks to General Scott Mackenzie, a man whom it now seemed had never existed at all.

As a younger man, Ethan Warner had served as a Marine with the 15th Expeditionary Unit in Iraq and Afghanistan before leaving the service to become a journalist. Working in some of the most dangerous countries on earth, he had forged a reputation for being able to find and repatriate lost souls, and in the process come to the attention of a secretive program run from within the Defense Intelligence Agency known as ARIES, that had been run by a former commander from Ethan's days with the Marines. Along with Lopez, a former DC police officer, Ethan had been drawn into the program as a lead investigator, and uncovered conspiracies around the world that had changed his views on just about everything: alien remains in ancient Peruvian tombs, free energy devices, computers that could literally read human minds, alien viruses and even evidence that the planet was routinely visited by craft that did not originate from Earth. Ethan had gone over the years from a sceptic to a true believer, but even that wealth of knowledge and experience could not have prepared them for what had happened when the CIA had hired them to investigate a series of bizarre UFO sightings that had occurred throughout Nevada and Arizona.

Ethan jogged out of the suburban street where he lived with Lopez and headed for the trails that ran alongside the river, a couple hundred yards to the east of town. He'd follow them north, then pick up Clear Creek before heading west back home.

The deserts stretched away to the east while to the west the Tahoe National Forest signalled the end of the desert and the start of California, Sacramento a hundred clicks to the west on the other side of the mountains. Ethan hit the trails within a minute or two and got into his stride, revelling in the solitude and the silence as he reflected on their predicament.

Put simply, during their last case both he and Lopez had been involved in a covert CIA investigation into the case of a man who had been able to predict when and where UFOs would appear. The case had been wound up in a way that neither he nor Lopez could possibly have predicted, and now they were facing the prospect of never knowing what had happened. The reason for that was that they'd suffered something known as "lost time". Everything that they had experienced over a period of several days had been, apparently, erased from not just their own existence but from everybody else's too. People they had met, spoken to, interacted with – all of them had recalled nothing and expressed considerable surprise that Ethan and Nicola knew anything about them at all.

Behind all of it was Mackenzie, a senior general within the CIA who had enlisted them to locate a man who was anonymously sending the agency crystal-clear images of UFOs. Panicked, the CIA had gone into lockdown while the individual responsible was located and questioned. Ethan and Nicola had tracked the man down, brought him to the CIA, and then…. Well, then, nothing. It was as if the entire episode had never occurred.

Ethan jogged alongside the river, the green water sparkling in the morning sunshine. He was out on the edge of town when he heard the first rumble coming in from across the desert. Ethan slowed, shielded his eyes with his hand as he sought the origin of the sound, and finally spotted the speck flying toward him from out of the flawless blue sky.

Ethan kept jogging, one eye on the helicopter as it thundered toward the town, and within a minute it flew overhead. Ethan looked up and saw the light blue-and-white insignia of Garrett Industries, a corporation he knew well. He changed direction and took a short cut across rough ground toward home. He was jogging up to his front door when it was opened from the inside.

Nicola Lopez let him in, as usual having just got out of her bed. He had never managed to quite understand how she maintained such a high level of fitness while barely making any effort whatsoever, and had put it down to genetics and her fearsome determination to achieve whatever goals she aspired to.

'Garrett?' she asked as she closed the door behind him.

'Just landed,' Ethan replied as he hauled his T-shirt off. 'Up at Carson City. He'll be here within a few minutes.'

Lopez headed off to make some coffee while Ethan showered and changed. Moments after he emerged, the door buzzer rang and Lopez answered it to a man younger than them who wore a tailored blue shirt, and casual slacks that probably cost as much as their home.

'Rhys,' Lopez grinned and hugged the man as he entered their home.

Ethan shook Rhys Garrett's hand, and ushered him into the lounge as Lopez brought the coffees and curled up in her favourite armchair.

'Well?' Ethan asked Rhys as they sat down. 'Did you find anything?'

Rhys Garrett was a billionaire, a real-estate developer who had turned a cottage business into an empire that spanned the globe. Ethan and Nicola had met him while investigating his father's murder of decades before, which had involved a government cover-up over a lethal, prehistoric virus that Garrett's father, a palaeontologist, had unearthed while excavating Tyrannosaur remains over in Montana's Badlands.

'Maybe,' Garrett replied.

'Stop pulling my chain,' Lopez urged him. 'We're drawing blanks here.'

Garrett sipped his coffee and spoke softly, as though even out here there were people listening.

'I got a few friends over at the State Department to have a rummage through anything that might ping regarding what you're both interested in. Turns out that something did come up, but I don't really know what to make of it.'

'We're listening,' Ethan said. 'Right now, we've got nothing on Mackenzie; where he works, what he's working on, nothing. Since the DIA operations folded and Jarvis went AWOL, we're out of the loop.'

Garrett nodded.

'Okay, well, I had to ask them to keep everything quiet. The moment I started mentioning things like UFOs and time displacement I got a lot of sharp intakes of breath, teeth sucking, nervous glances, you name it.'

'I didn't think the state department would have knowledge of anything like what we encountered,' Lopez said. 'What's their beef?'

'Turns out they hear about things like this more than you might at first think,' Garrett explained. 'A lot of what we call paranormal experiences get reported to the police, and those reports, as it turns out, are filtered up the chain of command and often reach the State Department and even the Pentagon. They of course deny any knowledge or interest in such reports, but quite often government officers show up and question witnesses of such phenomena, often within hours of the sightings, so we know there's a link between them. Folks who work admin' there are often told to keep their noses out of it all, so to speak, hence their aversion to talking about it to me.'

'But they did have something?' Ethan pressed.

Garrett nodded.

'One of my contacts there was able to pull a file that was held as a copy of another file than went all the way to the top. That's the only reason they remembered it, because of how important it was considered. The CIA confiscated all copies, but forgot about the original and basic report at the State Department. Turns out the clerk at the time was fastidious about preserving records, so they double-copied everything: in this case a copy for the department, a copy for the CIA and a third reserve copy that was archived. The CIA didn't know about the archived report, but my contact did.'

Garrett produced a slim folder from a briefcase and handed it to them as he spoke.

'This is a report filed six days ago on the island of Majuro, in the Marshall Islands. It was made by a resident doctor who treated an elderly American male, who was delivered by the crew of an un-named trawler working somewhere north of the island. The details are scarce, but the doctor's affidavit claims that the crew of the trawler swore that the man appeared on the surface of the ocean in a flare of light.'

Ethan glanced down at the file, which contained some brief photo-copied notes and an old photograph.

'Okay,' Lopez pressed, 'so what's the big surprise with this one?'

Garrett gestured to the image.

'The man said that his name was Ernest Walker, and that the year was 1954.'

That got their attention real quick. Rhys gestured to the image.

'This man, whoever he was, claimed that he was present at Bikini Atoll during what we now know was the "Castle Bravo" nuclear test detonation that vaporized the entire atoll in a blast one thousand times more powerful than the A-bombs dropped on Hiroshima and Nagasaki in Japan. The ship he was on got hit by the blast because it was too close, and he went overboard and into the water to avoid being burned to death. When he came to, he was picked up by the trawler. For him, over fifty years had passed in the blink of an eye.'

***

V

Ethan sat for a moment and looked at the image of the sailor. An Ensign, Walker was thirty-one years old at the time of his disappearance, recently enlisted after losing his job at an auto factory in Norfolk, Virginia, which explained his choice of the Navy given the big yards there.

To most folks, Walker's story would have been an enigmatic mystery, a folk tale, a myth found on the Internet that was compelling but disregarded as the stuff of fantasy or fake news. To Ethan and Nicola, it was something else entirely.

'Okay, so, this is what we've been looking for but where is Walker now?'

'That's the trick,' Garrett replied with a tight smile. 'The CIA obviously learned about this guy because it confiscated all known material pertaining to his experiences. However, I had my people do a little digging on my way out here and it turns out that Walker was never taken into custody. Before the military or CIA or whatever could get out there, Walker dismissed himself from the island's hospital and hasn't been seen since.'

Ethan felt his hopes sink again as another dead end presented itself. Over the past year he and Nicola had researched countless cases of supposed time dilation, time displacement, time slips and other related phenomena. They had travelled the country and spoken to witnesses, many of them honest people, many others charlatans and fantasists. The one thing that they did not have as a result was evidence to pursue their own case and find some foundation to what had happened to them.

'So, it's a dead loss,' Ethan said, closing the folder.

'What about family?' Lopez asked.

Garret smiled. 'A son and a daughter, now in their seventies but living in Virginia.'

Ethan's heart leaped in his chest. 'You've spoken to them?'

'Briefly,' Garrett explained. 'I can't say much right now because they didn't trust me. The moment I mentioned their father they got quite nervous and said that he had died during nuclear tests in the 50s. When I said that I believed that he'd survived and was in fact still alive, they hung up.'

'Great,' Lopez smiled. 'Call 'em up and scare 'em off.'

'What can I say? I'm a realtor, not a psychologist.'

'Makes me wonder why they'd be afraid of talking about their father if he was long dead,' Ethan said as he glanced at Lopez. 'The CIA might have been looking for him all along, and if he does make contact with his own family…'

'They'd want to keep it all quiet,' Lopez agreed, and re-opened the file to look at the image. 'He must have missed out on his entire life. That's gotta have pissed him off too.'

'His children are old enough that they might also need caring for, and who better to do it than their father, despite his own age?'

'The CIA must know about that and will have drawn the same conclusions,' Garrett warned. 'They'll have one eye on Walker's family, waiting for him to show up.'

Ethan looked at Lopez.

'Somebody like Mackenzie will be all over this,' he suggested. 'After what happened in Nevada, he'll be searching for similar cases.'

'If we find the Walkers, we find Mackenzie, or at least somebody who's working for him.'

Ethan nodded. 'What I don't get is the connection with Castle Bravo?'

Garrett took the file back from Ethan.

'I've got just the man to talk to you about that. You can meet him when you land in Virginia. I'm no rocket scientist, by I recall enough about physics to know that Einstein's theories as applied to nuclear power were also applicable in some way to time and gravity. Maybe something happened to Walker as a result of the blast?'

'Only one way to find out,' Ethan said.

Garrett looked at them both for a moment. 'How are you both coping?'

Ethan knew what Garrett was referring to, but not for the first time he felt reluctant to discuss what had happened to himself and Lopez. Sure, they both recalled it all well enough, but it was the following weeks and months that had haunted them the most.

After chasing down the CIA target and believing that their mission was over, both he and Lopez were effectively betrayed by the agency and left to die in the deserts of Nevada. Ethan had often since given the event a mental shrug and told himself that he should have known better: the CIA was not renowned for its loyalty to covert operatives of any kind. Still, their survival had both been a result of the possible benevolence of Mackenzie and something else so bizarre that Ethan was struggling to get his head around it.

Both he and Lopez had been mortally wounded, and they'd pretty much realised that they were going to die. Alone, too weak to move, abandoned miles from anywhere out in the lonely deserts, their long partnership had come to an end. He could recall the irony of being able only then to tell Nicola how he really felt about her, right at the moment where it wouldn't do either of them much good, but as the cold of death crept upon them, he had felt warmth from her, and had been able to face his passing without fear. He hadn't been alone.

Then the light had appeared. Right over them, blinding bright, as intense as a bursting star. Moments later, they'd been driving down a highway, following a route to the home of a young family whose daughter was suffering nightly abduction events that were threatening her health. They had been driving along, both of them feeling not quite right, enveloped by an aura of *deja-vu* so strong that they had pulled over and managed to piece together a few meagre fragments of their lost past.

The entire incident had been so strange that even now he could barely comprehend it. Had somebody else told him the story he would have believed them mistaken or the victim of fantasy, and yet both he and Lopez had the same hazy memories of Mackenzie and the young computer hacker named Kyle who had started the whole damned thing in the first place. They'd followed their path to the home of the young family, but learned that there were no abductions taking place, no strange events, and that their daughter was absolutely fine. Ethan and Nicola must have made a mistake.

He could have left it there, but Ethan knew facts about the family that he could not have possibly learned from the outside, a confusing reality that provoked Lopez to end the conversation and get them out of the area as fast as she could.

'It's not easy,' Lopez replied to Garrett, as ever more easily able to talk about her feelings and struggles than Ethan. 'We still get the dreams.'

Garrett nodded, looked at Ethan. 'You too?'

Ethan nodded, not really wanting to talk about it.

Ethan wasn't somebody who had normally dreamed much, or, to put it more precisely, he'd never really recalled many of his dreams. But now he did, all too many of them, all pretty much the same. Bright light, a sense of being in the wrong place, like those dreams where he'd wake up with no clothes on in the middle of a shopping mall or something and have to find his way home, but the displacement in these was more severe, more frightening. There was a sense of true dread, a fear of something overwhelmingly powerful that was descending upon them, as though somehow the entire universe knew that they should not be where they were and its vengeance was coming closer with every passing second. Headaches, sharps pains behind the eyes, fatigue at strange times of the day, and worse, the occasional moments where they would realize that a few minutes had skipped by in a matter of seconds, a television drama reaching the end only moments after it had begun.

'Time keeps slipping,' he said finally, deciding not to dwell on the dreams. 'Here, there, little bits of it. It's not as bad now as it was then, like it's wearing off, but when one hits you it pretty much knocks you sideways.'

Garrett nodded.

'I've been doing some work on that for you,' he said, 'and you'd be amazed what we turned up.'

Ethan leaned forward now. 'Such as?'

'It's pretty bizarre stuff, but as it turns out slips in time are not all that uncommon. There's one place in England where it's happening all the damned time, so we were led to believe.'

'Seriously?' Lopez asked, intrigued. 'We thought we were the only ones suffering this stuff.'

'You're not alone,' Garrett assured them. 'There seem to be hotspots around the world where time slips constantly affect their surroundings. I've assigned you a jet, which you can use to get around a little easier. This one's going to take some chasing down and if the CIA really did subject you to this, then there's a good chance that we'll be able to figure out whether they left any actual evidence behind.'

'Evidence?' Ethan echoed. 'What evidence could there be of something like that?'

Garrett stood up. 'You're gonna need a bigger brain than mine to explain it all to you. I know you want to go after this Mackenzie guy, but he's burrowed down deeper in the agency than an Alabama tick and he's not going to want to talk to either of you. Right now, we don't know if he organized the event that saved your lives or if it was orchestrated by somebody else, so I reckon it's safer to assume that he's the enemy and to be avoided right now. You turn up on his doorstep, and he'll have a SWAT team after you before you can blink.'

'We've faced worse,' Ethan growled, angry at the thought of General Mackenzie bolt-holed behind closed doors somewhere up in Langley.

'Yeah,' Garrett agreed, 'I know. But the way through this isn't going to be with brute strength, it's going to be through guile. We need to understand the enemy on this, and to do that we have to figure out what they know or what they're really after. My guy can show you that. The plane leaves in an hour: are you both in?'

Lopez and Ethan glanced at each other, and she got up from her seat.

'We're in.'

***

VI

Palo Verde Generating Station,

Tonopah, Arizona

Jim Anderson stood near a watch station on the east side of the vast nuclear power plant and cupped his hands to conceal the glow of a cigarette lighter, which he knew would be visible for literally miles around in the absolute darkness of the Arizona desert. The smoke hit his lungs and he closed his eyes and exhaled, letting the blue smoke spiral up into the starlit sky.

His watch told him it was just after two in the morning, so another six damned hours to go before his shift would end and he could get the hell home for a cool beer and a shower before bed. Jim hated the night shifts, had never been able to get used to sleeping through the day, and so he spent one week of every month just as miserable and grumpy as his long-suffering wife did.

The nuclear station around him was, by output, the largest in the United States. It was of such strategic importance that it was a focus of Soviet targets for a nuclear conflict back in the days of the Cold War, and even now the facility was a key focus of Homeland Security. Some of Jim's fellow guards were armed with rifles, while X-Ray machines, sniffer dogs and guarded turnstiles such as the one Jim was now watching prevented anyone who shouldn't be inside the plant from getting inside the plant.

Jim was smart enough to know that his role was important, even though he was always stuck out here on the east side by the senior guards. He disliked them intensely, most of them former Army guys with combat experience who viewed civilians like Jim as wannabee soldiers not worthy of serious security roles. Jim was not allowed to carry a firearm and, socially, was excluded from their "club". Not that he cared all that much, but carrying a weapon would have been so much cooler than just asking for identifications and watching the main entrance. Everybody knew that the action, were it to take place, would be on one of the more obscure desert tracks where the bad guys could sneak up on the place unobserved, or so they thought. Jim still fantasized about al-Qaeda terrorists attempting to take control of the facility, and the heroic steps he would take to stop them in their tracks and…

A movement in the heavens caught his eye. He stared at a star that he could have sworn had moved, momentarily, just a moment ago. Jim squinted up at it. He could tell that there was something different about this one, but he wasn't sure what it was, like a forgotten word balanced on the tip of his tongue. His old eyes might have been playing tricks on him, and he reached into his breast pocket for his glasses. Jim didn't like to wear them normally, as they might have made him look less threatening, but now he slipped them on and looked up at the star.

The first thing he noticed was that he could see ten times as many stars with his glasses on as he could with them off. The second thing he noticed was that the star had vanished.

Jim stood motionless for a moment, uncertain of whether he'd seen anything at all. Maybe he ought to wear the glasses more often, just in case. There was so much to see in these vast open skies, and he was surprised that he'd never noticed the dazzling array of twinkling stars spanning the…

There it was again! Jim sucked in a brief breath and held it. The star was still there, but it had crossed half the sky in what must have been a split second and was now hovering over the western horizon. Jim knew that no airplane could do that, and he also knew why it looked different to the other stars – they were twinkling, but this one was not. Jim was a smart guy, and he'd read once that the atmosphere of Earth had imperfections in it that caused the stars to twinkle as light was refracted by dust and haze and heat, their light faint enough to be affected. The planets of the solar system did not twinkle as their light was stronger and closer.

But planets didn't fly across the night sky in seconds.

Jim stared at the star as it hovered low over the mountains to the north west, and with his glasses on he could see that it was not one color but seemed to pulse with lights, like a distant sparkling firework that didn't stop burning. He watched it for several seconds, and then it blinked out and promptly reappeared a few miles to the north of its position.

Jim blinked. For a moment he wasn't sure what to do. Maybe it was some kind of energy release from seismic events far below the earth, or gases burning up in the atmosphere and fading out, only to be replaced by another elsewhere? He was about to chalk the unusual object up to just some atmospheric oddity when suddenly it zipped forwards, rushing toward the facility at tremendous speed and then stopped dead.

Jim's cigarette fell from his mouth and landed on the dust at his feet.

The light was brighter now, enough that he squinted and threw his hands up to protect his eyes. Through the flaring, pulsing light he could see something, something solid and disc shaped, but it was too bright to be sure of anything. He heard a humming sound and felt the air around him vibrating, the hairs on his head rising up as a static charge built up.

Moments later, he saw a pencil-thin beam of red light emerge from the bottom of the object and slowly begin to reach down toward a spot on the earth that was no more than a hundred yards from where he was standing.

Jim grabbed for his radio and hit the transmit button.

'Control, gate four, do you copy?'

The radio burst back with a squawk of static, nothing like an audible response coming back to Jim. He clipped the radio back onto his belt and did the only sensible thing: he ran.

He got four paces when he threw his arms up in the air as he stared down the barrel of an assault rifle. Jim's eyes widened in shock as he saw no less than eight men, all concealed in black camouflage smocks, boots and balaclavas, all heavily armed and all of them watching the light behind Jim. He saw cameras arrayed among them, all filming the same light.

Jim opened his mouth to speak, but then a gloved hand clamped over it and he was dragged to the ground with incredible force as he smelled something acrid in his nostrils. His vision blurred and he drew in more breath with which to scream for help, and the moment he did so his consciousness slipped away from him.

*

'Cameras all running,' came the whispered report. 'We've got this one in the frame.'

General Scott Mackenzie crouched in the darkness and nodded once, not risking the chance of exposing their position even further. He could see the facility guard lying on his back as he was dragged out of sight by one of Mackenzie's men, suitably comatose now for the duration.

Their team tonight was eight men strong, plus Mackenzie himself. Six of the team were highly trained paramilitary Special Forces soldiers attached to the CIA, the remaining two men skilled technicians capable of operating the advanced cameras and surveillance equipment they had brought with them. Dressed all in black, they moved in utter, practiced silence.

The light in the sky before them was brilliant, like an arc lamp, too bright to look at directly without being momentarily blinded. Mackenzie slipped on his sunglasses and watched the object closely. Although he could now see nothing around them, he could clearly see the shape of the object hiding behind the light. Smooth, disc-shaped, oval on top just like the disc they'd seen the previous night in Nevada, probably metallic and certainly solid just like a normal aircraft. This was something that Mackenzie could instinctively tell was manufactured, constructed by someone, or *something*.

The object was extending a line of red light like a laser beam, the beam sweeping this way and that as though searching for something. Mackenzie wasn't sure what the strange beams were yet, although he'd seen them several times now. They seemed to be made of light, and yet they sometimes moved slowly, creeping out of the objects that emitted them and gradually reaching the ground. He knew that the speed of light, in a vacuum, was a constant of the universe, a foundational principle of known physics, so the beams bothered him immensely.

'It's moving.'

A crackly whisper through the communications system, just strong enough at short range to burn through the electromagnetic fields now swirling around them, emitted in vast quantities by the craft. Mackenzie saw the craft start to move to the left, gradually easing toward the main reactor buildings.

In the distance, he saw vehicle headlights and heard shouts from security guards as they began reacting to the object now hovering over one of the country's most sensitive nuclear establishments. Mackenzie judged the movement of the object and the position of the guards and spoke softly.

'Maintain position.'

The team were arrayed in absolute darkness alongside one of the big turnstiles that blocked the entrance to the facility. Mackenzie had no need to break and enter, his team equipped with cameras and sensors that would be able to observe the object without the additional issues of dodging angry, and armed, security personnel. If the idiot on the gate hadn't fled his post right into their position, nobody would ever have known they were there.

'Massive energy spikes in all spectrums,' came a report from one man on an infra-red camera. 'It's responding to the security teams.'

Mackenzie slipped off the sunglasses so that he could watch the monitors attached to the cameras instead. The bright light in the sky virtually made visual observation impossible, but the cameras revealed a plethora of information. Even now, Mackenzie found himself amazed at the sheer volume of energy pouring out of the object before him. Ultra-violet light that was invisible to humans billowed in kaleidoscopic clouds on one camera, while the IR lens showed the object itself glowing a vivid white against the black sky and gray horizon. In contrast, the amount of energy produced by the most powerful nuclear facility in the country was paltry, barely registering on the cameras.

'Keep tracking it, see if it does anything interesting.'

The men kept their cameras trained on the object as it drifted west across the facility. Mackenzie watched as the security teams in their jeeps drove toward it, and their vehicle lights promptly went out as the trucks and jeeps were hit by the cloud of electromagnetic energy around the craft and their engines failed.

Lights flickered across the base, the air humming with energy, and Mackenzie felt the first twinge of concern as the craft neared the cooling towers and the nuclear facility itself, the three reactor chambers large, oval humps against the night sky. The danger of failing electronics in such a place was obvious to all, and Mackenzie recalled what had happened to the Russian city of Chernobyl decades before when the reactor there had gone into meltdown: thirty thousand people had been evacuated from their homes, and entire cities now lay in ruins, nature creeping back all over them in a post-apocalyptic wasteland devoid of humans.

The craft stopped somewhere between the towers and the reactor chambers, its red beam of light again sweeping this way and that. The guards were out of their vehicles, some of them aiming rifles up at the object. Mackenzie knew that they would not stand a chance of doing any damage, their rifles the equivalent of Stone Age men hurling spears at an aircraft carrier: whatever this thing was, bullets were not going to penetrate its defences.

The red beam suddenly drew back up into the craft, and as Mackenzie watched it rise up and away from the facility, slow and steady, not in any rush at all. Sometimes, it seemed as though the objects barely noticed that there were people around at all.

Then, quite suddenly, it vanished. The base was plunged back into darkness, the lights flickering back on in buildings and on the security vehicles. The air was no longer quivering with restrained energy, and Mackenzie heard car engines cough into life once more. He glanced at the camera monitors, but they too were dark and silent. The craft had not simply flown away – it had vanished from existence entirely as though it had never been there.

'Pack it up,' he whispered into his microphone.

The team worked quickly and quietly, camera tripods folding up into tiny cases, cameras slipping into backpacks, solid-state recording drives packaged carefully away. Within two minutes, the team were slipping away across open ground to where their vehicles awaited, hidden behind bluffs near the highway.

'Anything?' Mackenzie asked.

Kyle Trent was with the team this time, and he replied instantly.

'Fourteen milliseconds,' he said. 'Less than the last three sightings, but it's still present.'

Mackenzie nodded and briefly checked his watch. That their discoveries were ground-breaking was beyond doubt, but the general knew that he could not sit on this forever. Sooner or later he would have to debrief Langley, and his biggest concern now was how to impart what he knew and not have them discharge him from the service as insane.

***

VII

Punggrye-ri Nuclear Test Site,

Hamgyong Province,

North Korea

Jae-Hyuk Pak stood atop a muddy ridge and overlooked the test site, his collar turned up against the bitter wind. Snow was falling in silent sheets that obscured the mountains soaring into the slate gray sky, coating the valley in a pure white veil that hid the dirt and the misery beneath.

Behind Jae stood ranks of soldiers and officers of the People's Army, resplendent in their uniforms, their weapons held across their chests, oblivious to the cold. Their great leader, Marshal Kim-Jong-Un, would be watching from a heated box that the men had erected to the west the day before, overlooking the valley in which the test would take place.

The site, that of a nuclear facility capable of forging weapons-grade uranium, had been dismantled and destroyed sometime before in an effort to appease the Great Satan, which demanded no other country have the right to nuclear weapons, while hoarding thousands of such weapons within their own borders. Such hypocrisy, such bigotry, was the fuel that fanned the flames of hatred in Pyongyang and the provinces, the fuel which had driven Jae to the pinnacle of his career, here on this cold and windswept ridge.

While the main nuclear establishment had indeed been destroyed, the extensive underground facility beneath it had remained, and in fact flourished. Hidden from the cold black eyes of America's spy satellites, the great Korean People's Army had overseen the construction of a new facility, concealed by the dismantling of the old one. Trucks and construction vehicles had brought materials in under cover, before driving out with the debris from the dismantling project. No foreign journalists were allowed to view the site, no international inspectors permitted to survey the project until it was deemed that the subterranean facility was properly concealed. Only then had Marshal Jong-Un allowed inspectors to witness the final blasts that had destroyed the old site.

'It is time.'

Jae turned to his left to see the old General Hyung-Joon gesture to the site with one trembling hand, weak with age.

'As you wish.'

Jae glanced over his shoulder and nodded to one of his lieutenants. In turn the command was sent down the line, and from alongside the troops a bedraggled, chained line of men, women and children were jostled into motion through the thick snow. Each had a number painted on their chest and back.

Most were dressed in rags, their bodies trembling in the frigid wind as they were hustled past the troops. Drawn from the nearby Hawsong Concentration Camp, each was a traitor, a fraudster or a relative of one, imprisoned under the patriotic laws of guilt by association. More often than not, those found guilty of treason or other capital crimes were executed, but only after being told which concentration camp their entire families were being sent to, to serve out the rest of their lives enduring endless hard labour.

Some fell to their knees as they passed, only to be whipped and bludgeoned into motion by their guards. The great leader was watching nearby, just visible through the reflections in the glass of his observation post, flanked by his family.

Below them, in the valley, the prisoners were ushered into a tunnel hewn into the living rock, protected by a thick steel and concrete door designed to keep radioactive toxic waste sealed inside. The door was a ruse, of course, and in fact the entrance to the underground facility.

As soon as the prisoners were inside, Jae gave a signal and led the officers down the hillside and into the entrance tunnel. Once around one hundred troops were inside, the heavy door was sealed shut and their great leader would watch the proceedings on screens in his observation post.

The interior of the tunnel was cold, concrete walls supported by steel beams that descended down into the mountain. Harsh white lights countersunk into the ceiling illuminated the way as the prisoners ahead were led into a facility filled with enormous overhead pipes, offices, computer banks and other workstations. It looked like NASA's mission control, mixed with an oil rig and buried beneath a mountain, and at the far end was an enormous Tokamak Chamber.

Jae himself understood little of the physics behind the device, certain only that the donut-shaped chamber was capable of generating the temperatures and pressures found inside the hearts of stars, where hydrogen was crushed to such incredible pressures that nuclear fusion took place, creating helium in the process. Nuclear fusion had not yet been achieved in this chamber, but then that was no longer the purpose of this facility.

'Send them in!'

Jae climbed a gantry that overlooked the Tokamak with his officers around him. Before them, arrayed across the facility, were a series of spiral contraptions that surrounded rows of numbered cages. Twenty gigantic transformers, each as high as a house, were pointed at the cages, into which the miserable prisoners were shoved. It took several minutes to do so, during which Jae could hear the wailing of the women and the soft cries of the children as they were forced inside the cages and then locked within, twenty people to each cage.

Jae glanced across the facility to where another row of cages was arrayed across the back wall, perhaps a hundred yards from where the prisoners were now huddling together, hugging each other and weeping.

'Start the power converters, engage the chamber!' he snapped.

From the back of the facility a hum of energy spread outward toward the watching officers. The cold was instantly displaced by a warmth as atoms in the air were excited into motion. Jae felt his stomach quiver as vibrations passed through metal and air and skin and bone but he kept his posture erect and his expression stoic, forcing his men behind him to do likewise. This was what he had prepared for, this was what he had staked his reputation on, and right now he knew that if he failed, he'd be among the next test subjects cowering in the cages below.

The discovery that had been made in these tunnels three years before had changed the course of the country's foreign policy and might perhaps ultimately change the course of humanity's future. That the discovery had been made during a disastrous nuclear test had been fortuitous in the extreme, as had the fact that Jae had not been present at the event, which had killed over one hundred scientists. What was remarkable was that the scientists had not been killed by the blast. It was what had happened to them afterward that had sparked within Jae an extraordinary idea.

'Temperatures rising,' came a report from one of the scientists nearby. 'Reaching critical density.'

The immense Tokamak chamber before them was filled with a plasma that was heated to literally millions of degrees, and the energy generated now revealed itself through apertures in the chamber as a soft blue glow, deceivingly serene.

'Prepare the electromagnetic field generators.'

Jae spoke the words almost autonomously, having become deeply involved with the project over the past three years. While he was no scientists and could not hope to understand the deeper physics behind the creation before him, he could understand the basic principles when they were explained to him by those who had built this amazing and yet terrible thing.

The Tokamak chamber was like many used in attempts around the world to generate nuclear fusion, the power source of the sun and all stars in the universe. However, this one was the result of measurements made not of the fusion process within but of the blast that had followed the accident which had claimed so many lives out here in the mountains of Hamgyong Province.

During the detonation sequence, an unexpected chain-reaction had increased the yield of the previous Tokomak by ten-fold, utterly overpowering even such a robust machine. That detonation had blasted its way out of the containment chamber and resulted in great destruction and the deaths of most of the team working on the project. However, when the site had been cleared in the aftermath, it was realized that something extraordinary had occurred: all of the surviving clocks in the facility had been precisely seventeen seconds slow.

But that was nothing compared to the state of the victims of the blast.

'Ten seconds!'

Jae glanced at the Tokomak and saw the glow growing brighter before them, shafts of flickering electric-blue light slicing through the relative darkness of the facility as the lights began to fail. The humming noise grew louder, and it felt as though Jae's body was beginning to disassemble itself. His hands and fingers grew numb, and his vision blurred as though his eyes were vibrating within their sockets, but he held his ground and silently prayed for a good result, or at least one that would not kill everybody in the facility.

'Five seconds, four, three, two one...'

From the Tokamak a searing light as bright as a supernova ripped through the facility. Jae closed his eyes but for one terrible moment he could still see the chamber before him and the entire facility, the light burning right through his eyelids to score the image directly onto his retina. A rush of screams burst out and then the brilliant light vanished and the entire facility was plunged into darkness.

Jae opened his eyes, and for a moment he could not see a thing, could hear nothing save for the whining down of the generators as the power was reduced. Terror ripped through him as he feared that he had been permanently blinded, but then he blinked and he realized that in the wake of that fearsome blast, everything seemed far darker than it normally would. Gradually his pupils began to expand once more and he saw the facility around him as the humming noise faded away.

'Output reducing, power being re-diverted back to the generators.'

There was a moment's pause, and then the lights flickered back into life and Jae looked down at the cages.

They were all empty.

A rush of gasps filled the gantry as the officers stared in amazement at the empty cages, wondering where the prisoners had gone. Jae turned to his right, and his heart plunged into his stomach, flipping over and over in a supernatural awe as he saw the tangle of bodies in the cages across the wall.

Moans and cries drew the attention of the other officers, and Jae heard more horrified gasps as they caught sight of the carnage before them. Slowly, Jae stepped down off the gantry, brushing his own arms and chest with his hands, trying to make sure that he was fully intact.

The cages were the same size and shape as the ones in which the prisoners had been locked, each numbered in the exact same sequence, and Jae was pleased to see that each prisoner had ended up in the same cage number as they had started. However, that was where his pleasure ended as the moans became screams.

The bodies were as tangled as before, but now they were tangled *within* each other. He saw a woman with her head poking from the spine of a man, who was himself writhing in agony, his arms both lost somewhere within another man's body. Heads poked from within chests and torsos, and at least three of the prisoners were partially impaled by the bars of the cages in which they were trapped, their hands clawing ineffectually at the metal.

Behind him he heard two scientists' vomit while a third passed out and slumped to the ground.

'Guards!'

A handful of armed men rushed down onto the facility floor, their weapons drawn as they ran to the edge of the cages. Each raised his rifle and took aim at the horrific mess of limbs and hair and skin, but none fired.

Jae walked past them to the side of the cages, and saw a child's face twisted in agony, eyes wide with confusion and horror and fear. He looked down at the child with interest, one he knew to be the son of a former politician who had been found guilty of treason, after he'd been caught accessing the Internet. Jae felt no compassion for the traitor's child, for they were as guilty as the father and had only their family to blame.

He watched them all slowly dying, losing consciousness one by one as their brains were starved of oxygen, their internal organs either absent or unable to function correctly. There was absolutely no chance of most of them surviving, but one emaciated man was clutching the bars of his cage, the metal passing through his left shoulder. There was no blood, no trauma at all other than the understandable pain that he was enduring.

'That one,' Jae snapped. 'Cut him free and take him to the hospital. Kill all the others.'

Jae turned and marched away from the cages. He heard the man screaming as his cage was lifted without ceremony and carried out of the facility. A moment later, and the deafening cacophony of machine gun fire ripped through the facility as the remaining survivors were killed.

The noise irritated Jae and disturbed his thoughts. He had to find out what had gone right and also what had gone wrong, and explain it to the Dear Leader in just the right way that he turned a partial success into a victory, because right now his life depended on it.

***

VIII

Majuro, Marshall Islands

Ernie Walker crouched down beside the base of a palm tree and shivered as he waited for the light to return. The darkness shielded him but his Navy uniform was of little use against the sea wind gusting in off distant waves beyond the reefs. Although the islands themselves were hardly cold, he had not eaten properly in two days and he was exhausted.

He could see a series of low homes built along the beach nearby, no lights within, no sound of movement but for the endless whisper of the Pacific's relentlessly marching waves. Ernie crept along the edge of the beach, staying close to foliage and fences for cover, and peered over a low fence into the nearest garden.

Within there was little grass, a couple of rickety old benches and a washing line upon which were strung out various garments, all of which belonged to a woman with a considerably larger waistline than his own. Ernie kept moving, tracked along the back fences until he saw a line with clothes that he could take seriously: jeans, shirts, socks.

Ernie had never stolen a thing in his life, his father a disciplinarian who believed that a strong spine belonged to a strong mind and vice versa: breaking the law would have invited the lash of his belt. Ernie felt bad but he knew that he had no choice, and he told himself that he would return the clothes as soon as he could, or pay for them if he couldn't.

He pulled on the jeans, socks and shirt, rolled up his uniform and carried it under his arm as he hurried away from the homes toward the twinkling lights of the town nearby.

For a small settlement, Majuro sure was big. Ernie had never seen so many streetlights, and now he could see vehicles that looked like something out of *Imagination*, a science fiction magazine he'd seen recently during a stop-over in the Solomon Islands. Trucks were not battered and dusty, but glossy and metallic, much bigger and smarter than anything he'd ever seen. The ships in the harbor were more conventional looking but also a little sleeker and bigger than he was used to. He could see fishing trawlers leaving the bay as the first rays of light speared the eastern horizon, their running lights drifting like stars across the universe of the ocean.

Ernie knew that time had changed around him, but he was struggling to accept it. Something had happened to the ship, and he felt certain that they were around somewhere – an entire aircraft carrier couldn't have just vanished overnight. He hurried past shopping malls and warehouses, saw more of the shiny vehicles, most of them moving in near-silence compared to the rattling Army jeeps and trucks that he was used to.

He spotted a trash can near the sidewalk and was about to toss his Navy uniform into it when he had second thoughts. Right now, that uniform was the only evidence he had of what had happened to him. If he tossed it and it was lost or destroyed, he'd never get anybody to believe who he…

Ernie thought for a moment. He and his shipmates had often had their photographs taken, on shore leave and even on duty aboard the ship. There had to be a record somewhere, and more than that, his shipmates also had to be somewhere too. If he could get back to America, maybe he could find one of them. He thought of Cooper, and Henry Coleman, and wondered if he might be able to look him up somehow without attracting the Navy's attention.

The light was coming fast now, the warmth of the sun streaming across the town as Ernie hurried along the road. He needed food, water and shelter, and he needed some way of contacting Henry. He walked past a shop and then stopped dead in his tracks, staring at the wonderful television sets within: every damned one was *full color*, and one of them would have filled an entire wall back home.

Home.

Ernie felt a wrench in his guts as he thought of his wife and their children. Then he heard a great roar in the sky and almost ducked as he turned and saw an airplane rush overhead, as big as anything he'd ever seen before but built from shiny metal and splashed with a colourful livery. Jet engines that left no smoke trail howled as the airplane flew off into the distance, and Ernie could just make out the glittering lights of a runway further around the atoll.

'Where the hell am I?' he uttered, felt grief pinch at the corners of his eyes.

'You okay man?'

Ernie whirled to see a big, black man with biceps the size of coconuts looking at him with great concern. Ernie realized in an instant that the man was not a threat, merely a concerned citizen.

'Yes, thanks,' Ernie replied. 'Just very tired. I've got no money, no food, no nothing and I'm not even sure where I am.'

The big man raised an eyebrow, then smiled broadly as he spotted Ernie's uniform tucked under his arm. 'Big night out with the guys, huh? You from the base?'

Ernie wasn't sure which base the American was referring to, but just as long as he could keep talking to somebody he'd have nodded if the guy had said "moon base", which Ernie then reflected might actually be a possibility.

'Sure. Just gotta get myself sorted and then I can go report in.'

The big man clapped his shoulder. 'You're old for a sailor, man, but if you're wearin' the uniform, you're welcome here. C'mon, I got some food and somewhere to get your head down.'

Ernie felt a rush of gratitude as the man led him to a pick-up truck parked in a lot off the main street.

'Sorry 'bout the mess,' the man said as Ernie climbed in. 'Haven't had her cleaned this week.'

Ernie saw no mess, other than a couple of candy bar wrappers. The interior of the truck was immaculate black plastic, chrome fittings and glowing displays that lit up a mesmerising blue and green as the man started the engine, which purred as softly as Ernie's wife's cat. The seats were as soft as a bed, and Ernie almost closed his eyes right there and then as he sunk back into his seat, the soft hum of the engine lulling him as the truck headed west toward the airport.

'I got a buddy who runs the local motel, you can stay there in the spare rooms they run when it's off season. He won't charge nothin', so long as you don't mess up the room.'

Ernie nodded, so tired that he could barely do more to respond. The driver watched him for a moment.

'You've been out longer than one night, pal,' he observed with a knowing eye. 'You wanna tell me what gives? You're too old to still be servin'.'

Ernie rubbed his face, too exhausted to concoct much of a lie.

'Let's just say that I could really do with laying low for a day or two.'

The driver chuckled. 'Man, that's what most people come to the Marshall Islands for, I'm with you there. You stick with Papa D, which is me by the way, and there ain't nobody gonna find you, 'less I say so.'

On a better day, Ernie might have thought that there was something oddly sinister about what Papa D had said. As they drove, Ernie heard the sound of another airplane coming in to land at the airport. Papa D leaned out of his window to look up at the airplane as it soared overhead, flaps and gear down to land.

'Man, that's two this mornin' already. Wonder what they want?'

Ernie peered up at the airplane, and saw that unlike the last one this was a dull gray in color and bore the unmistakable barred-star of the United States military under its right wing. Ernie slid back into his seat as he watched the airplane touch down a mile ahead of them, and wondered just how close Papa D was taking them to the airport.

Mercifully, he turned off the main road less than a minute later, just before a sign that said Majuro Bridge, and drove up a side street lined with non-descript condos surrounded by palm trees. At the far end of the street, and backing onto a strip of beach, was a tired-looking two storey motel. Papa D pulled up outside and killed the engine.

'Here you go buddy,' he said. 'Just ask for Matteya, he runs the joint, tell him I sent you here for some shut eye and food. He'll take care of the rest, and you'll be right as rain come tomorrow mornin'.'

Ernie thanked Papa D, got out of the car and walked into the motel, keen to escape the military airplane that had just landed barely a mile away.

The interior of the motel was cool and dry, air conditioning supplied by the ocean breeze wafting in through open shutters. A native woman sat behind a desk, surrounded by leaflets for diving companies and boat tours. She greeted him with a broad smile.

'Hi,' Ernie offered wearily. 'Papa D sent me to see somebody called Matteya?'

The woman rolled her eyes and shouted loudly enough to make Ernie jumped. 'Matty! Another one of D's losers here to dry out!'

From a back room emerged a rough-looking guy with a shaved head and a permanent scowl. He looked Ernie up and down for a moment, grabbed a key from a hook on the wall, then gestured to a nearby staircase.

'Back room, end of the corridor. Make a mess and you don't leave until it's cleared up.' Matty tossed the key to Ernie, who caught it despite his weariness and smiled his thanks.

'I won't,' Ernie replied, and turned for the stairs. He climbed up and walked to the last door.

The key turned in the lock and Ernie walked in to see a room almost empty but for a bed, a sink and a latrine. The floors were bare, the shutters open to a view over the beach, the cool air and the whisper of the waves drifting in through the room.

Ernie locked the door behind him, and then on an impulse he grabbed a chair that was to one side of the room and pulled it until it rested beneath the door handle, preventing it from opening easily. Then he turned and walked to the window. Carefully, he leaned out and looked to his left. A mile away, he could see the airport, and there on the apron was the military airplane, personnel filing out of it in brisk fashion. Even from almost a mile away, Ernie could see that they were carrying rifles, and that from the back of the airplane a ramp had been lowered and two jeeps were being driven out onto the asphalt.

Ernie leaned back in and closed the shutters, then staggered to the bed and slumped onto it.

Moments later the cool darkness and the whispering waves lulled him into a deep sleep.

***

IX

Lawrence Livermore National Laboratory, California

'I feel like a lab rat.'

Lopez sat in a glass cubicle with several electrodes stuck to her temple, while outside her transparent prison several scientists analysed computer screens and mumbled to themselves.

'It doesn't take long,' Ethan promised as he removed scraps of adhesive tape form his own forehead. 'Doesn't even hurt, all that much.'

Lopez narrowed her eyes as she glared at him, but said nothing as she sat and watched the scientists bustle around print outs and screens, jabbing at graphs with the tips of their pens.

Ethan and Nicola had flown out to California the previous day, and as soon as their feet had touched the ground, they had been hustled into the laboratories for tests that had lasted ever since they'd arrived. They'd even been required to sleep over in carefully prepared rooms, their brain waves and other vital functions monitored to detect whatever the hell it was the scientists were looking for.

Lopez's test ended and the doctors opened the door of the cubicle, ducking aside as Lopez rushed out and ripped the electrodes off her head.

'Enough,' she snapped. 'Anybody else tries to probe me with anything I'll take it and shove it up their as…'

'As a matter of fact, the tests are complete.'

Ethan saw a rotund man with a white beard and keen eyes walk into the laboratory, an iPad in one hand and a pen in the other.

'Your results are most fascinating,' he added as he shook Ethan's hand. 'Doctor William Goldberg, I run the nuclear test facility here at the laboratories.'

Lopez also shook Goldberg's hand, somewhat cautiously. 'What do you mean, *fascinating*?' she demanded.

'Come this way,' Goldberg enthused. 'I'll explain while we head to the ignition facility.'

Ethan and Lopez followed Goldberg out of the laboratory and down a long corridor, passing offices and other laboratories as they went.

'Ignition?' Ethan echoed. 'Hope that doesn't apply to us.'

'No, no,' Goldberg promised. 'The only thing you've been exposed to is low-level X-rays and electrical impulses designed to measure the levels of activity in your brains.'

'Did you find any in Ethan's?' Lopez asked. 'I've been searching for years.'

Goldberg grinned as they walked. 'At a fundamental level both of your brains appear normal, but closer inspection revealed a number of anomalies for which I do not have a proper explanation. Have either of you been having trouble sleeping, bad dreams, things of that nature?'

'*All* the time,' Lopez grumbled. 'I used to love sleeping, now it's a chore, I'm always tired and irritable.'

'She was like that anyway,' Ethan murmured from one corner of his mouth.

'You're both suffering from a chronological anomaly,' Goldberg explained. 'Put simply, your brains are out of synchrony with your bodies, a bit like a chronic form of jet lag.'

Ethan frowned. 'We haven't travelled much in the past few months, and certainly not overseas.'

'I know,' Goldberg said, 'Rhys Garrett told me of your history and what led you to this point, which makes the anomaly all the more interesting. If I didn't know better, I'd say you'd popped out of one time-frame of reference and into another. It's this way.'

Ethan and Nicola exchanged a glance but said nothing as Goldberg led them into a vast facility. They were required to pass through several security sections to get inside, and both Ethan and Nicola donned protective lab coats, goggles and hoods before walking through a sealed hatch that was closed behind them.

'Welcome to the target bay of our National Ignition Facility,' Goldberg said with a grand sweep of his arms.

Ethan felt like he was standing on what looked like a mixture of the engineering deck of the star ship *Enterprise* and the boiler room of a warship. A circular room with a polished floor surrounded them, the walls enveloped in pipes and cables like creepers in a steel jungle. In the centre was an enormous, blocky contraption festooned with more cables, ladders and pipework. Ethan could see that around a central device were several large, rectangular contraptions that came out of the ceiling and all pointed toward the center.

'What the hell is it?' Lopez asked, bemused.

'This is a place where we use lasers focused on atoms to recreate the conditions found in the hearts of stars,' Goldberg explained. 'Here is where nuclear fusion takes place, albeit on a tiny and temporary scale. In the future, it's our great hope that society's electrical needs will be powered by the fuel of the stars; clean, safe and nearly limitless energy for all.'

Goldberg gestured to the rectangular arms protruding from the ceiling and into the central device, a chamber as large as a house.

'One hundred-ninety-two lasers are fired with extreme precision down those chambers and collide at precisely the same moment on all sides of small targets, compressing them to the conditions required for thermonuclear burn. The only other places in the universe where these conditions can be found are in the stars, or exploding nuclear weapons.'

'Okay,' Lopez said, 'so it's a big toy gun. What does that have to do with us?'

Goldberg leaned on a support rail as he replied.

'On this scale, nothing at all. But on the grander scale, everything. I take it you've both heard of Einstein, of his famous equations.'

'Yeah,' Ethan replied. 'But we're not physicists, so keep this simple.'

'General and special relativity *are* simple concepts,' Goldberg replied, 'it's just the math which describes them in detail that's insanely complex. In essence, Einstein's work showed that time, space and energy are all different manifestations of the same thing. You can't have one without the other. The sun has mass, converts a few billion tons of that mass into energy every second because its huge gravity causes nuclear fusion at its core, and it takes that energy a few minutes to reach the Earth when it breaks free of the sun's corona: mass, energy, space and time all in one conveniently packaged event. However, the sun's mass also bends space around it a little, just as the Earth does, which results in what we call gravity. But when it bends space, it also bends time with it, because the two are related: relativity, or space-time as it's sometimes referred to.'

Goldberg gestured to the ignition chamber nearby.

'When we compress matter in this facility to initiate thermonuclear burn, and when we accelerate particles to the speed of light in the Large Hadron Collider and crash them together to see what spills out, we create gravitational events that also bend time in the vicinity of those collisions. The periods measured are infinitesimally small, but they *are* measurable. We bend time, all the time, right here.'

'You're saying that time is something that can be altered?' Lopez asked. 'That we can already do it?'

'We all experience time in a different way,' Goldberg explained. 'Soviet cosmonauts, who spend up to a year aboard orbital stations, return to earth a few seconds younger than they should be. GPS satellites in orbit have to account for that same time dilation as otherwise they would be wildly inaccurate – their high velocities in orbit mean time moves at a different rate for those up there than for us down here. Earth's gravity is also stronger at the surface than up there in orbit, further increasing the dilation.'

'So how could we lose time?' Ethan asked. 'How could we experience something, and then find ourselves in a place where those things had not taken place?'

Goldberg sighed, folded his hands across his belly as he considered that problem.

'That's something that we cannot do, and I have no mechanism in mind that would allow one party to alter the timeline of another. As a scientist I can *hypothesise* how something like that might be done, but I can't prove any of it. What I can tell you is that your brains are showing residual signs of running on a thirty-six-hour clock, and not the normal twenty-four-hour clock we're all used to.'

Lopez blinked. 'What?'

Goldberg shrugged.

'I'd say that you're experiencing something directly that is deep within all human beings but is barely understood. Our natural, primal biorhythms do not equate with the planet on which we live.'

***

X

'Seriously?' Lopez uttered. 'I'm not following here.'

'It's what we would normally call insomnia,' Goldberg explained. 'The study of circadian rhythms in primates and mammals suggest that we operate on a sleep cycle that matches the coming and going of natural light, from our sun. But before our twenty-four-hour lifestyle, electric lighting and so on, we used to sleep in two natural shifts: a few hours' sleep after dusk, a couple of hours awake, and then back to sleep until dawn. People who struggle with insomnia shouldn't fight it at all, they're just more naturally attuned to primal rhythms that are much older than the lighting and television and so on that keep us awake later in the night than we evolved to be used to.'

Ethan frowned. 'That's not quite saying that we don't match our planet's natural environment.'

'It is, when every other species *does* conform to a twenty-four-hour night and day cycle,' Goldberg replied. 'There's something about us that is slightly different to all other species: when humans are deprived of light, they revert to a natural twenty-five-hour circadian rhythm, and some people reach a natural thirty-six-hour rhythm, far different from Earth's day and night cycle. It could perhaps have been an evolutionary adaption to fend off nocturnal hunters like big cats and so on, back when we would have been vulnerable while asleep, but the fact that it still occurs is of interest to science. Anyway, I digress. That you have both developed this chronological insomnia, when none was previously present, suggests that both your bodies and your brains were subjected to some kind of alteration in their perception of time that threw your rhythms out, and they have yet to recover.'

'It fits,' Ethan agreed, 'but is there anything that you learned that we could follow to find out what actually happened to us?'

Goldberg opened his iPad and the screen lit up to reveal a series of charts, each with Ethan's or Nicola's name alongside them.

'There's only one thing that I can show you that supports the notion that you were somehow, as difficult as I find it to admit, shifted in your timeframe of reference. These are charts from your medical records taken shortly after your experience. The doctors you saw noticed nothing unusual in your records, but I did see something in your bloodwork: the levels of both sugar and iron were both extremely low.'

Ethan and Lopez exchanged a glance. 'We were exhausted,' she said, 'and we'd both been shot.'

'Blood loss would cause such a dramatic dip,' Goldberg agreed, 'and your bodies had not yet recovered from the damage, although you yourselves were no longer afflicted externally by the injuries. I can't explain any of this – if you travelled through time, you would have carried your injuries with you, yet you did not: only a residual effect of those injuries remained.'

'Is there any mechanism that you can think of, no matter how crazy it might sound, where something like that could happen?' Lopez asked.

'Oh, sure,' Goldman replied. 'If you orbited a black hole near its event horizon for a few hours, you would come out the same age but years would have passed in the rest of the universe, perhaps decades. But even then, I would have thought that an injury you had that was taken with you would also still be there. While I accept that you believe you were somehow zapped from one place to another, and that physics does support the notion of the malleability of time and space, the energy to perform such an act is far beyond human capabilities at this time. Our best and brightest simply could not cause what happened to you to occur, at least not without vaporising you both on the spot.'

'What do you mean?' Ethan asked.

Goldberg closed the iPad. 'Back in the 1950s, when America was testing nuclear devices, it was noted that at the moment of ignition, even extremely precise atomic clocks would exhibit tiny time dilations. The cause has never been found, but we do know that it has something to do with the relationship between time, mass and energy. About the only thing I ever found in the literature that seemed to have a place in the discussion was electromagnetic energy, which is always emitted in high energy events like nuclear blasts, supernovas, black hole events and so on.'

'Castle Bravo,' Lopez said.

'Yes,' Goldberg agreed, 'that was one of the test project names of the period. The Ivy Mike detonation was one of the largest in history, and Castle Bravo detonated with a far higher yield than planned, causing the discovery of nuclear fusion.'

Ethan knew that they could not talk to Goldberg about Ernest Walker, but that there was a tangible link at all was enough to kindle a spark of hope that they were onto something.

'Thanks for your time,' Ethan said as he shook Goldberg's hand.

'Not a problem,' came the reply, 'and if you do learn something, please do let me know. There would be a Nobel attached to anybody who was able to figure out the science behind what you believe happened to the both of you.'

It took more than twenty minutes to get out of the facility and into the warm Californian sunshine once again. Ethan walked with Lopez to their hire car, deep in thought about everything Goldberg had said.

'He doesn't believe us,' he pointed out, 'but then I don't blame him. For me though, the evidence said everything: we weren't imagining it all.'

'Never thought for a moment that we were,' Lopez agreed. 'Right now, our only hope is that Ernie Walker will talk to us, provided we can find him.'

'He's on the run,' Ethan said, 'and the CIA are looking for him. I'm sure he's gonna head right home, but I don't know how he's going to do it without being caught.'

'Hiding in plain sight?' Lopez surmised. 'He's got to have figured out some smart way of putting himself right where he wants to be without being identified.'

Both Ethan and Nicola had long experience of operating without being noticed, of blending into a crowd, but the longest they'd had to do so was about six months and that had been hard on both of them.

'How do you hide in plain sight, when everybody's looking for you?' Ethan asked rhetorically. 'And when everybody knows what you look like?'

Lopez shrugged, but Ethan's mind briefly went blank, something tugging at his imagination like a word on the tip of his tongue that he couldn't quite grasp. Then, it hit him and he stopped beside their hire car and smiled. Lopez rolled her eyes.

'I hate it when you do that, 'because I just know you're gonna come out with something all super-clever, but you're gonna make me wait to hear it.'

'*Moi?*' Ethan said as he opened his door.

They got in, Ethan closing his door and switching on the engine. Cool air from the air conditioning unit billowed into the interior as Lopez sat with her arms folded and an expectant expression on her face.

'Don't make me kick your ass, Warner.'

Ethan smiled.

'The guy shows up forty years after he disappeared, the government knows about it, probably tries to locate him after he goes AWOL from the Pacific. Ernie's never found, but we all figure he wants to be close to his kids as they grow up. So, he's heading back to Virginia.'

'*And?*' Lopez snapped.

'The family would have to be complicit in it all, they'd know who he was because they'd remember and recognize him, but they wouldn't be easily able to show it, in public at least.'

Lopez shook her head. 'Okay you got me, just spit it out, will you?'

Ethan put the car into gear and eased out of the parking lot.

'Ernie Walker might have leaped half a century into the future, but Goldberg said it himself, when you move something through time, that doesn't mean that time itself changes for the observer. I'm taking that to mean that Ernie Walker would have aged over that time period.'

Lopez thought about that for a moment.

'The CIA records show Ernie Walker from his shots in the 1950s.'

'Which means that they're…'

'… looking for the wrong guy. They should be looking for an old man. But surely the Barn must have thought of this, must have realized?'

'Maybe,' Ethan agreed, 'but the early mistake might just be enough to have given Ernie a chance to slip by undetected. From there, he could have done anything, gone anywhere. We don't know how he felt about it, but having been exposed to a nuclear blast and seen half his ship mates burned alive by the Castle Bravo detonation, he probably isn't a fan of our government or the military of the time. He'll keep himself well hidden, and it's my guess that he'll put himself in the one place the CIA would never expect to find him.'

'His own family,' Lopez replied as she finally got it. 'He could be the cousin, the brother, the uncle, anything.'

'And he'd look like one of the Walker family, yet not look *quite* like Ernie,' Ethan agreed. 'I'm wondering whether Ernie might try to hide in plain sight in Norfolk, Virginia.'

***

XI

Pyongyang, North Korea

Jae-Jayuk Pak stepped off the train onto the platform of the city's main station, and marvelled once again at the stark difference between the North Korea that the rest of the world saw in the capital city, and the one that existed throughout the rest of the land.

Pyongyang was a jewel situated on the Taedong River, surrounded by a landscape that was almost medieval in its poverty. Jae was a patriot, without reservation, but even he knew that his country's prosperity was limited. The military were equipped with obsolete weapons, ships, armor and aircraft, and while there was the country's alliance with China and Russia, both were increasingly inclined to distance themselves from Kim Jong-Un's more militaristic impulses. Only one branch of the military was seeing the kind of progress that the country needed, and that was the one Jae found himself now caught up in as he was met by a military escort of the every-present Korean People's Army.

The Yokchong-Dong district of the city was as Spartan and spotless as ever, but even under a flawless blue sky something of the Soviet gray still seemed to permeate everything with a fog of misery. Jae marched in time with his escort out of the station, beneath metalwork letters that pronounced the longevity of their Great Leader and the glory of the Worker's Party, onto a large asphalt area where a bus awaited. The brilliant sunshine and immaculate buildings were the only things ever seen on television by the outside world, nobody ever seeing the endemic poverty in the hinterlands. The country had barely recovered from its last famine, and even Pyonyang seemed unusually quiet, which despite its size was home to just three million inhabitants.

Jae boarded the bus, which was escorted by armed police on motorbikes. There was no fear of crime in the city, the escorts were all just for show, the power of the state ever on display to its civilians.

The bus turned toward the Mansudae Assembly Hall, the seat of the Supreme People's Assembly, the parliament of North Korea. Jae sat in silence, his escort ignoring him or at the very least pretending to. Nobody knew whether he would return from this particular journey, least of all Jae.

The Supreme Leader had been intrigued by the results of the most recent test, that much Jae knew. Whether Kim Jong-Un was intrigued by what had happened or intrigued by how a senior officer could fail so spectacularly before him was uncertain. Jae had ensured that the remains of the unfortunate victims had been burned, and all required tests performed on the sole survivor before he too was committed to the flames. The tests had learned little, other than the fact that the survivor was genetically and physically identical to the samples taken before the test. His displacement had not caused any detectable injuries, other than the obvious ones that had so hideously deformed his fellow traitors. Jae had not been able to solve that particular conundrum, and despite a healthy supply of traitorous souls from the concentration camps he was reluctant to waste more electrical power generating another test until he could understand what it was that had gone wrong.

The bus pulled up outside the Assembly Hall and Jae stepped out, flanked by his escort as the hall's armed guards waved them through. Jae said nothing as he walked into the hall's grand interior and felt the first warmth since he'd boarded the train nine hours before.

The hall itself was vast, with enormous statues of previous leaders arrayed behind it. The interior was a maze of meeting halls and conference rooms but nobody simply walked where they wanted. Jae was guided with laser-precision to a particular conference room dominated by a long, polished table around which sat several high-ranking officials from the Worker's Party.

The escort stopped at the doors and Jae continued inside, heard the doors close behind him with a resounding thump as twenty or so old men turned to look at him. Jae stood to attention at the end of the table and waited to be addressed.

'Colonel,' said the leader of the Worker's Party, 'thank you for travelling so far to meet us at such short notice.'

'It is my honor,' Jae replied, meaning nothing of the sort but knowing that anything but absolute deference to the men in the room before him could end his career, and probably his life, in the blink of a politician's eye.

'We would like to know what happened at the test facility, and why the experiment so utterly failed.'

Jae did not hesitate in his reply, for to do so would be interpreted as having absolutely no answer for the question, which in some respects he didn't. Speaking, saying *something*, was better than a confused silence.

'The failure was in the containment of the individual's positions with respect to each other,' he said. 'As a test of the capacity to move a person or persons through time, the experiment worked very well. Clearly, there is much for my team and I to learn before we can move on to the next phase.'

There was a long silence as the Worker's Party leaders digested this information. Jae knew that none of them had the faintest idea of how to move forward, that not a man among them had anything tangible to offer in terms of advice or knowledge or even wisdom. They were simply there to decide who lived, and who died.

'The experiment killed almost everybody involved,' came the response. 'There will be no next phase as long as we're in any doubt that your work has produced the results you have so clearly insisted are possible.'

A direct accusation, the first. The committee before him would no doubt answer to Kim Jong-Un himself, thus being able to place blame elsewhere would be their top priority.

'There will be no repeats of the failure in the next tests,' he assured them. 'Of course, we must remember that we are using the least capable test subjects, those weak of mind and body. More robust comrades will fare much better, but we must not move forward until we can be sure that our finest patriots are safe to do so.'

The leader of the worker's party leaned forward on the table and eyed Jae testily.

'Indeed,' he replied. 'Perhaps, Colonel, it is time to put yourself and your reputation on the line for this experiment of yours. Much has been sacrificed to support it. Our Great Leader has suggested that, should the next experiment not go according to plan, that any further tests should be conducted with yourself as the sole subject.'

Jae felt his stomach flip inside him as he thought of the horrendously disfigured bodies he'd seen as a result of the last experiment. Then he thought of his family, his wife and their two children, of the fate that would befall them should he fail.

'I would step into the cages willingly,' he replied without hesitation. 'It is not the experiment that is at fault, merely our understanding of how to control it. Believe me, gentlemen, this technology could change everything for our country. Imagine, if for only a moment, the ability to step back in time, to know our enemy's actions before they are undertaken, to pre-empt their responses. We already know how to hack into their networks, their homes, their lives; with this technology we could do the same and then utterly confound their responses, to the point that we could disable an entire country overnight and bring them to their knees before our…'

'Or we could turn our best people into that mush you created in Punggrye-ri,' one of the officials interjected. 'We saw the videos, Colonel, and we're wondering just whether it's worth doing anything more with this.'

Jae felt panic rise like hot pins striking his neck.

'Without it, we are at the mercy of our enemies.'

The conference room felt as though the air had been sucked from it, faces staring at him aghast, that he should in a single sentence render the great North Korean nation as somehow inferior to its southern neighbor.

'You stain our nation with your insults?' the speaker uttered.

Jae knew that he'd gone too far, even though he'd spoken nothing but the truth. There was no going back now. He tossed his cap onto the table, took a deep breath and spoke from his heart.

'This will never work as long as we're all pretending that our great country is leading the world. We are behind, gentlemen. The Great Satan leads, followed closely by Europe like a pack of wild dogs picking up the scraps that it drops. We have infiltrated some of their infrastructure using hackers but they're always onto us before long as we have not secured any form of political or military advantage. What's more, each and every one of us lives under the threat of instant death should we make a single misstep.'

The silence around Jae seemed heavy and oppressive. He might as well have been insulting their great leader personally, but he knew that if he did not win the party over then he may as well draw his service pistol and shoot himself right now.

'But, imagine if that we no longer had anything to fear,' he whispered. 'Imagine if every mistake could be corrected, *before* it ever took place.'

Jae stepped away from his place at the end of the table, speaking quietly but with the force of a man dedicated to his mission.

'There would be no more fear. We could do no wrong, for we would know the outcome and be able to change it. We would be able to bring our country to the fore without ever firing a single shot against our enemies. While America seeks ever more control and power over sovereign nations with their nuclear weapons and their aircraft carriers, we instead could simply focus on the greatest technology the world has ever seen, the control of time and space, and forge ourselves as the *ultimate* power on the planet.'

Jae looked across them all, convinced now more than ever that if they united behind his project, they would be able to achieve the impossible.

'We cannot win a war against our enemies on the battlefield,' he insisted. 'We have the numbers, but not the equipment nor the tactical position to achieve victory. But with our minds we can achieve *anything* if we end this culture of fear and replace it with one of endeavour.'

There was a long pause as the committee reflected on the opportunities Jae was describing, and the risks, but Jae was convinced that his success would allay any risk to any of their lives. The leader of the Worker's Party cast a steely eye at Jae, unimpressed.

'Your patriotism is admired, but you lack the wherewithal to execute this plan with any measurable certainty of success. That is going to be a problem when the United States catch up with us.'

Jae felt his heart briefly stop inside his chest. 'What?'

The speaker gestured to the State Security Officials sitting opposite him at the table.

'Several days ago, our sensors detected an electromagnetic impulse from a remote region of the Pacific Ocean, very close to an area once used by the Americans to test their nuclear weapons. The signature of this pulse precisely corresponds to those measured during your own experiments.'

Jae felt his guts plunge within him. 'The Americans, they have a facility there, something that can generate that kind of energy?'

'No,' the speaker replied. 'But intelligence suggests both an interest in the event, and links to a nuclear accident from 1954. Our agents have learned of rumors from the area about a sailor who may have appeared out of thin air where he once vanished, over half a century ago.'

Jae felt momentarily off balance, trying to keep up with what he was hearing.

'They brought somebody *forward* in time? Even we cannot do that yet, we can only move them slightly.'

'They may have already surpassed our capabilities,' the speaker corrected him. 'Their sanctions continue to cripple our ability to build more modern equipment, whereas they suffer no such hinderance. Should these failures continue, it could be our country that forever is beholden to a past of America's choosing. Perhaps, some are suggesting, it already is.'

Jae knew that he had no answer and no solution to a problem that was occurring half way across the world. If the Americans were also experimenting with the same technology, then it was almost inevitable that they would seek to both dominate the field and hinder any other nation with similar plans.

'We need help,' Jae insisted. 'We should bring our allies in, purchase supplies from them, give ourselves the chance to even the race with the Americans.'

'No,' the speaker said, 'the time is past for that and there is no guarantee that they would not wish to obtain the technology for their own ends. This must remain with us and us alone, and for that to happen we must bring the American program to an end.'

'How?' Jae asked.

The speaker smiled, his expression almost cold, his eyes black like a shark circling its prey.

'You will lead a team to America to sabotage their work, while at the same time learning as much about their advancements as you can. You will start with this mysterious American sailor. We have information that he was found by a vessel that is now bound for Manila. You will intercept it there, find out what you can, then move on to the United States.'

Jae felt the world tilt awkwardly beneath him at the prospect of travelling to a land where he and his countrymen were so avidly demonized.

'Of course,' he answered automatically, 'it will be an honor. Might I have the chance to say goodbye to my family before I leave for...'

'The glorious nation is grateful for your sacrifice,' the speaker cut across him. 'As will be your family, if you are successful.'

Jae snapped to attention, saluted, then spun on one heel and marched from the conference room. As he heard the doors close behind him, he cursed silently to himself. The Worker's Party and security services had done their work well. His mission would take him away from home soil, into the lair of the enemy to commit international crimes, and if caught he knew that North Korea would disown him and his family would be sent to the concentration camps for his supposed treachery.

If you are successful.

Jae stiffened his resolve. If that was their plan, then not only would he execute it perfectly, but he would return triumphant and take his rightful place at their head. Then, and only then, would he exact his revenge upon each and every one of them.

***

XII

Norfolk, Virginia

Stakeouts were much easier to do when there were two sets of eyes on the target. It had not been hard to locate the homes of Ernest Walker's children, both of them living within a few blocks of each other in a quiet suburb of the city. Ethan had chosen to take the day watch, Lopez much more of a night owl. He'd split his watch according to the ages of the children, who would of course be Ernest's grandchildren, knowing that if the old man was going to be about it would be when the children were at home. Hanging around a school for them or avoiding the family at what would be considered normal times would have marked him out, so Ernie would have to be around at weekends, here and there, something an uncle or similar would be expected to do. He'd have had to change his appearance somewhat, but not so much that he wasn't evidently family, and there would presumably have to be forged documents somewhere along the line so that when the CIA went looking, they'd find what Ernie wanted them to find.

Ethan leaned back now in the seat of his car and read a magazine, his eyes on the pages but his focus always out onto the rows of homes a hundred yards from where he sat in a parking lot down near Greenbrier East. There was no way that he could stake out this particular home directly, so instead he was parked at one end of the street and watching the vehicles coming and going. Sooner or later, he figured, and Ernest Walker would have to show up.

But he hadn't.

Ethan had been there for three days now and still the wily old guy hadn't shown his face. Lopez had a pretty good watch on the night shift and was certain that she hadn't picked him up, and they'd identified everyone else in the family, everybody except Ernie himself. He should have been around, and Ethan began to wonder whether they had been right in deducing what Ernie would do. Would he not have feared for his family and decided to do the tough but honorable thing and stay away, perhaps in another country, far from them?

Ethan sighed as he saw Ernie's son, Clive, walk out of his home for the third morning in a row to check his mail box. Sure, three days wasn't all that long to stake out a family in the hopes of catching one individual: Ethan hadn't seen his sister Natalie for over six months and that wasn't considered unusual. Well, not for him anyway.

Clive Walker took a couple of letters from the mail box and walked slowly back up his drive. As he did so, Ethan heard his cell phone buzz and glanced down to see a message from Lopez pop up on the screen.

The hell with this.

There had been a time, once, when Ethan would have panicked at seeing such a message from Lopez. Now, he merely shrugged and got out of the car. She was around somewhere and clearly had decided that they weren't going to just stumble into Ernie, so they'd have to go see him themselves.

Ethan walked down the street and saw Lopez coming the other way. She'd probably only managed a couple hours sleep and was now on a mission, her long black pony tail of hair swinging from side to side as she crossed the street and called out.

'Mister Walker?'

Clive turned and saw her coming toward him. Ethan approached more slowly, knowing that guys took a warmer shine to Nicola, a petite and attractive Latino, than they did himself. Lopez smiled brightly.

'Sorry to bother you sir,' she purred. 'My name's Nicola Lopez, I'm looking for somebody named Ernest Walker.'

Clive tucked the mail under his arm and smiled. 'That would be my father, ma'am.'

'Is he around? Can I speak to him?'

Clive shook his head. 'I'm sorry, my father died some years ago.'

Ethan approached them and Clive spotted him.

'It's okay,' Lopez said, 'he works for me. We're just following up on a cold case from a few decades back.'

'You're cops?' Clive asked.

'We work for a private company,' Lopez explained. 'We try to locate lost souls, people who have disappeared. We were running through some older cases, and your father's popped out as unusual.'

Clive seemed uncertain, glancing back and forth between the two of them. 'My father was reported missing back in the 1950s, why would you be looking for him now? He was officially declared dead in the late 80s.'

'Well,' Ethan said, 'there's official and there's *official*. Ernest's body was never found and he was assumed to have been the victim of some kind of accident. But it could have been foul play.'

'We're not here to dig up the past unwarranted,' Lopez pressed, 'or open up old wounds and grievances. We just like to hunt out the truth, wherever we find it.'

Clive Walker nodded.

'I'm sorry, really, I would love to help you but we don't know what happened to our father and he's been gone so long now that we've kinda put it to rest and moved on. Thanks for reaching out to us, have a good day.'

Clive turned and walked up the steps to his porch. Ethan spoke up before he could open the porch door.

'Ernest didn't just vanish, did he, Clive? Something happened to him while he was at sea, and the government covered it up.'

Clive slowed, one hand on the porch door, but he didn't turn around.

'Same thing happened to us,' Lopez added. 'Not on the same scale, but similar. We're trying to get to the bottom of it, and we'd really like to know anything you can tell us about your father's disappearance.'

Clive hesitated for a moment with his back turned to them, and then his shoulders sank slightly and he walked away from them into his home. Ethan watched as Clive left the door open behind him, and with Lopez he walked up the porch and into the home.

Clive led the way out back, to where an open-air swimming pool backed onto a broad garden filled with well established trees. Clive gestured to some chairs around the pool as he eased himself into one and put the mail to one side on a table.

'My father disappeared in 1954, after jumping overboard from a burning vessel in the South Pacific. He was never seen nor heard from again, and I very much wish that were different. I don't know anything about what happened, as the government has kept the events classified for over half a century, but I do know that other members of the crew were afraid to speak out about what happened. When our mother asked them, when they returned from the voyage, they refused to speak to us.'

'That's the lead we're following,' Lopez replied. 'The issue we have is that the government still won't talk about what happened aboard USS *Bairoko* and the official record states that her crew suffered only minor burns from the Castle Bravo accident.'

Clive sighed and nodded. 'We've heard the rumors. We even once had a visit from the government about them. The only thing that we heard for sure was from one of the crew, one of Ernie's friends, who confided that many of the crew were burned alive. He said that Ernie went into the water and simply vanished, was never seen again.'

Ethan leaned closer to Clive. 'We've been hearing reports from the Marshall Islands that your father was seen after the blast, alive.'

Clive humped, shook his head and waved them away with a dismissive gesture.

'You don't believe any of it,' Lopez suggested.

'I don't believe that my father would have ignored us all of these years were he still alive,' Clive replied. 'He wasn't that kind of a man, both I and my brother remember him as a kind, family man who did all that he could for us. If he were somehow still around, he'd be sitting right here with me now.'

Ethan wasn't sure how to take that. He believed everything that Clive was saying, but he felt certain that if Ernie was around then he *would* be watching everything that had happened to his family.

'You said that something similar happened to you?' Clive asked. 'What did you mean by that?'

'It's a long story,' Lopez explained, 'but we were involved in a government operation and as a result, we lost some time.'

Ethan saw it. There was a quiver in Clive's reaction, the slightest tremor in his eyes at the mention of lost time. Ethan leaned forward.

'This is what we know so far,' he said. 'Your father was exposed to a nuclear detonation test in the South Pacific that got out of hand, the Castle Bravo event of 1954. The blast radius was much larger than anticipated and his ship got caught up in it. There was some kind of secondary event, perhaps caused by the original blast, that Ernie got hit by. He then surfaced and was picked up by a passing trawler. The crew sailed him to a nearby island to have him checked out, and after that he vanished, never to be seen again.'

Clive raised an eyebrow. 'And how does that relate to you?'

'We didn't lose fifty years,' Lopez replied, 'only a couple of days, but there's something going on and we've become a victim of it. We're trying to track down the people behind it all but so far we're coming up empty.'

Clive sat for a long moment, his hands folded in his lap as he stared down at them. Ethan wondered what might be going through his mind, and the fact that if he truly knew nothing and did not believe the stories about his father, why he was having to think about anything at all.

'I want to know who I'm really talking to first,' Clive said.

'I'm Ethan Warner,' Ethan said. 'I served with the Marines in Iraq and Afghanistan, before I became a journalist. I got hired by the Defence Intelligence Agency. This is my partner, Nicola Lopez, former Washington PD. We've been working together for several years now.'

Clive peered at them both for what seemed like a long time. Maybe he was sizing them up, maybe he just wasn't sure what to say, but then he sighed and nodded as though satisfied.

'Sometimes I get asked about this kind of stuff by government folks who come here and ask questions, and I don't like 'em. Can't trust them somehow, like their agenda doesn't concern you and they don't really care about the people they're talking to.' He looked at Lopez. 'They often send a pretty lady to soften the heart, too, but I get the sense that you two are different somehow.'

Lopez rolled her eyes. 'Oh, we're that all right, and I can assure you we're here for selfish reasons: we want to know what the hell happened to us. If we can figure out what happened to Ernie along the way, all the better.'

Clive seemed satisfied, and he thought for a moment before speaking.

'My father was stationed aboard USS *Bairoko*, which was steaming through the South Pacific just at the time you said. The Navy never told my mother what happened to dad, but a fellow seaman who saw what happened got in touch with us a couple years later when he left the service.'

'Was he able to detail what happened to your father?'

'Some,' Clive said. 'The Castle Bravo detonation was far more powerful than expected and they were caught up in the outer areas of the blast zone. According to dad's shipmate, the carrier was hit by flames and high winds, a real apocalypse, and the heat was enough to set clothes on fire. Crew members went over the side to protect themselves, but as my father jumped, he was seen to hit the water just as a bolt of some kind of energy hit about the same spot.'

'Energy?' Ethan asked. 'Like lightning?'

'Something like that,' Clive replied. 'Right after the shockwave passed, the ship got back under control. Many of the sailors were burned, but all were put under strict orders to never speak of what had happened. I don't think that dad survived the blast, simple as that.'

Ethan decided to take a leap of faith. 'You said that government people show up sometimes, ask questions here?'

'Yeah, sure, now and again.'

'When did that start?'

Clive thought for a moment. 'Couple of years ago, I guess. Why?'

Ethan took a breath.

'The sightings of your father after the blast,' he said, 'they didn't occur in 1954. They occurred last week.'

Clive stared at Ethan. 'Get out of my house.'

'It's true,' Lopez said. 'We know how crazy it sounds, but the reports are real and the US military has just sent a bunch of airplanes and personnel out to the Marshall Islands in a real hurry. Something's happened, Clive, and we think that it has something to do with your father's disappearance.'

Clive frowned, stared thoughtfully at his hands for a long time. 'How do you know this?'

'Reports say a man wearing the uniform of a sailor called Ernest Walker was picked up by a trawler south of Bikini Atoll,' Ethan said. 'The ship that reported him in was never identified, was probably up to no good, so the crew would have remained anonymous. I guess the trail ran cold after that and so the military are swarming the islands trying to track your father down before he disappears again.'

Clive didn't say anything for a moment, still thinking.

'The people from the government,' he said, 'they always asked us if we've heard from our father. Why would they ask that if he's officially listed as dead?'

'Do you know who they are?' Lopez asked. 'Do they give you identification?'

'Never,' Clive replied, 'although there's no doubt that they're the real deal. That they also believe something happened to my father is obvious, but they only ask questions, never reveal anything, and believe me, I've asked plenty.'

'You got anything we can look at that might help identify them?' Ethan asked.

Clive nodded, and stood. They followed him back into the house, Clive speaking as they went.

'We had security cameras set up a few years back, motion-sensor activated. Last time somebody came calling, I pulled the camera footage and saved it. Don't know why, I suppose I just wanted some kind of evidence of what was happening.'

Clive opened a drawer in the lounge and pulled out a six-inch by nine-inch high resolution photograph that he must have printed from the camera footage. He handed it to Ethan.

'Well,' Lopez murmured, 'whaddya know?'

The black and white image showed the Walkers' drive and the street outside. A dark car with government plates was parked outside, and walking from it was a tall man with gray hair in a military uniform that bore no unit insignia. General Mackenzie had been captured mid-stride, in broad daylight.

'How old is this image?' Ethan asked.

'Three months,' Clive replied. 'That's the last time he came here.'

***

XIII

Groom Lake,

Nevada

There was a solitude to the silence of the deserts that was comforting to General Scott Mackenzie, the main reason why he chose to drive to his post rather than take the twice-daily "Janet" flight out of Vegas. The drive gave him time to think, to be alone and away from the bustle and stress of his job, and remind him that regardless of rank or power he was just one man on a vast planet, a member of just one species that didn't know half as much as they thought they did about this world upon which they lived.

Nobody much drove out here. The nearest inhabited town was called Rachel, a haven for conspiracy theorists hoping to gain a fleeting glimpse of what had once been the most secret airbase in the world, but was now ironically one of the most famous. He'd made the drive north out of Vegas, turning onto the 375 and eventually reaching a dusty track known as Groom Road. It traced a thin line toward mountain ranges to the west, their peaks faded by heat haze and distance.

Mackenzie had driven for ten kilometres down this lonely track, plumes of dust coiling from his vehicle's tires up into the hot blue sky behind him. Multiple signs lined the road, warning of the danger to trespassers that lethal force would be used to deter anybody from entering the airbase unauthorized.

Even with his rank, driving into Area 51 without clearance would have resulted in several gunshots and flowers being sent to his wife, such was the classified nature of the facility. As he drove, so a pair of four-by-four trucks with silver bodywork appeared, having waited for him on a dusty slip road near the base.

The trucks led him over the ridge of hills, following the winding contours of Groom Road until it descended on the far side. The deep shadows gave way to brilliant sunshine once more and revealed the vast salt flat of Groom Lake. On its far side, roofs and metal-clad buildings twinkling in the fearsome sunlight, was Area 51.

The airbase dominated the far side of the salt flats and the runway was almost ridiculous in its length, running alongside the entire airbase and then north-west across more of the salt flats. All of the hangars were low slung, the buildings around the base all on the western side of the runway and equally innocuous. To an observer, even from this close range, it would appear that the base contained nothing at all remarkable. Mackenzie knew that was because what was remarkable about Area 51 was not the base itself, but what was concealed beneath it.

The vehicles pulled up in a parking lot at the northern end of the base, Mackenzie spotting a pair of Apache attack helicopters parked nearby and an F-16 *Fighting Falcon*, armed and ready for immediate flight and intercept should any pilot be foolish enough to try to guide his plane within visual distance of the base.

Mackenzie parked and got out of his vehicle, and was immediately flanked by silent armed guards who escorted him toward a non-descript metal-clad building on the airbase's north-west corner. Designed to look like nothing more than an ancillary storage shed, the construction was arguably the most important building on the base.

The armed guards accompanied the general to the doors of the shed, where they stood off to one side. Mackenzie entered an access code onto a panel on the wall, and a door lock clicked automatically open. Mackenzie walked into the building and closed the door behind him.

The interior of the building was filled with old shovels and pick axes, rusting barrows and other paraphernalia that disguised the building's true purpose. In the centre was a rickety looking interior shed. Mackenzie opened the shed door to reveal a simple elevator shaft, similar to ones sometimes seen in old coal mines, rusty metal shutter doors and a dirty interior. The elevator looked like a car that had been disconnected from its original location and dumped in the building, rusty metal cables dangling from its upper mechanism, severed from the engines they had once been connected to. Large enough only for two people, Mackenzie stepped inside and entered another code onto a small pad within the elevator as soon as he'd shut the doors.

The soft whine of modern, well maintained generators that belied the elevator's tatty construction filled the small hut and the elevator dropped gently away, descending into a shaft of rough-cut rock and hard desert mud. Mackenzie knew that the real lifting mechanism was beneath the elevator car, not above it. It slid smoothly down the shaft for some one hundred feet, the shaft lit by the occasional passing light, until it reached the bottom. Mackenzie input a third code, this time aware of security cameras watching him from just outside the car.

A perfectly formed metal panel slid aside to reveal a corridor, and Mackenzie stepped out of the elevator car and walked down the corridor. Another security door before him opened automatically, and the general walked into the Area 51 that few people alive on earth knew about.

Essentially a research and development site, Area 51 had earned its name from its location on maps dating back to the previous century. Throughout the 1990s and into the next century, the base had become probably the most famous in the world, and high-security work normally carried out above ground had been transferred into subterranean areas constructed for that purpose.

The public was fickle, something that the military and governments understood well. In order to draw their attention away from Area 51, operations were transferred to other classified installations at Dulce, New Mexico, and Joint Base Andrews in Maryland. This created a mystique around those areas, while the draw-down in activity at Area 51 allowed the construction of underground facilities to go ahead with minimal observation by the media or the public. As the focus of the conspiracy theorists was drawn to those other high-security installations, so the most classified operations were returned to Groom Lake's remote location. Now, the base was once again in full flow and its work was of the highest security and most disturbing in nature.

'Sir.'

An officer snapped to attention as General Mackenzie walked between ranks of offices and laboratories, all sealed under strict security protocols. Nobody knew what went on in neighboring offices, each team working in isolation and rarely seeing other operatives on the base.

'Where are we with the EMIT program?' Mackenzie asked.

The officer accompanying him slipped naturally into line alongside him, his uniform devoid of signature or name. Here, personal security was almost as important as the security of the operations themselves.

'Right now, we're at an impasse. Theoretical physicists are working on the problem but we don't anticipate a solution any time soon. They're at the limits of what we can literally understand with our own senses, let alone calculate with the math we have to hand. It's no wonder Project Montauk was cancelled.'

Mackenzie had inherited a program that had operated decades before under the Project Montauk title, which had involved serious military study into the nature of time and space. The aim had been to gain whatever advantages could be had in order to further dominate the Soviet Union, and although some remarkable conclusions had been drawn over the nature of existence itself, those working on the project had not possessed the technology needed to monopolize on those discoveries. Now, they did, and the EMIT program was the resurrection of Project Montauk in modern form.

'We're waiting for a breakthrough sir, but right now I don't have anything to tell you other than we're still trying.'

Mackenzie nodded but said nothing more. This facility was not a place where staff were reprimanded for a perceived lack of progress. It wasn't a place where failure resulted in resignations or apologies. The progress of discovery at this scale of science was not linear, and nobody knew that better than Mackenzie.

The officer led him into a large chamber, where a nuclear Tokomak was being tended to by legions of scientists in white lab coats, their faces covered by masks along with their hair. Separated from the chamber by thick glass windows, Mackenzie could see a young but brilliant man named Kyle Trent working among the team.

The EMIT program, which stood for Electromagnetic Manipulation of Interspatial Time, was right now the most classified project in United States history. More carefully concealed even than the Manhattan Project, the president himself did not know of its existence, much less Congress or the Senate. Funded by the Black Budget and controlled by the Central Intelligence Agency, the project was staffed by a private aerospace company, thus ensuring protection from the Freedom of Information Act. General Mackenzie's success in tracking down its chief architect, a wildly intelligent kid of just twenty-two years of age, and of obtaining the remarkable knowledge he possessed about the true nature of UFOs, had put Mackenzie at the head of the project and, privately, way out of his depth.

'Get Pioneer One out here, I need to speak with him,' Mackenzie ordered.

There were no names down here, only numbers preceded by a code-reference to their role within the facility. Sierra referenced general, civilian staff. Mackenzie was Alpha Zero One, with obvious reference to his superiority.

Kyle was called out of the chamber, and was alone with Mackenzie in the control room within a couple of minutes. A gangly youth with a cunning intellect and wild imagination, Kyle Trent had a year previously come up with an algorithm that correctly predicted both when and where UFOs would appear, and in doing so revealed much of their true nature to the CIA. The call-sign Pioneer One had thus been applied to him.

'The test was successful?' Mackenzie asked.

'Sure,' Kyle replied, 'if you consider one quarter of a millionth of a second successful.'

'That's how far back you went?'

'That's how long it *lasted*,' Kyle replied.

Mackenzie leaned back against a desk and folded his arms as he looked at the chamber. 'That's a lot of energy for not a lot of movement.'

'Tell me about it,' Kyle replied. 'We're on the right track, but man we must be missin' something real big to be having such a hard time getting this to work.'

'Just run me through it one more time,' Mackenzie asked.

Kyle sighed, clearly exhausted. His team had been working seven days a week for months down here, and it was starting to show.

'Everything is energy,' he said wearily, and reached out to tug at the general's uniform. 'You, your clothes, rocks, the air that we breathe, everything is just energy. What we perceive to be solid matter is an illusion. We're made of atoms in the same way cigarette smoke is made of particles. Take out all the space between the atoms in our bodies and we could walk through the eye of a needle. The whole universe is like that, but what we can see of it is a mere fraction of what's actually out there. Everything, though, remains a form of energy, whether we can see it or not. That's what Einstein was getting at; mass, gravity, light, heat, they're all different forms of the same thing and each affects the other.'

Kyle turned and gestured to the Tokomak chamber.

'When we run this thing up and create the nuclear fusion that occurs in stars, at a tiny level there is a change in time and space. Gravity is created, masses are altered and thus so is time itself, just on a tiny scale. Build this Tokomak on the scale of a star, and its mass and gravity will bend light and time around it a little, something that Einstein predicted when he said that the planet Mercury, which orbits our sun very closely, would not appear to be where it actually was – the light from it being bent by the sun's mass and making it appear someplace slightly different. This was later, along with most of his predictions, proven true, and that's the nature of space and time. We see the night sky as it used to be, far in history, because the light from distant stars takes so long to get to us. In some respects, we're all able to see the past, but never the future.'

Kyle was reciting his little piece from memory, almost by rote, trying to help Mackenzie understand.

'Take this process to its extreme, such as around the periphery of a very massive object like a black hole, and things get out of hand. Time is warped so heavily that it stops for an observer outside the hole watching events within, and yet for someone falling into the black hole time speeds up relative to the rest of the universe and they see the future of the entire universe play out before they're consumed.'

Mackenzie blinked. 'I don't know that I'll ever get the hang of this.'

'You don't need to,' Kyle said, not for the first time. 'You just need to know that the science is solid. What's missing is our understanding of what occurs *in between* those two extremes, at the fine line between our timeline and that of the black hole, the point of no return. That's what we're doing here, trying to replicate that environment. We're trying to make tiny black holes to figure out what happens at the point known as the Event Horizon.'

Mackenzie had read about the Event Horizon many times, and still it seemed so bizarre that he could not comprehend it.

'The point where nothing, not even light, can escape the black hole,' he recalled.

'Yes,' Kyle replied. 'What we're trying to do is measure the energy and the nature of the event horizon, because what we can learn from it may help us understand how the hell it is that UFOs can do what they do, because as you know, we're pretty sure that they're not a manifestation of aliens travelling through the universe. We think that they're travelling through time.'

***

XIV

Mackenzie had spent much of the past year thinking about nothing else but what Kyle had just outlined. The revelation, when he had considered it for the first time, had been so explosive, so utterly amazing and yet terrifying, that he had seriously questioned whether the military should dare investigate it at all.

The conundrum of UFOs had been one that had fascinated humanity for centuries. Popular culture upheld it as a modern phenomenon, but Mackenzie's introduction to EMIT had included a general history of the sightings of UFOs around the world, and it had become abundantly clear that they had been seen by humans for hundreds, and perhaps thousands, of years. The question had always been: *what are they?* Now, the question had changed.

How are they doing what they're doing, and why?

A year previously, the CIA had been sent a series of crystal-clear images of UFOs appearing across the United States. Initially dismissed as some kind of elaborate hoax, it had soon been realized that somebody, somewhere, had learned how to predict the appearance of these strange entities, and those sightings included ones over military installations. Shocked into action, Mackenzie, who had been attached at the time to the CIA at Langley, had found himself at the head of the search to locate and apprehend the man responsible. Kyle Trent, eventually, had been tracked down and brought to the CIA, and in time he had proven far worthier as an asset than a foe. Now, he was at the forefront of EMIT's mission to unveil the mystery of UAPs as they had now come to be known: Unidentified Aerial Phenomena.

There had been a long-standing fascination with UFOs not just within the public but within the intelligence community for almost as long as it had existed. That such a phenomenon could exist for so long, and be virtually acknowledged as real by most of humanity and yet continuously denied by successive governments was to Mackenzie a liability, or at least it had been until he had joined EMIT. By then, he understood just why the US military wanted the subject to remain out of the public eye, and to be ridiculed and dismissed when it did appear.

UFOs were not alien craft. They were *human*, and they were coming here from elsewhere in time.

Mackenzie, when he finally understood what a UFO was, began to realise that the conclusion removed all of the mysteries surrounding the phenomenon. The craft did not have to cross galaxies from worlds as yet unknown; their occupants' humanoid forms became not an unlikelihood of natural evolution on another world but a natural evolution of mankind on this one; the technological advances required became less science fiction and more of an expanded version of things that already existed on Earth. The only mystery that remained was how they were appearing from the future, and why?

Kyle had been remarkably blasé about the subject.

'It makes sense,' he'd replied, after he'd recovered from his own exposure to the remarkable revelations. 'We'd all like to see human history, so we'd travel back in the blink of an eye if we could. As for the technology, there's nothing in Einstein's theories that prohibits travel into the past – time can run both backwards and forwards in the equations that govern our entire universe. Maybe someday we figure out how to do it and that's why UFOs appear in our skies and seem able to defy the laws of nature.'

What had shocked General Mackenzie the most was Kyle's grasp of the UFO's agenda and methods.

'I don't think they're travelling through time,' he had said finally, after months of work on the EMIT program. 'I think that they're *looking* through time, and we're able to see them doing it. It's that breach of their past and our present that causes the human viewer such distress, and it's the spill over of energy required to do such a thing that makes humans so sick afterwards.'

That single line, spoken in front of the Joint Chiefs of Staff in a meeting at the White House to which the President was not invited, had sent the EMIT team in new directions. There was one thing above all that witnesses to UFO sightings reported: a humming noise accompanied by large volumes of static electricity, along with the failure of vehicle engines and communications equipment. Kyle had been able to provide a clear and unequivocal answer to what would cause such manifestations.

'Electromagnetic energy,' he had said. 'Lots of it, and I mean *lots*.'

Mackenzie had only the most basic grasps of electromagnetic theory, and knew only that a magnetic field could generate electricity, and vice versa, that the two were connected. Kyle's explanations of Relativity and energy's interconnectedness with everything had enlightened him to the importance of electromagnetic fields witnessed around UFOs and suggested an important clue: whatever they were using as a power source, that allowed them to travel at tremendous speeds and perhaps through time itself, either was electromagnetic in nature or created an electromagnetic trail or exhaust.

That had led to the EMIT program's remit, and the more recent successes that had led to an understanding of how electromagnetic energy could affect everything around it, perhaps including time itself. A former Navy sailor by the name of Ernie Walker, Mackenzie had soon learned, had mysteriously vanished during the Castle Bravo detonation in 1954, which had created a bolt of electromagnetic energy that had struck Ernie directly when witnesses said he had hurled himself over the side of his ship. Images of the detonation had captured the bolt itself, and simple triangulation from the known source had provided the point where the bolt had hit the water right alongside Ernie's aircraft carrier. That blast of concentrated energy had propelled him through a tiny gap in the spacetime continuum, right into the present day.

'The tests aren't showing enough movement though,' Kyle repeated. 'We're generating fields here that are strong enough to lift a car off the ground and hurl it across a field, but we're not seeing anything like the energy required to effect time and space. There's something missing, but we can't figure out what it is. About all I can tell you is that whatever is behind the technology that they're using, it's not based on energy as we know it. There has to be something involved that we just don't yet know about.'

Mackenzie nodded.

'Fine,' he replied. 'Gather the team and set the Disclosure Protocol running again. We need to gather more data.'

The Disclosure Protocol was an unofficial name for Kyle Trent's original algorithmic program that predicted the appearance of UFOs. Mackenzie had adopted the name in deference to Kyle's original work, although the CIA now owned the operation. For Kyle, it had been the choice between seeing his work continued and becoming part of the team at Area 51, or dreaming about it for thirty-to-life in a Colorado Super Max Prison. He'd taken the smart option.

'There's only so much we can get,' Kyle said. 'We can witness these things appearing and record them, but what we're missing is something other than straight out technology. You've seen them yourself, they're metallic, they're something that's been built by intelligent life. Doesn't matter whether they're ours from the future or something from another world: they're manufactured by someone. They're highly advanced, but in principle there's nothing they're doing that's not beyond our capacity to learn or understand.'

'So?' Mackenzie asked. 'That doesn't answer what it is that we're missing.'

'No, but it tells us what we're *not* missing. I think that what we've got set up here would work, if only we can find whatever secret sauce it is that we haven't put in yet. We can create the energies we need, but it's as if we haven't plugged the right cable in someplace.'

Mackenzie wasn't sure where to go with that. He knew well enough that they were chasing a black cat in the dark here, but the recent North Korean tests had created a far bigger impetus for them to get results. There was simply no way that the reclusive dictatorship could be allowed to gain the upper hand in this race, and Mackenzie suspected that the administration would not rule out military strikes should they fail to prevent a North Korean advantage. The consequences of such a strike could be all out war, and if China and Russia got involved…

At that moment, another technician hurried into the room, his face flushed with excitement as he waved a print out in his hand.

'We've got another one!' he gasped.

'Another what?'

'Another emission, same as the one in North Korea!'

Mackenzie felt his guts plunge. Could it be that other countries were also discovering this incredible technology at the same time?

'Where?'

'Near Bikini Atoll, in the Marshall Islands.'

Mackenzie and Kyle exchanged a glance. They had worked on cases of time slips and mysterious disappearances for the past year, even those that remained classified even after decades, and one name popped simultaneously into both of their heads.

'Ernest Walker!'

Mackenzie took the report and read it, which didn't take long as it was only a few lines of data that identified the location, strength and duration of the emission. He handed it to Kyle.

'What do you make of it?'

Kyle shook his head in wonder. 'Right location, the very spot where USS *Bairoko* was hit in 1954. There's nothing else out there that could do this, it's open water, no industry, no weapons installations. Nothing. You know what that means?'

'No, what does it mean?'

'It means that this was natural. We need to look into this, find out what the hell happened out there because if this is what I think it is, Ernest Walker might just be the missing link we're searching for. I think he's come back.'

Mackenzie didn't hesitate. The United States military had significant resources based in the Marshall Islands, and he knew that he'd be able to direct search teams onto Ernie Walker.

He was on the phone to Pacific Command within minutes.

***

XV

The sound of passing vehicles and a sense of being too hot woke Ernie Walker from a deep sleep. He opened his eyes and for a few moments he did not know where he was, his brain struggling to recall the events of the past few days. Suddenly he realised that he must be late for duty and he rolled to one side and out of bed, rather than banging his head on his shipmate's bunk above.

All at once he realised that he wasn't in his bunk, and his memories reconnected themselves: the blast, the fishing trawler, the years that had somehow vanished, and his arrival on Majuro. Ernie reached up and massaged his head, dehydration now a problem as he recalled he had not eaten nor drank anything since leaving the hospital the previous night.

Ernie got out of bed and walked to the shutters, opened them onto a stunning sunset glittering across the bay. He squinted, threw up his hands to shield his face and instantly remembered the Castle Bravo blast, the searing light, the officer whose eyes had been burned to a crisp, then the terrible heat and noise.

The Navy!

Ernie stepped back from the shutters, searched the beach for any sign of soldiers, but there was nothing to see. The tourists were all back in their hotels, presumably preparing to go out for the evening, and the beach was almost deserted. Ernie remembered Papa D, and his consternation at entrusting his safety to a man he'd never met. Ernie looked over the window ledge and saw that the hotel backed onto the beach, the ground maybe twelve feet below.

He clambered out of the window and lowered himself down until he was dangling by his fingers, and then Ernie pushed away and dropped down. He landed on the beach and let himself fall into a crouch to absorb the shock of the fall. He felt no pain, but his old joints creaked it seemed with the impact, his body far less able than the one he was used to.

He waited for a moment, looked left and right, and then as casually as he could he set off down the beach, away from the airport, heading back toward the town. Despite his hunger and thirst he was thinking more clearly now and he knew that he had to get home, that he could not survive alone here. Things seemed so different, so much better and yet so much worse at the same time.

The scent of cooked food wafted tantalisingly across the beach as Ernie made his way north up the island, and he drifted closer to the road. There, he could see rows of restaurants serving food and cold drinks. Ernie had never been homeless before, and he suddenly realized how being so must have felt for people, even here in a tropical paradise: hunger and thirst felt just as bad no matter where one was living.

Ernie hurried up onto the main road and skirted the restaurants, then cut in down a side alley and around to the backs of the buildings. There, he could smell the scents of food more clearly, and in the fading evening light the lengthening shadows gave him greater cover. Ernie crept along behind the buildings, saw kitchens with doors open to let out the heat, heard foreign voices gabbling as cooks hurried to prepare meals for hotels and eateries.

Ernie spotted one kitchen with a lone cook hurrying this way and that within, filling plates and then rushing away through double doors to serve the tables beyond. He waited until the cook rushed out with another order, then Ernie dashed into the kitchen. There were plates everywhere, food cooking on grills, wonderful looking coolers with glass doors, all filled with bottles of soda.

Ernie grabbed a plate, yanked a steak off the grill and shovelled a handful of fries onto his plate. He opened a cooler and grabbed two cans of Coca Cola, the only brand that he recognized, and then he hurried out of the kitchen and over a low bluff to the where palms swayed over a secluded patch of sand.

Ernie shovelled down mouthfuls of fries and steak as though they were the last ones on the planet, chewing as he turned his attention to the cans. He pulled the unfamiliar ring-pulls and saw the top peel open, revealing the drink inside. Ernie guzzled it down, finally sated after so many long hours.

He finished his meal and then turned his attention to where he was going to go next. He knew that he wouldn't survive for long like this, and stealing from people made him feel real bad. What he had noticed was call boxes around the place, but he had no money on him and he wasn't sure where to call. About the only thing that he could think to do was to try to find a working passage home to Norfolk.

There was a marina and some docks on the island, and he already knew from the trawler that had picked him up that he might be able to earn a passage east to

America. All he needed were a few more clothes and he could head out, and he was certain that he could find those along the way. He ate the rest of his food, watching as another airplane stencilled with U.S. military markings sailed overhead and touched down at the airport to the west.

His belly finally full, Ernie got up and hurried away from the seafront. The night was upon him now, but he wasn't concerned. Ernie knew from experience that seamen would normally congregate in bars when they weren't on duty, and many crews got jobs working ships in the merchant navy just by hanging around in the right places. Ernie figured that such a fundamental truth probably hadn't changed all that much over the last fifty years, so he headed north up the atoll in search of the nearest place where he might be able to pick up some kind of working passage home to Virginia.

*

'Where are we?'

Mackenzie asked the question as soon as his plane landed and he stepped onto the asphalt of Amata Kabua International Airport, the night air fresh and cool after the airplane's stuffy interior. He was exhausted, despite trying to snatch some sleep on the flight, and he kept himself alert and upright by force of will, years of experience sleep deprivation as a soldier maintaining his focus.

The sergeant who met him at the foot of the step way replied with military efficiency.

'We have teams sweeping all sides of the atoll, working in fours and covering every single abode and building. It's going to take time but there aren't many places that he can hide on an island this small.'

'What about routes off the island, the docks and the airport. Is it possible he's already slipped away?'

'No likely sir, not in the time that's been available to him,' came the reply. 'However, the shipping here is largely unregulated and there's the chance that he could island-hop his way out of the Pacific.'

Mackenzie smiled ruefully. 'So, he could be anywhere and we don't have a fix on him yet?'

'That's correct sir.'

'And the trawler that found him, Atoll Angel?'

'It left the islands before we arrived,' the sergeant replied. 'As soon as it puts ashore or comes within range of a battle group, she'll be boarded and her crew questioned. If somehow Mr Walker is still aboard, we'll find him then.'

Satisfied, Mackenzie dismissed the sergeant and made his way to a small pre-fab hut that had been built on one side of the runway, alongside the small terminal and guarded by a pair of armed soldiers. They saluted the general as he passed by and walked into the hut to find a desk, chair and some papers arranged for him. His aide-de-camp, Saunders, a corporal, saluted and reported with brisk efficiency.

'Updates as requested sir, accommodation likewise. Will you be eating at the hotel or here, sir?'

'Here is fine,' Mackenzie replied, barely looking up. 'At ease, Saunders. Get some rest, things are going to get busy once we track this guy down.'

'Yes sir, thank you sir!'

Saunders saluted again, spun on one heel and marched off into the night. Mackenzie sat down behind the desk and reviewed what little information they had been able to collate on Ernest Walker. There wasn't much beyond what the sergeant had told him: Walker was here, had been seen, and those sightings had been made *after* the trawler that found him had departed. A nurse had treated him briefly at a medical station near the dock, recording that he seemed to be "mentally disturbed" and highly confused, which she had put down to an "undisclosed period of exposure at sea". The nurse had made no mention of the sailor's antiquated uniform, and Mackenzie figured that if Walker had said anything about what had happened to him, that would have been likewise recorded as a resulting factor from his mental disposition at the time.

There was nothing that Mackenzie's team could not cover up here; a sailor found after days or weeks at sea, dehydrated, starving, blabbering about time. Nobody would raise an eye to the story, and life would move on as though nothing had happened.

Locating Walker would prove more difficult, and Mackenzie's greatest confusion was over why Walker had not handed himself in already or sought the Navy's help.

Mackenzie noted that the nurse had recorded signs of "scorching or burning" on Walker's uniform and on patches of skin, consistent with what Mackenzie knew of what had happened aboard the *USS Bairoko*. He wondered what he would have done in the same position, and felt certain that he would have approached the nearest law enforcement officer or Navy station to ask for help: as wild as his story would have been, he would have soon been identified and his story proven true, and thus would find himself at the very least looked after and protected.

Mackenzie halted his train of thought. He was thinking like a general in the twenty first century, not a seaman in the 1950s. Walker did not have high ranking, nor the benefit of fifty years of exposure to advanced science, science fiction, computers, social advances and other factors that made anybody in the modern world just a little more capable of handling something as incredible as a leap in time. Walker had none of those things, and what had happened to him would have been both terrifying and confusing. He might have considered himself insane, and there was no telling how long he had actually been at sea before being found by the crew of the trawler. Walker might also have considered what happened to *USS Bairoko* to have been an attack of some kind, perhaps by his own people.

He might think that we're the enemy.

Mackenzie glanced outside the hut to where two large military aircraft were parked, one of which he'd flown in on only minutes ago. If Walker was still on the island, he could not have failed to see the airplanes land.

Mackenzie picked up a phone and dialled into his staff's communication lines. Moments later, a lieutenant answered.

'Yes sir?'

'Pull all uniformed men back into the perimeter of the airfield and prepare all troops for departure. Leave only our undercover assets in place.'

'We're leaving already? Have we found the target?'

'No,' Mackenzie replied. 'If we can't locate him here, I want him to make his way home. We'll be ready for him when he arrives. I want agents staking out any location that Ernie Walker might visit: homes, family, friends, you name it. He'll head for somewhere familiar.'

***

XVI

University of Virginia,

Charlottesville, Virginia

Doctor Richard Boltman was a diminutive man who worked at the University on quantum loop theory, which Ethan figured was something that he didn't need to know about right now. Boltman shook their hands when they arrived in his office, which was uncluttered but for rows of books on shelves, a small desk and two chairs that he'd set out for them on the opposite side of his desk.

Ethan sat down and Boltman looked at them both with some interest.

'Rhys Garrett sponsors much of our work here so I'm happy to help, but you don't look like the kind of people who would be interested in the study of time,' he said after a moment's pause.

'We're not, usually,' Ethan admitted. 'We're working on a missing persons case that has some unusual qualities, and wanted to know whether you could shed some light on them?'

'I'll do my best,' Boltman promised. 'What's the case?'

Lopez spoke, and over a few minutes she outlined the Castle Bravo test of 1954 and the vanishing, and alleged reappearance, of Ernie Walker. After she had finished, Boltman stared at them both for several long seconds, and Ethan wondered if the doctor was about to order them out of his office for wasting valuable time.

Instead, Boltman leaned forward, his hands clasped before him.

'Fascinating,' he said finally. 'And have you spoken to anybody yet about how this could have happened?'

'Doctor William Goldberg in California,' Lopez replied, 'but a lot of what we're hearing is pretty confusing, and we don't have much evidence to support the likelihood of someone being somehow transported a few decades into the future.'

Boltman raised his eyebrows and shrugged.

'It would seem impossible, but then most people don't really understand the nature of time.'

Ethan allowed a faint smile to curl from the corner of his mouth. 'You don't think that this is a waste of time?'

'Not at all!' Boltman insisted. 'Time slips happen to people every day, but this case is extremely interesting in its longevity.'

'What now?' Lopez asked. 'Time slips?'

'Yes, time slips,' Boltman replied, as though everybody knew about them. 'You know, when people accidentally find themselves a few years back in time.'

Ethan and Lopez looked at each other. Boltman chuckled.

'Okay, maybe a lot of people haven't heard of time slips, but it's surprisingly common and there are hundreds of documented accounts of people experiencing extraordinary glimpses of the past all around them.'

'Okay,' Lopez said slowly. 'Fire a few off and we'll see if they match anything that Ernie Walker supposedly experienced.'

'Well, none of them are quite that long-lived,' Boltman said, 'but they're no less fascinating. The best documented cases that I have are those that occurred in a place called Bold Street in Liverpool, England. The area seems to have an unusually high concentration of time slips, with multiple reports over the past half a century or so.'

'Since about the same time as America and Russia's nuclear tests,' Lopez noted.

'Yes, now that you mention it, although they're not the only instances,' Boltman said. 'The first concerned a young thief who had robbed a shop in Bold Street and was fleeing a police officer. The youth turned into an alleyway just ahead of the officer, but when the officer reached the alley the youth had vanished.'

'Maybe he went over a wall?' Ethan offered.

'The officer said at the time that it was impossible for him to have done so, as the alley was between two tall buildings and far too long for the youth to have reached the far end. Besides, things got stranger when the youth handed himself in the next day. Turns out that he was terrified not of being caught, but of what had happened when he'd reached the alley. He'd decided to give himself up right there and then, but when he stopped and turned, the officer did not appear in the alley behind him. The youth walked out and saw cars from the 1950s driving around, people wearing old clothes, you name it. The shops were different and there were less people around. The boy walked up the street and suddenly found himself back in "normal" time, but when he looked over his shoulder, he could still see the past playing out behind him. The experience so unnerved the youth that he handed himself in to the police the next day so that his experience could go onto a public record. He claimed that his vision of the past was as real as now, but it seemed a little hazier, like the sun was partially obscured, and he felt a sense of heaviness or depression while he was there, as though something was profoundly wrong that he could not put his finger on.'

Ethan leaned forward, recalling his and Nicola's own symptoms in the wake of their lost-time experience.

'What about the other examples?'

'A Merseyside policeman in the summer of 1996 found himself in what he described at the time as a strange "oasis of quietness" on Bold Street. He noticed that the cars around him appeared to be from the 1950s, and he was almost hit by one with *"Caplan's"* written down the side, as he suddenly realized that he was unexpectedly standing not on the sidewalk but in the middle of the road. The shops around him had changed, such as one modern book store named *"Dillons"* suddenly appearing to be a woman's clothes shop called *"Cripps"*. He then noticed a young woman in modern clothes entering the clothes shop and followed her, but as they entered the shop it suddenly became a bookshop again. The girl was as confused as he was, both of them appearing to have entered the time slip at the same moment. They spoke to each other, confirming what they had experienced.'

Boltman folded his hands in his lap before him as he spoke.

'Later research revealed that *Cripps* and *Caplan's* were both based in Liverpool during the 1950s, and both had long gone out of business. The point is that these are two examples of ordinary people encountering time slips that appear to be spontaneous, and for which they were completely unprepared.'

'Sure,' Ethan agreed, 'and they're also based on testimony that can't be checked. Do we have anything more solid, something that's been verified?'

'Sure, we do,' Boltman replied. 'In 1935, a British Royal Air Force pilot, Air Marshall Sir Victor Goddard, was flying to Edinburgh in a Hawker Hart biplane from his home base in Andover, England. He chose to overfly Drem airfield on the way up, and saw it as it was, abandoned and used as farmland. However, on the return flight some days later he encountered a strange storm in which he described seeing brown or yellow clouds, and within which he struggled to maintain control of his aircraft. As he descended, he reported that he came out of the clouds overhead Drem and into sudden, bright sunshine. This time, there were new hangars, bright yellow monoplanes that he didn't recognise, and the mechanics were dressed in blue overalls when they should have been brown. Goddard continued his flight home and reported the event to his fellow officers. Nobody believed him, until 1939, when RAF training aircraft were repainted yellow, mechanics switched to blue overalls, a new monoplane called the Magister entered RAF service and Drem airfield was refurbished.'

Lopez leaned back in her seat.

'It's better, but it's still not something that can be quantified or checked.'

'Miami pilot Bruce Gernon's account from 1970 was verified,' Boltman replied. 'Flying a Beech Bonanza light aircraft from Andros Island to Miami Beach, his airplane encountered anomalous atmospheric phenomena very similar to that reported by Air Marshall Goddard. The difference here was that Gernon was in contact with air traffic control in Miami for much of his journey. They passed through the cloud, and once clear reported their position, however what Gernon described as a dense "electronic fog" was messing with the instruments and he couldn't confirm his position visually. ATC came back and identified him over Miami beach. When they checked the logs, they'd flown two hundred fifty nautical miles in forty-seven minutes, a distance far greater than they could possibly have achieved in that aircraft type. Their watches were also out of synchrony with clocks on the ground. But even that is nothing compared to the event that got me interested in the study of what time actually is.'

Boltman gestured to an image on the wall of what looked like the world's most complex DVD player, a silvery box with multiple digital displays filled with glowing red digits.

'What is it?' Lopez asked.

'That is a Caesium Time Generator, accurate to a tenth of a millionth of one second per year, on Kwajalein Island in the Pacific Ocean, north of the Marshall Islands. It's a United States military base, and it's the location of the only officially recorded time slip in human history.'

***

XVII

'An atomic clock registered a time slip?' Ethan asked, guessing the gist of where Boltman was headed.

'It did,' Boltman confirmed. 'As abhorrent as it is for me to admit it, given that I've spent my life studying physics, the most accurate clock in the world confirmed something that is both alien to our understanding and yet, in the world of general relativity, fundamental: time does not flow along a linear path, but is both fluid and flexible.'

Boltman gestured again to the image.

'The clock is a Master Timing Center operating around three Hewlett Packard timers of Caesium Beam standards. Their primary purpose is the millisecond accurate timing of enemy nuclear ICBM launches, giving the USA the chance to intercept and destroy the incoming missiles with extreme accuracy. Its time is checked and correlated against orbiting satellites and the U.S. National Observatory in Washington DC. It's *that* accurate. But between November 1973 and October 1974, that clock lost synchrony by three tenths of a microsecond, then returned to normal, no less than three times. While that may not sound very much, to a clock of that accuracy it's like you waking up tomorrow and finding a hundred years have gone by – it's huge.'

'How could that have happened then?' Ethan asked. 'Haven't they figured out what caused the slip?'

'Well, that's the interesting part,' Boltman explained. 'Since the event, what was already a highly classified base has become part of the military's Black Budget. Literally nothing gets in or out of that atoll without them knowing about it. The base has grown in size and, being out there in the remote Pacific, it's not an easy place to get to.'

'And not all that far from where the nuclear tests of the 1950s took place,' Lopez noted again. 'I'm seeing a pattern here.'

'Yeah,' Ethan agreed, 'that's where Ernie Walker had his experience. I'm starting to see why the government covered up the event.'

'I've heard rumours,' Boltman said. 'Something about some of the crew being adversely affected by the blast, some hints of minor time dilation around the periphery of the site, but nothing concrete.'

Ethan nodded.

'Same as us, but the way we see it there's no smoke without fire and there was something that happened back then that in some ways matches what happened to us. Now you say that even atomic clocks have been affected by such things, it at least confirms that we're not losing our minds.'

'Indeed,' Boltman agreed. 'It has been pointed out in the past that time slips are not considered to be paranormal events by scientists, although they would not dare to go on the record for saying such things. Careers have been lost by those willing to speak out on such matters. Time slips are, by their nature and by our understanding of the fluidity of time, considered to be a natural phenomenon, something that may occur far more often than we think.'

'How so?' Lopez asked.

'Well,' Boltman said, 'let's assume for one moment that time slips do occur and that the events I've outlined are not hallucinations or mistakes, that people really did witness other moments in time. The events we know about tend to be those that are easily identified: people seeing cars from fifty years ago, or old shops, or other archaic forms of transport or dress that make the slip really easy to spot. But what's to say that yesterday you were walking down the street and inadvertently walked into a time slip from a week ago? Would you even have noticed?'

Ethan smiled at the devious nature of the physicist's question. He had never even considered the possibility that time slips could be all around them, and that people just never even noticed.

'Take the situation of looking at distant hills,' Boltman suggested. 'They're five miles away, and you can see a crowd of people on the hills. Although it's only five miles, you're technically looking back in time, because there is a measurable distance between you and the crowd, and it takes light a measurable time to reach you from them. You're looking into the past, and so are they. In fact, the further you can see at any point in space, the further back in time you're looking. The moon is seen as it was just over a second ago in the past, the sun about eight minutes, the planets hours and even our nearest star some four and a half years in the past, each long enough that it's not actually occupying the spot we're looking at, where we perceive it to be. Look at Saturn, and you're actually seeing it where it was a few hours previously.'

The mind-bending truth was both understandable and tough for Ethan to get his head around.

'So even you're in the past, to me,' Ethan said.

'Yes, by an amount so small that it doesn't affect us, but none the less I occupy a different time and thus space to you. What seems to happen in some forms of thermonuclear event is that the difference increases, and it seems to have something to do with electromagnetic energy. I've spent the past two decades researching this, even going so far as to step outside of classical physics and into theoretical physics to try to see if relativity and other well-proven theories can help me understand what might be going on. Trouble is, the math is so complex it's taken me years.'

Boltman glanced at a row of books on a shelf nearby, all of them on advanced physics and other mathematical issues that Ethan considered way above his pay grade, not to mention his head.

'Almost every encounter we've heard about involves some form of energy like you describe,' Ethan said. 'And that same energy seems to manifest itself during UFO sightings and even sightings of ghosts and other things that are thought of as paranormal. Is there any chance that energy in some form is responsible for all three?'

'Absolutely,' Boltman said, 'it's a conclusion that I reached many years ago, although proving it mathematically or even through experiment is proving far beyond my means. I do have one rather interesting example of the idea in practice however, and it's a classic time-slip experience that occurred in 1901, when two Englishwomen of high standing visited the Palace of Versailles in France. One was a Doctor Eleanour Frances Jourdain, and the other an Annie Moberly who was a Principal of St. Hugh's College in Oxford. While there, they briefly got lost in the grounds and near the Grand Trianon witnessed numerous people and events believed to have occurred in the late 1780s, before returning to the palace. Although the events have been greatly embellished since in the retelling, there are two very important points to note: firstly, that both women experienced a sense of foreboding, a darkening of the atmosphere, a "flattening" – as they described it – of reality and a sense of depression or lethargy.'

'Which matches some of the other experiences,' Ethan noted. 'And the other point?'

'Unrelated documents record on the same day of the women's experience electrical storms over Europe of an unusually high intensity, and an atmosphere likewise laden with electrical energy.'

Lopez glanced at Ethan. 'So, that ties in with all the others too. High levels of electromagnetic energy, storms reported of one kind or another, or in the Castle Bravo tests a nuclear detonation.'

'There's one other final point of note,' Boltman added. 'The unusually high number of time-slip events in Liverpool's Bold Street also coincides with the same theory. All of Bold Street's time slips seem to revert people back to the 1950s or 1960s. What's interesting is that beneath that area of the city are three concentric circles of high-voltage rails, centred roughly under Bold Street. They were only electrified in the 1920s, and nobody has ever reported a time slip in the area that precedes that date.'

Ethan thought about that for a moment. Man-made time slips, inadvertently caused perhaps by the rail system in Liverpool's subways, might explain both the high incidences of time slips and present a limit on how far back a person could be taken. Lopez got to the punch before he did.

'Storms could potentially take people back as far in time as storms have existed,' she said.

'That's what I believe is happening,' Boltman replied, delighted at her insight, 'although as I said I cannot prove it, but human nature is littered with examples of how storms seem to affect things in ways that we used to call *supernatural*. How many movies or books have you read that set a spooky tone with pouring rain, thunder and lighting in the dead of night? Is that because such storms are inherently frightening, or because mankind has become used to seeing supposedly supernatural phenomena during such storms?'

Ethan wasn't sure which way that would be, but he knew already that there was enough to tell him that what had happened to them had happened to others, and that there was a mechanism in place that might just explain how.

'Storms,' he said finally, recalling the night when he and Lopez had nearly died. 'There were storms that night, electrical storms out over Nevada.'

Lopez nodded. 'We figure out how far Mackenzie has got, we might be able to figure out where they're going next. I figure that sooner or later, that's going to be Kwajalein Island.'

***

XVIII

Jae Hyuk-Pak stepped off the flight from Pyonyang to Manila and paused on the jetway for a moment to smell the air. It was laden with the scents of aviation fuel, lubricants and metal, the odor of the decadence of the west, not like the clear air of his homeland. He tried not to let the thought into his head that North Korea's clean air was mostly due to the fact that nobody could afford motor vehicles. Instead, he headed toward the airport terminal.

Unlike North Korea's main airport, Manila was a bustling hive of activity, filled with thousands of people rushing this way and that. Jae negotiated the crowd alone, although he knew that his team were with him, shadowing his every move as he made his way toward passport and security control.

Travelling outside of North Korea was problematic because security control would always take special notice of North Korean travellers, and treat them with suspicion. Jae was ostensibly a businessman from Pyongyang looking to meet other business leaders in Manila for new trade deals to help circumvent American sanctions. The cover was good and Jae was used to travelling overseas, but this time it was different. He would have liked to have travelled direct to Hawaii and from there to the American mainland, but doing so would have exposed him to detailed searches and security checks that might have spooked the Americans and exposed his true identity. Instead, he would overnight in Manila before flying east across the Pacific to San Diego under a new identity, one that he had used before to successfully enter the United States.

Manila's security teams gave him some special attention, but a combination of good false paperwork and Jae's well-practiced always-smiling act saw him through the checks. Minutes later he was outside the airport and straight into a car that was waiting for him, already arranged back in Pyongyang.

The driver nodded in his mirror to Jae but otherwise said nothing. Jae knew that the regime of Kim Jong-Un had agents operating in countries around the world, although their strongest presence was in the Far East and the Malay where they could of course blend in the easiest. Those who travelled further afield were the children of the Dear Leader's *honey-trap* scheme, who were trained from birth to serve the regime in countries far from home. Attractive young North Korean girls were plucked from schools and universities and trained to become spies, operating as tour guides and translators to foreign businessmen and political figures. They would seduce their charges, and were then forced to carry any pregnancies through on behalf of their Dear Leader. The program had two main benefits: the children would be brought up to revere North Korea, and the foreign dignitaries would be contacted and informed of the child, and of their fate should the dignitary not ensure cooperation with the Dear Leader. The information and assistance gained by the scheme, from foreign politicians terrified of their illegitimate children being revealed to the world, or perhaps cast into the North Korean *gulags* for life, had been elementary in ensuring the survival of North Korea's leadership through hard times. They were also effective in ensuring the deaths of those not loyal to their Dear Leader, such as his own brother, who was murdered by two North Korean *honey-trap* agents in 2017. The memory of that event reminded Jae that nobody beneath the rule of Kim Jong-Un was safe, not even members of his own family.

The car drove Jae to a hotel in the city, where he walked into the foyer and was directed by the staff to a room on the eighth floor. Jae knocked on the door, which opened and revealed a North Korean agent who ushered Jae inside and closed the door behind him.

The room was non-descript in every way, but for the other three agents awaiting him. There was no welcome, no sense of friendship, only duty. Jae was here to learn of his next steps, and the agents were here to pass that information on.

'You will overnight here in Manila,' the oldest of the four men informed him without preamble. 'Then, you will fly to the San Diego in the United States. From there, you will connect a flight to Norfolk, Virginia.'

Jae raised an eyebrow. He knew better than to question the new orders, to ask for more information. His orders came down from their Dear Leader, and to ask questions would be to question the Dear Leader's judgement or intelligence, something which was done only on pain of death. None the less, he was curious to know why he was being sent to Virginia when he was certain the subject of their mission was somewhere in the Pacific.

'The mission has changed,' the man said by way of an explanation. 'Our sources in Langley have detected unusual orders for troop movements that have deployed simultaneously to opposite ends of the globe, and our Dear Leader believes that these two missions are in some way connected.'

On one wall of the room, a large map of the world had been tacked. The older agent now used a thin cane to point to areas of interest on the map, tagged with colored markers.

'The initial emissions of interest occurred here, in the South Pacific, however we have detected a second more recent emission here, in Nevada. Within a few hours of this emission, officers whom we know to be working for the Great Satan's black projects dispatched an aircraft from Nellis Air Force Base in Nevada to Majuro, in the Marshall Islands.'

Jae's interest was now piqued. He knew from his work that Majuro was not far south of Bikini Atoll, one of the Great Satan's nuclear test zones in the 1950s and the epicentre of the beginning of the search for the nature of time. A second emission could mean…

'Something happened right there and they're checking it out,' Jae said, momentarily forgetting himself.

Jae's error did not result in admonishment, however. The agents knew the stakes, and they could also see the immediate enthusiasm for the chase in Jae's eyes. The older man nodded.

'We can not be sure what, but we can be sure that it was important enough for their personnel to drop everything and fly half way across the Pacific. If it's important to them, it's important to us and the Dear Leader.'

Jae, sensing a moment of humanity in his handler, dared a question.

'What is the connection with Virginia?'

Now, the older man smiled and reached down to a briefcase that was laying open on the bed. From within he produced a photograph, one that was new but depicted a much older image, a copy of some original shot. The old man handed it to Jae as he spoke.

'This is the *USS Bairoko,* an aircraft carrier stationed near the Marshall Islands in 1954. It is believed that the carrier was struck directly by a bolt from the Castle Bravo detonation, and that the impact caused a time dilation sufficient to propel at least some of its crew elsewhere in time. We think that that time is now.'

Jae felt his heart race as he looked at the image. Instantly, his mind was working overtime.

'We could trace the crew,' he said, 'and if any of them were not seen after the Castle Bravo voyage….'

'Then they might be a person of interest to us,' the old man smiled. 'We have been working while you were travelling here, and have already obtained a crew manifest. The wonders of the western Internet have allowed us to identify and locate over ninety per cent of the ship's crew and rule them out of the events. However, there is one man who embarked with the ship's company, but was allegedly lost at sea during the event. His name was Ernest Walker.'

The old man had some trouble pronouncing the name. Jae had another image passed to him, this time one of four American seamen posing in front of the immense guns of one of their battleships. The uniforms of the men were of a vintage form, and the image itself was yellow with age. The third man along was ringed with red pen, smiling at the camera, his arms around his fellow sailors, the sun shining.

'The Great Leader believes that this man will try to travel either into the arms of his Navy, or the arms of his family. With the US Navy already hunting for him, and given what little we know of what happened during Castle Bravo, it's likely that he will seek home.'

Jae nodded, relieved that for once the Great Leader's judgement did indeed appear to be sound. This man, Walker, suddenly stranded in a place fifty years in the future, would be afraid, desperately seeking some sense of familiarity. If he knew that he was indeed in the future, and perhaps trapped, he might seek home. Jae's only fear was that the man might be a patriot and would hurry to the nearest naval vessel and beg for assistance, but he could not voice that concern. He was here to obey orders.

'The Americans are weak, emotionally unstable,' the old man went on, 'they shout with belligerence when they feel confident, but collapse in tears at the slightest whimsy or offence. Ernest Walker will not seek to solve his crisis, but will seek comfort and the solace of home. You will be there to meet him, General, and then you will bring him to us. There will be a plane waiting, details will be sent to you once you arrive in Virginia. Your team will consist of the same three men with you now, two will fly out ahead, one will follow you.'

Jae nodded. He knew that the men were not just there to assist him. They were there to further ensure that he was not tempted to defect to the west as so many others had done in the past.

'Before you leave,' the old man added, 'you will visit the docks and locate this vessel.'

Jae was handed an image of an old trawler moored alongside a battered sea wall.

'The ship was present at the time of the recent event near Majuro,' the old man explained. 'Its crew may know something of what happened. Radio transmissions identify the vessel as being in the immediate vicinity of the event, and it left the area for Majuro before then sailing east for Manila. Ensure that the crew are…, cooperative.'

'They will be,' Jae replied.

'For the glory of the People's Democratic Front!' the old man snapped.

Jae returned the salute, and then the four men briskly left the room and closed the door behind them, leaving Jae to focus on researching everything that they had discovered about Ernest Walker.

***

XIX

Bangkalusi, Manila

Jae watched as he and three other agents were driven by a taxi north out of the city to the huge fish ports on the Philippine's west coast. Out here, it was as clear as ever, even at night, how shallow and vapid the Capitalist Dream truly was. Barely a mile north of Manila's glossy city center, beneath the harsh glare of aged and intermittently working street lights, the reality of life in the west was laid bare.

The roads were paved but lined with debris, shattered masonry and cranes presumably being used to carry out repairs. In the darkness alongside the freeway were vast shanty towns of corrugated iron, mud and fetid water where the poor and the sick scurried this way and that. The stench of raw sewage competed with the salty air of the Indian Ocean, swirling in a heady mix with that of cooked food from open barbeques and street vendors hawking their wares. Were it not for the electric lighting and the motor vehicles, he could have been travelling through Victorian times and not noticed a difference.

The docks were immense, a jumble of massive cargo vessels around which were anchored or moored hundreds of smaller vessels, right down to tiny wooden craft operated by subsistence fishermen who still plied the waters for a daily catch for their families. Jae breathed calmly and deeply, preparing himself for their work. The docks of any major city were an epicentre for crime, and he did not expect this to be an easy job. Men of the sea were invariably as tough as the environment in which they made their living, and would not comply quietly when Jae and his men arrived on their ship.

The taxi dropped them off on a slip road that led down into the docks and the markets that lined it. The stench of raw, rotting fish, stale water and sewage was overpowering, enough so that Jae's eyes watered as he forced himself to get used to the environment. This was where Manila's "bat people" lived, in shanties built beneath bridges where the ceilings of their homes were the undersides of the highways above.

The Novatas docks were fronted with a large entrance, around which were hundreds of floating houses, shacks built on brackish water where children scavenged for scrap metal in the dangerous, dark water. The squalor was almost unbelievable, and for a moment Jae saw in his mind's eye the poor and the suffering of his own people in the rural north of his homeland: no better, but no worse either. At least there they lived without the pollution, danger and disease that he saw here in this vast port.

Jae walked with his men along a massive jetty, lined with huge cargo ships and flocks of smaller fishing boats, until Jae spotted the blue-hulled trawler they were looking for. The ship was small, maybe sixty feet in length, and the kind of vessel that would hold a crew of perhaps three or four. She had lights in her rigging and her cages were neatly stowed, the ship old and battered but kept in running order, a sign of a competent crew.

Jae's men paused near the ship's bulwarks as Jae checked up and down the jetty. There were few people about here at this time of night, and the ones that were here would know better than to involve themselves in other people's business: this was a land of survival.

Jae reached beneath his jacket and pulled out a Makarov pistol, his men mirroring his actions. Jae pointed two men to the bows, the other to the stern, and then he reached up and hauled himself aboard the ship.

He could hear the sound of a television playing somewhere inside the vessel, and the sound of laughter accompanying it as he crept into the cabin and saw within a deck panel that led down into the ship via narrow metal steps.

He waited patiently as his men cleared the decks above, one by one returning to join him on the bridge. Satisfied that the upper decks were clear, Jae took a breath and then silently but swiftly descended into the vessel. The light was bright as he saw before him a narrow corridor lined with berths, smelled the scent of cooked food and saw ahead an open doorway into a large cabin. He hurried toward the sound of laughter and noise, and burst out into the cabin where four men were lounging around a table playing cards and drinking alcohol.

The men were all big and burly, thick forearms laced with old tattoos. Each man shot to his feet with remarkable speed as Jae rushed with his men into the cabin, but they were not quick enough to reach for their weapons as four pistols were aimed at their heads.

Jae spoke swiftly, hoping to defuse the situation and gain the men's trust as they were no good to him dead.

'We are not here for you,' he said. 'We are here to ask you some questions.'

There was a moment's silence as the men looked down at the intruders, and then one of them pushed his way out to confront them. He stank of American beer and strong cigarettes.

'You get your guns out of our faces, and we might think about not throwing you over the side.'

Jae kept his cool. He needed answers, not a massacre.

'Just some simple questions, and we will be gone.'

The big man peered down at Jae, leaned forwards on unsteady legs. 'We don't take orders from little shi…'

Jae's cool left him. He snapped his head forward and butted the man directly on the end of his nose, then stamped a boot down the inside of his knee. The big man toppled to his knees on the deck and as Jae pushed the pistol against his scalp.

'Let me try one more time,' he snapped. 'Answer our questions, or I'll put bullets into your brains one by one and dispose of your disgusting remains into the water, where nobody will notice or care.'

The man kneeling before him wiped blood from his beard, looked up at Jae, and suddenly burst out laughing, a great belly laugh that seemed to shake the entire boat.

'Now that's more like it!' he boomed.

Jae looked down at him, confused, saw the other sailors smirking at him, and wondered briefly whether all Americans were as suicidally inclined as these.

The kneeling man completely ignored the pistol and stood up. Jae's men pushed closer, but the sailor wafted them drunkenly aside with a sweep of his big arm.

'You should know that we don't care whether we live or die,' the big man growled, 'and the captain ain't here right now, so just as long as what's said down here, stays down here, you can ask us anythin' you want. Just make it fast, we got a lot of drinkin' to get through.'

The big man clapped Jae's shoulder, apparently genuinely unconcerned about the pistol still pressed to his head. Jae blinked as the big man sat down and picked up his cards as though nothing had happened.

'Now, what wash it that you fine *shennelmen* wanted to know?'

Jae lowered his pistol.

'Majuro island,' he said, 'you collected a passenger there, a man named Walker.'

The four men looked at each other and the atmosphere changed instantly.

'Oh, that,' the ringleader said. 'We're not supposed to talk about that.'

Jae smiled. 'Things have changed now. How did he come to be aboard your ship?'

The big man sighed, stroked his thick beard as he considered his reply.

'We picked him up out of the water,' he said finally. 'Looked like he was a survivor of some kind of accident, there was some debris around him, things like that. He was a mess, real screwed up, confused by everything.'

'What was he wearing?'

The answer almost knocked Jae off his feet.

'Navy uniform, an odd one though. Looked like something out of one of the old black and white movies, you know?'

Jae nodded slowly. 'Yes, I know. Did he have a name?'

'Walker, wasn't it?' the man asked his shipmates, and got a couple of nods in reply.

'Where is Walker now?'

The sailor shrugged his big shoulders.

'Who the hell knows? We thought he'd want to be handed in to the Navy or something, so we get him off the ship in Majuro. Captain took him to the hospital, and we heard later that he took off after being treated. That's the last we heard of him.'

'He ran?'

'Guess he didn't want to be around the Navy,' the sailor replied. 'Now, how about you boys join us for a round of Poker and a…'

Jae raised the Makarov and fired once. The bullet flicked the sailor's head back and sent most of what passed for his brains over the back wall of the cabin. Three more shots rang out as Jae's men fired a split-second after he had, killing the other three sailors outright.

Jae turned, and with his men hurried out of the ship's bowels and onto the decks, the air actually a little fresher outside the vessel despite the trash floating on the water all around them. He led them off the ship and they walked without hurrying back toward the dock entrance, Jae thinking fast.

The Great Leader had been correct: Ernest Walker had fled the Navy and was by now almost certainly heading for home. With only a few days having passed by since the event in the Pacific, he might only have just reached America, assuming that he had managed to find passage aboard an airplane. If, as seemed more likely, he had been forced to find passage aboard a ship, he would not arrive for a week or more.

'He's heading for home,' Jae confirmed to his men out loud. 'We need to be there when he arrives. We leave in the morning.'

***

XX

Hampton Roads,

Norfolk, Virginia

Ernie Walker stood on the prow of the cargo vessel *Independence* and closed his eyes, the familiar scent of home filling his mind with memories of how he'd left his wife and children a year – no, over fifty years, before.

The sun had not long risen and the air was brisk and cold, green water crashing around the ship's bow as she eased into the roads and turned slowly to port, passing Norfolk Naval Station as she did so. Ernie would have ducked inside to hide himself, but he could not bring himself to move as he saw the impossibly immense hull of an aircraft carrier twice the size of any he'd seen loom over the ship. She was utterly gargantuan, and he could see a sleek fighter jet of a type he did not recognize parked on her deck, the wings folded up to save space. The *USS Bairoko* had been a minnow in comparison to this leviathan of a ship. As they sailed past, he spotted the carrier's name proudly emblazoned upon her stern: *Nimitz*. Ernie smiled; the old fleet admiral would have been proud to have seen his name upon such a magnificent ship.

The naval station passed by and there was no scrambling of soldiers or fighter planes to intercept him, no port authority vessels rushing out to them.

'Ernie, you wanna gimme a hand buddy?'

Ernie turned to where Sam "Sweats" Chandler was hauling cargo deck doors open and securing them, ready for the cranes of Norfolk's terminals to unload the huge shipping containers within, and began locking the hatches open.

Ernie had been correct in his assumption that he could find a working passage off Majuro and into the eastern Pacific. He'd joined a fishing vessel for two days, free board and a little pay, then jumped onto a cargo ship out of Majuro, bound for Lima, Peru. From there, he'd joined *Independence*, laden with shipping containers that had once held American cars sold into Peru. They'd sailed home via the Suez Canal and up through the Caribbean, Ernie all the while longing for home and to see his family once again.

Ernie knew that once they docked, he would be paid, although it had been something of an effort to get the captain to agree to pay him in cash. Ernie did not have a bank account and had told the captain that he liked to move freely from job to job, to not be tied down to such things. The crew of the *Independence* were good men and despite the fact that, apparently and amazingly, cash was rarely used to pay wages these days, the captain had relented. Ernie had busied himself with tasks befitting his age, despite wanting to get involved in the heavier work that his mind still believed he could do. The younger hands seemed to like his enthusiasm and he had soon become a welcome part of the ship's compliment.

Independence found her berth and docked a little over half an hour later, and Ernie shook hands with the captain and the crew. Despite the ship's size, he was constantly amazed at how few hands were needed to run her. Ernie had, considering his circumstances, enjoyed the voyage home and now was sad to say goodbye to his new shipmates, but thoughts of his family were overwhelming him as he took his pay and walked down off the ship.

Norfolk ship yards had grown considerably since Ernie had last been here, and were now as gargantuan as the aircraft carrier he'd seen earlier that morning. He craned his head up as he saw airliners cruising the blue skies, trails of white vapor high against the heavens, and other jets lower down making their way in and out of a major airport somewhere nearby. The roads were full of cars, all of them seemingly polished to a mirror shine, the sidewalks filled with people who wore clothes that ranged from the vaguely familiar to the outright bizarre: kids in jeans that seemed ready to fall off, others with black hair and white skin and make-up that made them look half-dead, others still wearing T-shirts emblazoned with names and logos Ernie didn't understand.

He fought his way through the crowds, heading toward the one place that he knew he would still recognize even a half century later – Norfolk's West Ocean View, the home he'd bought with his wife before he'd set sail aboard *Bairoko*. It took Ernie and hour to find his way there using the public bus service across town, the journey allowing him to marvel at just *how many people* there were, everywhere. It seemed as though the whole world had suddenly got into one real big rush, everyone hurrying to be somewhere else.

The bus pulled in and Ernie stepped off near the corner of Dupre and 1st, then stared around him. He could recognise the street plan, but that was about it. Homes were bigger, trees were huge, telephone wires criss-crossed the street and the lawns looked better kept than he remembered. Still, he felt somewhat at home as he made his way down the street to *9467* and hurried up the steps.

He took a breath and knocked.

There was a brief pause as he stood on the porch, and then he saw movement within. A petite, blonde woman just about Margaret's size hurried to the door, and Ernie's heart leaped as the door opened.

His joy was short-lived as a woman whom he did not recognize looked out at him, smiling but a little confused as she registered his disappointment.

'Hi, can I help you?'

Ernie opened his mouth to reply, but suddenly he didn't know what to say.

'Um, hi, I'm, er, I'm looking for Margaret Walker. She lived here.'

The young woman seemed surprised. 'I'm sorry, we've been here for eight years past and I don't recall the name of the family who lived here before that. When was Margaret here?'

Ernie swallowed. 'It would have been a while ago, ma'am, around 1954.'

'Oh, wow, I wouldn't know, but you could ask old Henry over the street, he's been here for decades, he might know where Margaret went. Sorry I can't help you more.'

Ernie's heart leaped again as hope blossomed within him. 'Henry, you mean Henry Coleman?'

'Yes, that's right, his house is right over…'

Ernie was already in motion as he waved and called a thank you over his shoulder. He hurried down the porch steps and managed to jog across the street to the house opposite as he heard the woman call to him.

'Nine four seventy-two!'

Ernie changed direction and jogged down toward a square house that sat on the corner of Dupre, and as he closed in on it, he slowed down. There, sitting on his porch in a rocking chair that looked as though it had been there since the war, was an old man with thinning white hair, dressed in slacks and a check shirt. He was reading a newspaper as Ernie slowly walked up the drive toward him.

'I don't want my windows cleaned,' the old man called from behind his newspaper, not even looking away from the page, 'and if you're back from the Jehovah's I swear you're gonna see God again real soon, because I'll kick your ass from here to Heaven myself if you don't…'

'Henry?'

The old man looked up as he lowered the paper. He peered at Ernie through his spectacles.

'How'd you know my name?'

Ernie walked closer. For a moment Henry didn't seem to understand, but then, slowly, his eyes began to widen. Ernie saw Henry's lip begin to quiver, confusion twisting his old features as he struggled to understand what he was seeing.

'Ernest?' he whispered, as though afraid. 'Ernie? Is that you?'

'It's me, Henry,' Ernie said. 'Honest to God, though I don't believe it myself, it's me.'

Henry's paper fell out of his hands and he struggled to his feet on legs rubbery with age. Then, to Ernie's dismay, he backed away toward his front door.

'That ain't right,' the old man whispered. 'It can't be. You died.'

Ernie froze. 'Henry, I don't know how this has happened. We were on the ship and we were hit with something, you know, you remember, right?'

Henry froze. 'The ship,' he echoed. 'What was it called?'

Ernie smiled. 'You know damned well she was the Bairoko. You wanna test me, at least try me with something tough.'

Henry hesitated. 'Who'd we share bunks with?'

'Jimmy Foster and Mick Jones,' Ernie replied, their memories fresh in his mind. 'Both snorers, we used tissue paper as earplugs the whole damned voyage.'

'Who was our commanding officer?'

'Captain Benjamin Reed,' Ernie replied. 'Took us all the way to the Marshall Islands, by way of Hawaii, and Greg Potter's *mistake* with the local ladies of the night.'

Henry slapped his thigh and cackled a laugh. 'Got himself the clap, had to be sedated!'

'So did what's his face, in Rio, what was his name? Marvin someone or other?'

'Marvin "Stand" Still,' Henry replied. 'And she wasn't even a looker!'

There was a moment's pause, as Henry looked Ernie up and down.

'Who was my date, at the dance, before we left?'

'Joanna Innes,' Ernie whispered. 'You'd been courting her for weeks.'

Henry's lips quivered again and he nodded, tears springing from his eyes. 'Married her when we got back,' he said. 'Had forty good years with her, before the cancer took her.'

Ernie closed his eyes briefly. 'I'm sorry, Henry, I didn't know. Look, I need to find Margaret. Do you know where she is?'

Henry stared at Ernie for a long moment, but his grief did not subside, and after a few seconds Ernie knew that he was too late.

'When?' he asked as his throat tightened and needles poked at the corners of his eyes.

'Few years back,' Henry replied. 'She had a good 'un, Ernie, but never got over you going missing.' Henry shook his head. 'How, Ernie, how is this possible? Where have you been?'

Ernie looked up and down the street and moved closer to Henry.

'I need your help, pal,' he said. 'Can we talk?'

***

XXI

CIA Headquarters,

Langley, Virginia

General Scott Mackenzie stood at the head of a briefing room buried deep within the agency, one that was absolutely impossible to bug. The room itself was suspended within another that was lined with materials designed to absorb all electromagnetic wavelengths, creating what was known as an anechoic chamber, effectively ensuring that what went on inside the room literally stayed inside the room.

Seated around a long table in the center of the room were the hierarchy of the CIA's Special Operations Group, which was a unit within the Special Activities Division. Each man was responsible for teams trained in specialized means of military operations that required the deniability of the United States Government. Each unit gained its personnel from elite units within Special Forces such as Delta Force, Navy SEALS and the 24th Special Tactics Squadron, itself normally attached to covert CIA operations. None of the men wore uniforms that bore any insignia, anything to betray the units for which they worked.

Mackenzie had flown direct from Majuro to Virginia, knowing that Ernest Walker would most likely make his way to the state from the Marshall Islands. Mackenzie did not have the resources to scour the island chains of an entire ocean, and he could not be sure whether Walker would head east or west as it would depend on what passage he could find and whether he would attempt to work that passage home. While Mackenzie's people had alerted CIA watch stations in the Malay to Walker's presence, he felt certain that waiting in Virginia and letting Walker come to them was by far the best policy.

Now, Mackenzie had enough information from the EMIT program, and enough data from the studies that they had conducted, that he felt it was time to bring their work to the leaders of SOG and request further funding for broader, and bolder, initiatives.

'We caught the signal seven days ago, at just after eight hundred hours Eastern Seaboard Time, emanating from the Hamgyong Province of North Korea,' he began. 'All initial signatures bear the hallmark of a nuclear detonation, but right now we have no seismic or other geological traces that would normally accompany a conventional nuclear test.'

The faces around the table were all carved it seemed from the same rockface, one of gray granite topped with white, experienced field operators now leading the CIA's operations overseas. Nobody was under any illusions of what this event meant for the wider and increasingly unstable geo-political situation in the far East and the East China Sea: a significant breach of North Korean nuclear disarmament agreements.

'Could it be a fizzle?' asked one of the men.

'A fizzle is unlikely, given North Korean advances in high-yield nuclear tests,' he explained, a "fizzle" the term given to a nuclear detonation that didn't generate the expected yield. 'Therefore, this is likely a smaller device detonated with higher efficiency and represents a leap forward in their potential nuclear capability. I don't have to tell anybody in this room that a device small enough to fit into a warhead is precisely what we don't want in the hands of somebody like Kim Jong-Un.'

A murmur of general agreement rumbled around the room, everybody more than aware of the dangers of a nuclear-armed Korean Peninsula.

'Our assessment is that the North Korean regime has initiated a series of low-yield tests either close to, or beneath, the old site at Punggrye-ri, presumably to avoid attracting the attention of our satellites or emitting seismic waves that can be picked up by our sensors in the North Pacific.'

Another SOG team leader leaned back in his seat, his arms folded across his chest.

'Then how did we come to know about this, if the detonation was designed to be undetectable by our sensor assets?'

Mackenzie gestured to the young man alongside him.

'Kyle here has developed a system that allows us to more easily detect electromagnetic emissions from subterranean sources, a second eye-in-the-sky if you will, that has proven very effective in monitoring covert nuclear and EM events.'

Mackenzie watched the SOG commanders closely, waiting to see what they would say. Most were military men, pragmatists, not scientists, and would not wish to delve too deeply into the "*how*". Their focus would be more on the "*why*"?'

'Why have you been monitoring these kinds of emissions? We have other agencies working on North Korean nuclear activities.'

Mackenzie hesitated. For well over a year now he had been working on the EMIT program, which was so classified that he spent most of his time checking his own words before he spoke them to ensure that he let nothing slip. Thus, to speak openly about it to the SOG was something that he almost had to force himself to do.

'We believe that the North Koreans are testing nuclear and electromagnetic devices, but not to build a warhead. We believe that they have an advanced program in place that is being used in an attempt to influence the flow of time.'

There was a long silence as the SOG officers stared at him.

'Say that again? You think that they're trying to control time?'

'Yes,' Mackenzie said. 'And we understand this to be so, because my unit has had some success with a similar method. Gentlemen, I'm here to request that my unit be allowed to test a new device which, if successful, could ensure American dominance over all nations in all theatres in the future.'

That got the attention of the uniforms present, but grand claims required grand evidence and Mackenzie knew that this was going to be one hell of a hard sell to military men of action.

'The device is currently undergoing small-scale testing at the Groom Lake facility in Nevada. Our requirement is for a location that is more remote.'

That raised a few eyebrows.

'Well, we haven't got anybody on the moon at the moment,' an officer said.

A ripple of chuckles fluttered around the table. Mackenzie grinned.

'When you hear about what we've got down at Dreamland, you might want to rethink our moon strategy.'

The chuckles died down. Mackenzie turned to a screen, which lit up with a map of the United States, a red line drawn across the 37th parallel. A moment later, hundreds of tiny pin-prick lights appeared down the line, all crowded around it from the west coast to the east.

'The 37th parallel North,' Mackenzie announced. 'Nothing special, you might think. I'd ask you all, however, to think about how many of our largest, most classified and sensitive military bases and nuclear installations are located directly on this line of latitude.'

For a moment none of the men moved, and Mackenzie could almost hear them thinking. Eyes began to widen a little, interest growing.

'Each of these lights is a verified recording of a sighting of what we now refer to as Unidentified Aerial Phenomena, UFOs in the historical vernacular. For decades now we have been studying these appearances, often learning very little at all about their nature, their origin, their purpose. Last year, that all changed.'

The screen altered to one of a perfect, crystal-clear image of a brightly lit flying disc captured descending amid dense forest, bathed in lights that were so colourful and vivid that every man in the room sucked in a breath. They knew, instantly, somehow, that despite all the world's computer-generated imagery, this was no forgery. There was something about the image that was other-worldly in a way that could not be described, colors that were not familiar or natural, a kaleidoscopic display that no *Hollywood* artist could ever conjure.

'Last year,' Mackenzie went on, 'we figured out how to predict when and where they would appear. I have had a team working for months now gathering data, images, video, sound recordings, everything we can think of to determine what these things are and how we can benefit from their technology.'

A Marine general finally spoke. '*How?* How have you done this?'

'With big data,' Mackenzie replied. 'We use a customized version of a law-enforcement program which gathers data in large quantities, called PredPol, short for Predictive Policing. It's been in use for some years in Los Angeles. It's a data-crunching program that lists all known crimes in a given area, compiles all the details about those crimes, and generates an algorithmic prediction of where future crimes will occur based on that data.'

There was a moment of silence from the men before Mackenzie.

'You're predicting the future?' one of them asked.

'In a sense,' Mackenzie replied. 'The data is gathered from years of UFO reports, especially from respected organisations like the Mutual UFO Network, or MUFON, along with reports from professionals like pilots, police officers and so on. This algorithm in effect allows us to intercept UFO appearances, and gather the data we need to put ourselves ahead in the technology race.'

'And what does this data tell you?' asked an Admiral.

Mackenzie gestured to the screen.

'Two things,' he said. 'Initially, it allowed us to set up cameras working in various spectrums to measure all radiation and energy sources coming from these objects, to understand something of their construction and their modes of operation. In truth, sometimes this has been difficult to interpret as those modes of operation are sometimes counterintuitive and often downright bizarre. It was only when we stopped looking at them from our own point of reference, as human beings, and simply took them at face value that we started making progress. Firstly, we confirmed the trend that UFOs often tend to appear at military and nuclear facilities around the world, but especially along the 37th parallel. The second was that these appearances come in rhythmic waves.'

Mackenzie pushed a button on a nearby computer and the map of the USA and the little lights began flowing, almost like a wave, across the country, pulsing as though it were something alive.

'UFO fanatics call these waves "flaps", and they occur all over the world. Some aspects of this might be sightings of the same craft appearing over different states, but a lot of it appears to follow a pattern rather than a flight path. Finally, we established that a large number of sightings occur in the western United States, specifically Arizona and Nevada.'

'That's due to our military bases and test, surely?' an Army general said.

'Some of it certainly is due to military traffic, but we had access to UFO reports from some of those military pilots, and it's pretty clear that whatever they were seeing, it wasn't other military aircraft, at least nothing that belongs to us.'

'So?' the admiral asked. 'Where are you going with all of this?'

'The measurements we took revealed that these objects were not just travelling at exotic velocities. Chronological measurements of extreme accuracy revealed that there were pulses in the flow of time around many of the closer sightings, recorded in real time.'

Mackenzie saw that the Joint Chiefs were not following.

'Time itself was warping around the objects,' he explained. 'They were travelling from another time period, visiting us not from another planet but from our own. They're not aliens, gentlemen. They're *us*.'

***

XXII

A long, deep silence filled the room as the SOG chiefs took this momentous announcement in. For a moment, Mackenzie feared that he might be laughed out of the room, that they would consider him to be insane and petition for him to be removed from his post. The silence seemed to last so long that the general almost continued his briefing, but then one of the JCOS finally broke the silence.

'So, this is what the EMIT program has been hiding? How long has this been going on?'

In truth, Mackenzie did not know just how long the agency had known about the nature of visitations by other forms of life, or what their agenda might be. The agency was so deeply layered, with so many covert operations, that for all he knew somebody working down the hall might be ten years ahead of his own research but be unable to share what they knew for fear of breaching security.

'It has been a subject of study for decades,' he replied.

The officers before him nodded quietly but again said nothing. It was something of a shock to Mackenzie that they were taking the news so well, but when he thought about it, mankind was far better able to deal with something like this than he would have been decades before. Television, dramas, *Hollywood* movies about alien invasions and other science fiction films and books, all had in some way helped to prime the human psyche for the inevitable day when, someplace on Earth, the truth about UFO sightings was revealed.

'How do we know *for sure* that it's us?' the Marine general asked.

'Well,' Mackenzie said, 'we can't be *absolutely* sure, but certain factors about how they're seen, how they affect their environment, and what we understand about the nature of time and space all point to that conclusion. That they have a clear interest in us is undoubted, as well as other life on the planet. The conclusion reached by our team also explains many of the other questions about supposed alien visitations, such as the distances travelled and the physical appearance of the supposed travellers: two arms, two legs, two eyes and so on, just like us. Evolutionary factors could possibly contribute to the rise of a species on another planet that just happened to look a little like us, but that they are some *future* form of us is a much more likely occurrence.'

More silence. The men were clearly thinking deeply about all that he had said, as he himself had thought deeply about it for many long months. It was a lot to take in, and he retained the suspicion that many of them remained sceptical but were unable to ignore the evidence he was displaying to them, nor the possibilities that they presented.

'What do you intend to do about this?' an admiral asked.

The big question, Mackenzie noted, the one he had both hoped for and dreaded: hoped, because it would mean that they in principal had accepted his conclusions despite their remarkable nature; and dreaded because he hadn't yet come up with a good answer.

'Our research into the nature of time around these objects suggests that, as amazing as their capabilities are, the technology required is not actually beyond our capacity to achieve.'

Now, every pair of eyes locked upon his.

'Say that again,' the Army Colonel said.

'We can build something that can do the same thing,' Mackenzie replied. 'With enough energy, the right tools, we think that we can put somebody back in time, to allow them to take knowledge of the future and put things the way we want them to be.'

The silence now was so deep that it was tangible. All eight military brains before him were working overtime as they thought about all of the incredible possibilities. Then, quietly, the Admiral spoke.

'How do we know that we haven't already done so?'

Mackenzie's carefully planned train of thought slammed to a halt. Nobody, not even Kyle, had yet thought to ask that question, and he was both relieved and alarmed at the admiral's forethought. *How could they know?* Perhaps, in the first iteration, the Nazis had won World War Two, or the Soviets had won the Cold War, or the Bay of Pigs had resulted in an all-out nuclear exchange that had wiped most life from the face of the earth. Maybe they had already gone back and altered things, at some point in the… future?

'We do not know,' Mackenzie replied, keen to speak before his own thoughts drove him into an endless cycle of logical contradictions. 'This conversation could be the first stage in a process that initiates a change in history as we know it, which leads me on to my next revelation.'

Behind Mackenzie, on the monitor, appeared an image of a young sailor sitting on the deck of an aircraft carrier.

'The man in the center of the image is Seaman First Class Ernest Walker, sitting aboard the aircraft carrier USS *Bairoko,* in early 1954. It's the last known image of Walker, as two months later the carrier was damaged when the Castle Bravo nuclear test went awry. Walker went over the side to protect himself from the heat of the blast and was never seen again.' Mackenzie took a breath. 'Two weeks ago, a man wearing Walker's uniform was found floating in the Pacific, near the site where *Bairoko* had been when it was hit. He claimed that he'd gone into the water, and when he'd come up, over half a century had gone by.'

The COG was listening intently, their gazes fixed on Mackenzie. Whether they thought him insane or were simply enraptured by the tale he couldn't tell, so he kept going.

'Walker vanished from a hospital in Majuro, Marshall Islands, and hasn't been seen since. My team is not large enough to track him down, so I'm here now asking for the support of every branch of the SOG to find this man.'

The Army officer frowned.

'Why would he be so important to this? Even if he is some kind of time traveller, if that's what you're implying, he probably doesn't know anything more about what happened than we do, right?'

Mackenzie inclined his head.

'You'd think so,' he admitted, 'but the leader of my technical team thinks otherwise. He's convinced that the reason Ernie Walker made it through time and others present did not is all to do with the man himself. Kyle believes that the one thing we've been missing in our work is the human component. I won't bore you with the technical details, but it's a known fact that key components of the universe, such as electrons, respond and react to observation by living entities. Something about our presence affects how the world around us is seen. Kyle thinks that Ernie, for whatever reason, is the final component: the one thing we would need to complete a device to send people back in time.'

Again, silence. Mackenzie knew of the stakes he was facing, and wasn't about to hide that from the COG.

'We know that the North Koreans are seeking the same technology as we are, under the guise of their own nuclear research. The evidence of electromagnetic emissions from former test sites support our suspicions that they're following the same lines of enquiry, and it's not impossible that they also are aware of Ernie Walker's apparent reappearance in the Pacific. Again, I don't need to elaborate on the dangers of allowing a reclusive, Communist state like North Korea to access this kind of technology.'

There were nods all around the table.

'What are your intentions?' the admiral asked.

'We want to build a test site out in the Pacific, away from prying eyes. Groom Lake is a good location for our work but right now we need to perform the tests elsewhere. Using a site in the Pacific virtually guarantees zero media coverage, and may also ensure we're not tipping our hand to any sleeper agents working here in the country. We also want support to hunt for Ernie Walker. If my team are right and he is needed in some way to complete our tests, then he's the only person on Earth right now that we can say with any certainty has travelled through time.'

The COG looked at each other for a few moments, and Mackenzie could see in their expressions that he had them.

'Very well,' the chairman replied. 'Consider the COG at your disposal. The Pacific fleet has a carrier battle group stationed north of the Marshall Islands, and there are a number of remote bases in the island chain that could serve well as test areas, well away from prying eyes.'

'Thank you,' Mackenzie replied. 'We should not reveal to the fleet what our true purpose is, nor of course should they know about any activities on the islands conducted by EMIT or the COG. We should only put them on call, and only request direct support as a last resort.'

'Agreed,' the chairman said. 'What about the North Korean site?'

That, Mackenzie knew, was going to be the tricky bit.

'We cannot afford to lose any advantage to the North Koreans, in any aspect of this research. Should they achieve the capacity to send operatives back in time with any kind of knowledge of the future, they would instantly leap-frog over the United States in technological and military prowess and our world, our history, would be changed overnight. I propose that any and all efforts should be made to neutralise their operations, permanently.'

The admiral drew a deep breath. 'Infiltrating North Korea is a one-way trip and you know it. I'm not going to commit men to a suicide mission, even though I know that they wouldn't hesitate to carry it out. There has to be plausible means for success.'

Mackenzie got that. If he couldn't send qualified men, then he could hardly expect the SEALs to commit to the same operation with any expectation of greater success.

'I don't think that infiltration is the right play,' he suggested. 'It's early days yet, but if we can confirm the North Korean operation is what it seems to be, I propose a surgical strike.'

There was another silence. Mackenzie knew that what he was proposing, an act of war against a sovereign state, could result in the worst of consequences should anything go wrong. A war on the Korean Peninsula would be almost guaranteed, and a global conflict, perhaps even a nuclear exchange, was possible should Russia or China become embroiled in the engagement. Fortunately, he also knew how to win the COG over as he'd practiced this briefing a hundred times before today.

'Of course, if we learn how to pre-empt any enemy's future plans, then a surgical strike would not be required…'

Mackenzie let the statement hang in the air for a long moment. He saw one or two of the senior offices restrain quiet smiles, knowing as he did that Mackenzie had won the day.

'Your point is taken,' the chairman said. 'Send a list of requirements, direct to me, and I will ensure they are in place. This meeting is now closed, and all present must sign the NDAs before they leave this room.'

The COG command team stood and filed out of the room, signing the NDA form as they went. Mackenzie was the last out of the door, and made his way up toward his office. He was halfway there when he was intercepted by Kyle Trent.

'Well?'

'EMIT was tightly packaged. They've cleared all funding for us.'

Kyle clenched a fist and breathed a *yessss* as they walked. 'Good, now we can test what we know so far and see if we really can copy what the UAPs are doing.'

Kyle spoke quietly enough that he wasn't overheard by other staff as they walked.

'How far do you think the North Koreans have got?' the general asked.

'Who cares? We get the jump on them, everything they've done becomes history, right?'

'Works both ways, Kyle,' the general reminded him.

Kyle looked suddenly nervous, and the general raised an eyebrow. Kyle knew the look by now and he didn't hesitate to speak.

'This is going to happen sooner or later,' he said. 'People are getting too well educated, there's too much information out there. You know it as well as I do. The Disclosure Protocol is going to be redundant within a few years anyway. Why bother covering this up any longer?'

Mackenzie was surprised, given all that was at stake.

'Do you really want it to be Communist North Korea that makes the greatest discovery of all human history? Would you rather the Russians had got to the moon first?'

'It shouldn't matter *who* does it,' Kyle replied, 'only that it is done.'

Despite a year with the CIA out in *Dreamland*, the pilot's call sign for what everybody else in the world knew as Area 51, Kyle still retained some of the idealistic vigor that he'd possessed when Mackenzie had first managed to recruit him to the team.

'Son, I get where you're coming from, and yes, sooner or later this will all become public knowledge and the whole world will change forever. Right now, though, it's a work in progress, and given the choice I'd rather it was our nation that announced to the world that we had come to understand how time works, than some tin-pot dictatorship where people still have to queue for bread in the morning.'

Kyle shrugged. 'I guess. Still, I know one or two people who I bet could get in and out of there without raising the alarm.'

Mackenzie knew at once to whom Kyle was referring, and he shook his head.

'Warner and Lopez are out of the game.'

'They survived,' Kyle replied. 'They saved my ass and they did a damned fine job of protecting yours until you decided that they were expendable.'

'Don't forget what the alternative to working for me was,' Mackenzie warned. 'A Colorado Supermax won't be half as much fun as working down at Groom Lake.'

Kyle veered off in another direction.

'And there was me thinkin' you'd learned how to win friends.'

Kyle opened an office door and walked out of sight. Mackenzie waited for a few moments, and the kid returned with a sheepish look on his face.

'End of the hall, turn right,' Mackenzie said with a jab of his thumb. 'I'll meet you in the lot.'

Kyle offered him a feeble thumbs-up and headed off out of sight again.

Mackenzie knew the kid was right, and he could admit it to himself, although only to himself. The stakes were too high to play around here. Mackenzie had his own family, two daughters and a loving wife, everything to play for. But he also knew that if North Korea beat his team to the chase, then everything that had happened up to that moment in time, quite literally, was up for grabs. The regime could not hope to win a military confrontation with South Korea when the USA was right behind its southern neighbour, so that meant they sought other means to undermine their enemies. Social media, fake news, war by guile rather than by strength.

If they won this covert battle, North Korea would win the war by changing history itself, and Mackenzie's team was the only thing standing in their way.

To his surprise, Kyle suddenly reappeared, an urgent look on his face.

'We just got word from a watch team in Norfolk,' Kyle said. 'They spotted someone hanging around Ernie Walker's old home.'

'Does he match Ernie's description?' Mackenzie asked as they walked.

'Well, kind of.'

'What's *that* supposed to mean?'

***

XXIII

'This is it, Dupre,' Lopez said.

Ethan pulled their hired sedan up near the sidewalk and killed the engine. The street was deserted, lined with trees that swayed gently with the breeze. The lawns were perfect, the houses whitewashed and gleaming in the bright morning sunshine.

'If I were Ernie, this is where I would head first.'

'If I were the CIA, this is where I would head too,' Lopez pointed out. 'What else do we have on his likely places to visit?'

'His wife died last year,' Ethan said, 'which is going to hit him hard. She was living in a care home in Norfolk, so you can bet the CIA will stake out that property, even though Ernie can't possibly know about it yet. He could have tried calling places, maybe figured out the new dialling codes, but none of his family live in the same places any more. That leaves here, the last home he knew.'

'Can't cover them all,' Lopez murmured. 'I get why he'd come here, but if he's decided to avoid the government then he's not going to just waltz straight down the street. He's gonna want to stay out of sight.'

'Right, but he'll do it 1950s style,' Ethan said. 'He's not going to know about orbiting spy satellites, drones, CCTV and who knows what else. He's going to be sitting on a park bench peering over the top of a newspaper. They'll be onto him within moments of him showing up.'

'So, what do we do about it?' Lopez asked.

Ethan opened his car door. 'Only thing we can do is beat them to it.'

Ethan walked across the street to Ernie's old home and knocked on the door. Moments later, a middle-aged woman answered.

'Hi, sorry to bother you.'

'You're not,' the woman replied with a smile as she glanced him up and down. Her interest waned as she saw Lopez saunter up alongside Ethan.

'We're looking for an elderly guy who's gone missing this morning,' Ethan explained. 'Goes by the name of Ernest. He might be seen around here looking for somebody called…'

'Margaret,' the woman replied.

'He's been here already?' Ethan asked in surprise.

'Yeah, said he lived here. I sent him over to old Harry's, thinking he might know where this Margaret was. I sent the Chinese guys over there too.'

'The who?' Ethan asked, as he was gripped by a sense of impending doom.

'The Chinese guys,' the woman repeated. 'They showed up right after Ernie did, at least I think they were Chinese. They said they were.'

Ethan frowned thoughtfully, thanked the woman for her time and then hurried down the drive with Lopez alongside him.

'Why would the Chinese be interested in Ernie?' Lopez wondered out loud. 'How would they know he was here, for that matter?'

Ethan wasn't sure, but now he began scanning the street up and down. He saw what he was looking for after a few moments, and Lopez caught sight of them at the same time: two men, sitting in a vehicle at the top of the street, perfectly positioned to watch the home where Ernie Walker had once lived.

'Let's go find out.'

They walked up the street together, staying on the opposite side of the street to the car to make it appear as though they were just an ordinary couple who had maybe parked outside the city center before heading in on foot. Ethan waited until they were almost perpendicular to the car, chatting amiably away in the sunshine, and then they both wheeled abruptly left and crossed the street.

The two men in the car were not Chinese, and Ethan could see through the lightly tinted glass of the non-descript silver sedan that they were Americans, both wearing suits and sunglasses. As he got closer, he noticed that they were oddly motionless and were ignoring his approach.

'What the hell?' Lopez uttered.

Both men were sitting with their heads leaning back against the headrests of their seats, both with what looked like bundles of fabric tucked under their chins. Ethan reached out and opened the driver's door, to see the man within sitting comatose, his eyes open and unseeing behind the sunglasses.

Ethan's eyes drifted down to the man's neck to see a wide, deep incision through the man's artery, his shirt stained a deep red beneath his jacket where he had bled out.

Ethan whirled away from the vehicle and ran back down the street to old Harry's house as he realised that the CIA had indeed been watching Ernie's house. Unfortunately, so had somebody else, and they clearly wanted Ernie in their custody real bad.

*

'Tell me how this happened.'

Ernie Walker sat down in a wicker chair on Henry's back porch as the old man joined him, two glasses of lemonade in his hands. The morning sunshine was warm, and for a moment Ernie realized that he could have been back in 1954 again, but for the sight of a modern airliner climbing like a white dove into the perfect blue sky.

'*USS Bairoko*,' Ernie replied. 'It got hit by the Castle Bravo blast.'

'I remember,' Henry nodded, glancing at his arms. Ernie could see there amid the old folds of skin the faint white lines of scars. 'Got myself burned half to a crisp.'

'How many died, Henry?'

The old man shrugged. 'Man, I don't know. We put into port right after, and everybody was sworn to silence. Half the damned crew were grilled by guys, I think they were from the army but they didn't wear any insignia. The put us under a lot of pressure, and we were under no illusions about what would happen if we talked about Castle Bravo – charges of treason, Court Martial, life without parole, you name it. The crew was split up after that, so I guess they didn't want us to know how many got out. My best guess is we lost maybe a hundred men.'

Ernie closed his eyes briefly as he thought of the lieutenant who got his eyes burned out.

'They covered it all up?' he asked.

'Sure they did,' Henry replied. '*Bairoko* supposedly enjoyed a blemish-free career and was broken up back in 1961, out in Hong Kong, I think. The only record I ever found of Castle Bravo said that a few crewmembers received beta-radiation burns from the blast test, nothing more.'

Ernie nodded. 'There's a lot more, Henry.'

'I can see that. Where the hell have you been?'

'Nowhere,' Ernie replied. 'I don't understand it but I went into the water to escape the flames, and when I came up out of the water half a century had gone by. About the only thing I can say is that the blast was the cause, but beyond that I just don't know. And I'm pretty sure the CIA or somebody else is looking for me.'

'How did you get here?'

'Fishing trawler picked me up,' Ernie replied, 'and I got a working passage out of Majuro, cash only, then another out of Lima, Peru. I don't think that they've traced me but they must be searching. Henry, I'm gonna need help. I've got some cash but I don't know half of what's happened to the world, and I'm afraid that if I go to my children's homes there'll be people waiting for me that I don't want to see.'

Henry sat up in his chair. 'Anything you need pal, what's your plan?'

Ernie smiled, but he hadn't had a chance to figure out what he hell he was going to do about all this yet. Mostly he'd been concerned with surviving, nothing more. When the answer came to his lips, he was surprised at it.

'I want to go back,' Ernie said. 'Back home, where I belong.'

Henry chuckled.

'Shucks, Ernie, can I come too? How the hell do you think that you'll be able to get back? They don't run tests like those anymore, it all got banned under international treaties after Bikini Atoll and others were vaporized. I don't think they even know for sure that what's happened to you, has actually happened. How would they?'

'A bunch of military planes showed up in Majuro before I got out,' Ernie said. 'Can't have been a coincidence.'

Henry frowned for a moment, looking at his old hands where they rested on top of his cane.

'Man, we could head back and take the past forty years' worth of lottery ticket numbers with us. I could put shares into Nokia and Amazon right at the start.'

'What's Nokia?'

'Never mind,' Henry said. 'Right now, we need to get you someplace safe while we figure out what the hell to do about this. It might be that the only way to protect you and get this done is to go public with it.'

Ernie hesitated.

'I don't know, that pretty much puts all my cards on the table and it'll take months, perhaps years to spread the word widely enough that the government doesn't just hide it all.'

Henry looked at Ernie and chuckled again. 'Buddy, you've got a lot to learn about the modern world. If we go public, it'll be on every living human being's lips by tomorrow morning, the ones that count anyway.'

Ernie blinked. 'Really? Is the wireless that good these days?'

Henry didn't get the chance to reply. His words dried up as the barrel of a pistol was pressed against his temple. Ernie leaped to his feet but was instantly surrounded by a group of four Far Eastern males, all armed but dressed in smart suits. One of them, a determined-looking and stocky man who was a little older than his companions, moved forward.

'Good morning Mister Walker,' he said in accented American. 'We've been looking forward to speaking with you.'

***

XXIV

Ernie Walker froze. There was no gun against his head, but frankly the idea of putting one to the head of a man who could hardly put up much of a fight was an abhorrent act that cemented in his mind that these people were an enemy to be despised like no other.

'Who are you?' he demanded. 'What do you want?'

The smaller man looked up at him, a cold, dark expression on his face.

'My name is Jae, and you will be coming with me.'

'I'm not going anywhere,' Ernie said. 'Put the guns away and tell me what the hell it is that you want. You might find that you get what you want that way.'

Jae offered him a thin, almost pitying smile. 'I get what I want, regardless.'

Ernie saw the man with the pistol held to Henry's head push a little harder. Henry pushed back, a snarl on his face.

'What? You gonna take my poor young life away from me? Ernie, tell them to go to hell!'

Jae's smile did not slip as from beneath his shirt he revealed an ornate dagger, one carved with murals of some kind, letters that Ernie did not really recognize but looked to be perhaps Japanese.

'This is what's going to happen,' he said. 'You're going to do precisely what I say, and if you do, I promise that I won't slice your friend open an inch at a time and make you watch his organs spill out over this nice clean porch.'

Ernie felt rage building inside of him. Henry's voice reached him from afar.

'To hell with 'em Ernie, I won't stay conscious long enough for it to matter!'

Jae turned to Henry and reached out with the blade for his belly.

'Enough!' Ernie snapped. 'I'll go with you, but if you so much as put a scratch on him, I swear you'll have to kill me to prevent me from taking that knife of yours and gouging your eyes out with it.'

Jae looked at Ernie appraisingly for a moment, and then he slid the knife back into its sheath and stood upright again.

'Good,' he said. 'In that case, you will leave with us now, and if you fail to deliver what we ask of you then you can be sure we will come back here to finish our business with your friend.'

Ernie did not dignify the men with a reply, instead glancing at Henry and offering him a fractional shake of his head, as if to say *"humor them, don't make things worse"*. Henry said nothing, scowling in silence as the four men surrounded Ernie and led him toward the front door of the home.

'You're an interesting man,' Jae said as they walked. 'You vanish from 1954, reappear here, owe nobody anything and yet you protect an old man who already suggested he has nothing to fear from dying.'

'It's called not being an asshole,' Ernie replied. 'You should try it someday.'

He sensed Jae tense up and wondered if he was Japanese, such an outright insult to his honor something that would normally be punishable by death. Ernie smiled.

'What is it Jae? Does being short make you feel inadequate, or is it your stubby little dic…'

'Coming from the time that you do, I would have thought you would have better manners,' Jae cut him off.

'Coming here with guns drawn and with the benefit of fifty years of social advances, I'd have thought the same of you.'

Jae's men moved ahead and opened the front door of the home.

'I don't need manners to…'

Ernie leaped back out of the way as two of Jae's men were suddenly cut down in a hail of blows. Two figures lunged into the home as the door opened, fists and legs flying as they disarmed the two men with a flurry of fearsome moves.

Jae reached out for Ernie but he batted the smaller man's arm aside and stepped forward and smashed his forehead into Jae's nose. Jae slammed backwards into the wall, his vision blurring and his limbs flailing as he slumped to one knee, and Ernie didn't look back as he turned and hurried back through the house and out into the garden.

He ran past Henry and scrambled over the fence into an adjoining garden, over another onto the sidewalk outside the homes, then started running for his life toward the city.

*

Ethan grabbed the gunman's wrist and twisted it sideways as he drove one knee up into his belly. The man folded over at the waist as the pistol was ripped from his grasp, as beside Ethan he saw another man hauled from the porch and collapse to his knees as he collided with Lopez's fearsome right hook.

Ethan saw Ernie break free from a third man and flee out back as the fourth gunman took aim at Ethan. Ethan turned the pistol he'd wrenched from his first victim and ducked back out of sight as the Oriental man fired a single shot.

Whitewashed wood sprayed away from the door as the bullet skimmed the edge and veered off across the street. Ethan stayed out of sight and poked just the weapon into the house and fired three shots, heard the sound of the man collapsing, and poked his head around the corner to see him slumped on his back with blood pouring from his chest.

'Three down,' Ethan said as he glanced at Lopez and saw her stamp on her victim's face and grab his pistol.

'Did you see Ernie?'

'He took off out back!'

Ethan and Nicola dashed through the house and out into the backyard. Ethan instantly saw a man in a wicker chair with a furious expression on his face, and ducked as a wooden cane flashed toward his head.

The cane swung wide and Ethan lunged in and gently stayed the old man's arm.

'It's okay, we're not here to hurt you. Is Ernie okay?'

The old man looked into Ethan's eyes for a long moment, then his gaze softened as he saw the genuine concern therein.

'He took off south,' the old man replied.

'Who are these assholes?' Lopez asked, gesturing to the unconscious men now lining Henry's hall.

'I don't know. They wanted Ernie.'

Ethan turned and rushed the fence, vaulted over it and landed with Lopez right behind him. They took the next fence and hit the sidewalk, and Ethan saw Ernie vanish around a corner at the bottom of the street.

They ran hard in pursuit, turned a corner and saw Ernie jaywalk across the street, seeking cover amid the rows of trees lining the streets and the busier roads of the city ahead.

'He's gonna try to lose himself,' Lopez said as they ran.

'He won't in the city, they'll be onto him in no time,' Ethan panted in response. 'We've gotta get him out of here.'

Ethan ran hard, but as ever Lopez pulled away from him, lithe as a gazelle. Lopez was like a racehorse and she was wearing sneakers rather than her more normal heeled boots, both of them having anticipated the chance of a chase.

Ethan managed to keep up as they hit Granby, and right away he knew that there was no way Ernie was going to make the city without being intercepted, the old man just not up to a prolonged sprint. Granby was a two lane north-south highway and the city was far enough away to not even be in sight. Ethan didn't know the area that well but he figured Norfolk would have to be two or three miles at least, so the only way Ernie would get there would be by bus, and that would put him firmly in the CIA's sights.

'I'll go for the car!' Ethan yelled at Lopez as she tore away from him. 'Try to get Ernie out of sight!'

Ethan doubled back, running as hard as he could back to Dupre. He heard sirens coming from somewhere nearby and he knew that the gunshots had alerted locals to what had happened. Oceanview didn't much look like a high-crime area to Ethan so he figured that local law-enforcement would take the reports seriously.

Ethan reached the car, started the engine and pulled out, his breathing ragged. He pulled onto Granby and headed south, spotted Lopez within sixty seconds as she ran down the street in pursuit of Ernie, who was still making good ground despite his advanced years.

Ethan drove a hundred yards past Ernie, then pulled into the sidewalk and shuffled across to the passenger seat. He stayed low, watching in the rear-view mirror as Ernie rushed toward him, and then at the last moment he shoved the passenger door opened and leaped out.

Ernie's eyes widened and he tried to veer past the open door, but Ethan blocked the way with his hands in the open.

'Ernie, we know what happened! We're here to help!'

Ernie didn't stop. He plowed into Ethan and the pair of them went flying backwards and thumped down onto a lawn. Ethan grabbed hold of Ernie's shirt and tried to roll on top of him to pin him down. He was halfway over when Lopez arrived and grabbed Ernie's collar.

'Ernie, we're on side. We know about Castle Bravo!'

Ernie kept struggling for his life and on an impulse Lopez took the pistol she'd pilfered from Ernie's would-be abductors and shoved it into his hand. Ernie stopped struggling and stared at the pistol for a moment, dumbfounded.

'We need to get out of here,' Ethan said to Ernie. 'Unless you'd like your foreign friends to catch up with us again?'

Ernie stared back and forth between them. 'Who the hell are you two?''

'People with the same problem as you,' Lopez said as she stood back and let Ethan get to his feet. 'We can talk about it, but not here. There are people everywhere looking for you.'

Ernie stood up, stared at the pistol in his hand again, then held it back to Lopez.

'I don't want this.'

Lopez took it, and Ethan heard the sirens getting louder. 'Come on, before they get here and this gets even more messy than it already is.'

Ernie hesitated for only a moment longer, and then the sound of the sirens got much louder and he darted for the safety of the car. Ethan got into the driver's seat, Lopez alongside him, and he pulled gently out into the flow of traffic heading south toward the city as the sirens of police cruisers heading north wailed past them on the other side of the highway.

***

XXV

'We got something.'

General Mackenzie sat in a mobile surveillance vehicle parked on an apron at Chambers Field and looked up as one of his staff, a former Army Ranger by the name of Brooker, strode in.

'Where?'

'Norfolk,' came the reply. 'Law enforcement were called to a shooting in Oceanview, found two dead CIA operatives in a vehicle and one dead Asian male, unidentified. They're questioning witnesses now.'

Mackenzie closed his eyes briefly. Two dead agents. It was not often that service personnel were lost in the field but whenever it did happen it was time to reflect on the sacrifice that they gave, often in complete secrecy, to the security and prosperity of the United States.

'Families will be informed,' Brooker went on, 'although circumstances will be changed to avoid exposing the operation.'

'What about the target?' Mackenzie asked, forcing himself to remain focused on the operation and not on its losses.

'There is only one positive identification,' Brooker replied. 'A local woman recognized Walker from the photofit. Says he was looking for someone, which we believe to be his wife, Margaret, deceased. Turns out a guy living on the same street was a former ship mate and school friend. Walker went there. About the only other thing that we know is that the witness insisted there were several Chinese people also looking for Walker that same morning, and two Americans, a man and a Latino woman.'

Mackenzie froze for a moment, his mind reeling from this additional information. He figured that the supposedly Chinese people were in fact North Korean agents, but he could not of course be sure. However, he had no problem identifying the two Americans that Brooker had said were present on the scene.

'Warner and Lopez,' he said softly.

'You know them?' Brooker asked.

Mackenzie smiled quietly to himself. Although he could not formally admit as much to his superiors, he had a nagging affection for the duo with whom he'd worked on a previous case, although the terms in which they'd parted company were less than ideal. He'd already known that Warner and his fiery partner were looking for him, trying to figure out what had happened to them in the wake of a violent shoot-out that had occurred out near Tonopah, and he knew also that he could not afford for them to figure out anything about what he was involved in at Area 51. That they had somehow worked out who Ernie Walker was and were already on the case both shocked him and yet somehow did not come as much of a surprise. Warner was tenacious, to say the least, and Lopez was every bit his match and a serious danger to the security of Mackenzie's operation if she was unleashed.

'Where is Walker right now?' Mackenzie asked.

'Disappeared,' Brooker replied. 'We're searching for him and have teams deployed across Norfolk.'

Mackenzie nodded. Ernie was nobody's fool, that much was clear, and he had already spent weeks evading Mackenzie's team despite being fifty years out of his familiar world. Sure, he could vanish from the Marshall Islands on a boat easily enough, but they should have been able to pick him up within hours of him arriving in Norfolk. Unless he had help.

'Keep watch for Warner and Lopez also,' he advised Brooker. 'They're almost certainly with Ernie and will probably try to keep him hidden until they can figure out their next move. Consider them a priority.'

'Yes sir.'

Brooker wheeled from the office, and Mackenzie leaned thoughtfully back in his chair. Warner and Lopez were obviously up to something, and about the only option open to them to expose Mackenzie's operation was to go public. Tangible proof that an American serviceman had been propelled fifty years forwards through time would be the most sensational news piece in human history. There were, of course, protocols in place already for just this sort of emergency. The crew manifests of *USS Bairoko* were being altered to remove any reference to Walker, and images from the time had been located and destroyed. Former crew members who remembered Ernie were still under no doubts about the charges they faced if they spoke out, but Mackenzie knew that they could not really be silenced. Most were so old now that they had nothing to fear from threats of death, and threats against younger members of their families were empty: Mackenzie wasn't about to start slaughtering innocent American citizens despite the stakes.

The presence of the North Koreans was problematic, as they were clearly following the same evidence trail as Ethan and Nicola. If another state actor was in play, that could cause real friction as well as further expose what was already mutating into a large, expensive and complex operation. Mackenzie did not like such operations because they invariably leaked like a sieve and despite best efforts were impossible to hide for long. He couldn't have operatives crawling all over Norfolk and expect nobody to notice, no matter how discreet they might be.

The only way to bring Walker, Warner and Lopez out of the shadows was to entice them out. Mackenzie reached out and picked up a phone.

*

Jae sat in the rear of a vehicle that was driving south towards Norfolk city and scowled, rage seething through his veins as he thought of his family back in Pyonyang, anxiously awaiting to see if he would return victorious and save them from the *gulags*.

The house in which they'd found Ernie Walker would by now be crawling with police, and it was only by the skin of their teeth that Jae and his team had escaped before the area was locked down by law enforcement. As it was, they had been forced to leave one of their number behind, an almost unforgivable failure. Jae knew that had he had been captured alive, they would eventually have been exposed as North Korean agents and the diplomatic row that would have ensued would have ensured the fate of Jae's wife and children.

Jae had simply removed that fate from the equation, for now, by putting a bullet in the wounded man's head even as he begged for his life. The remaining three men had fled the scene. Now, he knew that the country's law enforcement and military would be on high alert, as Jae had personally killed the two CIA agents watching the home before his team had infiltrated it.

He had no idea who the two Americans who had intercepted them were, but right now the face of the man was indelibly imprinted on his mind, not to mention Walker's on the bridge of his nose. Blood spilled onto his shirt and jacket as he held it pinched closed, and with a growl of rage he yanked it to one side to straighten it. Bright pain lanced through his face and tears streamed from his eyes, but he fought against the pain as he plugged his nostrils with tissues.

'Did any of you see where they went?'

His two companions shook their heads, each staring ahead and saying nothing. Jae knew that they were expecting repercussions for their failure, perhaps the loss of their lives, or the lives of loved ones back home. Jae knew that such threats could push people to excel, but he also knew that it could pummel them into abject dismay and apathy. They were all in this together, and he suddenly realized that they probably feared him as much as he feared the consequences of failing their Dear

Leader. He had, after all, just killed one of their team in cold blood rather than have him fall into enemy hands.

'Look, we got surprised. It happens, and we can't change that. What matters is what we do about it now.'

There was a moment's silence in the car as the other two men considered this.

'They were American, and they were trained,' said one. 'They knew that we were there, so we have to assume they know everything else about the American, Walker.'

The other man nodded.

'They fled the scene also, so they're not CIA or law enforcement. Walker took off, but they went after him and left us to it.'

Jae nodded, his thoughts clearing. His men were right, the two imposters were almost certainly working alone and were not part of American law enforcement. They too, then, were on the run. That could play into Jae's hands very nicely, as whoever they were, he could arrange for them to take the fall for the slaying of the CIA officers as well as Jae's comrade. They had taken the fallen man's pistol with them, and although it wasn't the same weapon that had killed the CIA officers, all of their pistols were bored identically, a measure to make it more difficult for foreign governments to tie any one weapon to any particular crime. The bullets used were custom made and bore no identifying marks.

'We need to ensure that the Americans become a target for law enforcement,' he said, his voice sounding heavy and nasal from the damage Walker had inflicted on him. 'We will call in a tip as anonymous witnesses, reporting the two Americans approaching a vehicle on Dupre Street and attacking the occupants. Local resident's descriptions of the two should support that and send law enforcement after them.'

His men nodded, but the driver seemed unconvinced.

'They saw us also,' he pointed out. 'That's not something that the Americans are going to ignore.'

Jae nodded in agreement. 'We can't cover everything, all we can do is confuse and distract until we have Walker in our hands. We will change clothes at the first opportunity, make the call straight after, and then start looking for Walker. Make sure you wear, what do they call them, hoodies? To make sure we are not identified on cameras. The Americans have them everywhere.'

Satisfied, Jae leaned back in the rear seat of the car and dabbed at his injured nose as he envisioned himself capturing the American who had hurt and embarrassed him so, tying him to a post, and slowly carving pieces off his body in a prolonged and intensely painful demise.

***

XXVI

Ethan drove in silence, keeping one eye on the rear-view mirror as he turned south on I64 toward Chesapeake. He had decided to avoid Norfolk, knowing that the CIA would be all over the city within hours and that there was a good chance that both his and Nicola's faces would be circulated to law enforcement.

'On the run again, huh?' Lopez said as she glanced at him.

Ethan nodded, but said nothing. It seemed they'd spent half their lives on the run from one agency or another, often CIA outfits working outside the normal boundaries of law and order. While that gave them a certain advantage now, the fact was that neither he nor Lopez enjoyed living off the grid. Forget the movies and the books about lone heroes wandering the wastelands of America righting wrongs: it was a hard, lonely and often traumatic experience that left even a natural loner like Ethan hankering for the comforts of a normal life.

'Where are we going?' Ernie asked from the back seat. 'And who the hell are you people?'

Ethan replied as he drove.

'Where we're going is up to you,' he said reasonably, 'but it might depend on what we have to tell you. As for who we are, that's a long story. This is Nicola, I'm Ethan, and we used to work for the US Government's intelligence agencies.'

'Used to?'

Ethan smiled. 'As you're discovering, they don't always have their operatives' best interests at heart. We were freelance for a while, walked away from it all two years ago, and were then approached by a general working for the CIA who wanted us to look into something for him. We did so, and got ourselves burned for our troubles. Turns out, we lost time, a few days' worth, and we're trying to figure out the how and why.'

Ernie peered at them both from where he sat. 'You lost time?'

'About three days,' Lopez confirmed. 'Almost slipped us by without us knowing it, but then we kind of recalled about half of what had gone missing. Point is, we know that you've experienced something similar and we wanted to find you to see if between us we can figure out what happened. We don't have any proof of our experience, but we think the government has been covering up what happened to you and your shipmates for decades, so going public with both our stories would force them out into the open.'

Ernie visible relaxed as he realized that they were genuine, that he wasn't alone.

'Damn, I thought it was me losing my mind.'

'You're not,' Ethan said. 'You're an unwitting victim in all of this, and it seems that everybody wants to talk to you about what happened.'

Ernie rolled his eyes. 'They could have just asked, but they broke into Henry's home and threatened to kill him and…. Do you think he's okay? Maybe we ought to go back and…'

'Henry will be fine,' Ethan assured him. 'There were police streaming in from every which way when we left, and those guys who threatened you wouldn't have had time to hang around to hurt Henry. They'd have run as fast as we did, and they won't be going back. Do you know who they were?'

Ernie relaxed a little again, and nodded.

'Koreans,' he said.

'You sure?' Lopez asked. 'How do you know?'

'Met plenty in Seoul in the Navy,' Ernie replied. 'You get to know the difference after a while. Pretty sure those guys were Commies, from the north.'

Ethan and Lopez exchanged a glance. 'That might explain why they're hostile to Americans, but it doesn't explain how they're here and how they know about you,' Ethan said.

Ernie replied softly as they drove.

'The Russians were always watching our exercises and our tests,' he said. 'They would have ships shadowing our fleets and battle groups at all times. The Korean War was only recently ended, so the Koreans themselves would have had an interest in what happened at Bikini Atoll. If they picked up any communications about the disaster, they would have known that something had gone wrong.'

'Yeah,' Lopez said, 'but what brought them here, now? How could they know that they should be looking for you, and not one of the other seamen who died? Why wouldn't they just think that you'd died out there too?'

'Surveillance and subterfuge,' Ethan guessed. 'We knew about Ernie because of the reports we got from Majuro. It's fair to assume that other countries might also have figured out what had happened and sent agents to check the story out.'

'What do they want from me?' Ernie asked. 'I don't know what the hell happened myself, so what use would I be to the North Koreans?'

'I don't think that they know themselves,' Lopez said. 'But they figure that having you in their custody gives them a better chance of understanding what happened to you, than letting you walk off with the CIA.'

Ernie seemed unconvinced.

'They don't want me talking,' he replied. 'They're keen to see this all hushed up. The crew of *Bairoko* were already under strict non-disclosure protocols even before the tests. I can't imagine what was said after the blast, when half the damned crew burned to a cinder when that thing went off, but Henry said they were all given such a scare that not one of them ever spilled the beans on what really happened.'

Ethan nodded. The witnesses would have been ordered, intimidated or both into absolute silence regarding what had happened. Although the event was unexpected, it still amounted to putting American service personnel in harm's way without warning them of the dangers. In modern times, the US Government would be facing a human rights calamity of unthinkable proportions, but half a century earlier, a battle group operating on the other side of the world was much easier to contain. There were no cell phones, no satellites, no optical fibre cables beneath the oceans, and a fleet running silent might be out of contact with the rest of the world for weeks at a time.

'There won't be many witnesses left,' Lopez pointed out, 'and most of them probably just thought you'd died.'

'Henry did,' Ernie confirmed. 'He couldn't believe it was me standing before him. How can this have happened?'

'That's what we're going to try to figure out,' Ethan promised. 'There's no way we want to hand you over to the CIA, let alone the North Koreans, but you can bet that they'll have us identified soon, so we're going to have to stay under their radar for now. There are one or two people that we can talk to, we'll check them out and see if they can understand what's happened, how it happened, and what we can do about it.'

Ernie nodded, looking somehow vulnerable and afraid now, perhaps as the magnitude of what had happened to him hit home.

'My children,' he said, 'I need to see them.'

'They'll be under surveillance,' Lopez promised. 'We won't be able to get within a quarter mile of them without the CIA picking you up, and I'll bet that the Koreans head the same way in the hope of picking up your trail.'

Ethan glanced in the rear-view mirror at Ernie as an idea crossed his mind.

'Ernie,' he said, 'don't take this the wrong way, but I need you to take your clothes off.'

*

General Mackenzie was not used to being out of uniform.

He watched from the rear seat of a sedan as the driver pulled into the sidewalk near a row of perfect lawns and whitewashed homes shining in the bright sunlight. Police cordons lined the entrance to Dupre, officers standing guard and detectives taking notes from witnesses.

Mackenzie climbed out of the unmarked car, his suit light on his shoulders compared to the snug fit of his uniform. He could not stroll into a crime scene wearing a four-star general's insignia without arousing media interest, but in a plain, dark suit and with sunglasses partially concealing his features, he looked like any other detective working a case in Virginia.

Mackenzie walked to the cordon and asked for Detective Amber Forsyth, who had caught the case an hour earlier. She had been informed that he would arrive soon, and Mackenzie was pleased to see her spot him without trouble and head over, waving him through the cordon.

'Detective,' Mackenzie greeted her with a handshake.

Amber Forsyth was petite, slim and looked sharp in a charcoal suit that contrasted with her long auburn hair.

'Sir,' she replied, both interested and cautious at the same time. 'Commissioner gave you access to my crime scene, which doesn't happen every day. What unit are you out of?'

Mackenzie smiled briefly as he walked with her. 'Tell me how this went down, please.'

Forsyth's green eyes peered sideways at him but she didn't press her question as she gestured to a nearby car that was sitting with its doors open.

'Two victims here in the vehicle, throats slit, neighbors didn't hear or see a thing. Pronounced dead at the scene, no identification. A third victim found at the home of one Henry Coleman, Asian origin, possibly Chinese or Korean, shot once through the belly, once again through the head. Locals heard those shots and the police were called.'

Mackenzie hesitated alongside the parked car and saw inside two bodies, both men in their thirties, both splattered with blood, eyes open and unseeing. Both had been killed with extreme precision and speed, and neither had time to draw their weapons.

'Both were armed,' Amber said as though reading his mind, 'both suited and booted, both carrying no identification. I'm sorry for your loss.'

Mackenzie looked at her directly now. Forsyth shrugged.

'Government agents,' she said, 'people working for you, obviously.'

'Obviously?' Mackenzie echoed.

'No badge,' she said as she gestured to the sedan he'd arrived in, 'and we detectives drive ourselves to crime scenes. We don't get chauffeurs, sir.'

Mackenzie cursed his own momentary lack of foresight. He'd been eager to get out here, but was so used to being driven it hadn't crossed his mind it would make him stand out among detectives.

'These men were patriots,' Mackenzie said. 'I need this to remain quiet.'

'Done,' Amber replied without issue. 'We figured who they were pretty fast, but we're keeping it from the media. Get your driver out of here and you can ride with us off scene, that should stop them from picking up on you.'

Mackenzie nodded. 'Do we have any potential suspects?'

'Locals identified two Americans and four Asian or Oriental men, all of whom were looking for a guy named Ernest Walker. Thing is, Ernest Walker turned up here a few minutes before them, apparently looking for his wife of all things.'

Mackenzie felt a chill run down his spine. 'He was here?'

Amber peered at Mackenzie again, interested. 'Sure, showed up at one of the homes here asking for a Margaret. I got a problem though – the woman's description of the man doesn't match the records we have of an Ernest Walker, who lived here decades ago. We're looking for someone who's described as about thirty years old, but Ernest Walker is registered as deceased and would have been at least seventy by now.'

'It's probably a son, or somebody impersonating Walker,' Mackenzie replied smoothly, his story developing on the fly. 'We're investigating an international fraud ring that uses out-dated personal identification papers to forge new identities based on deceased American citizens, a technique often employed by drug cartels but also by foreign agencies spying in the United States.'

Amber nodded as they walked to one of the houses. 'Sounds about right, given the nationalities of some of the supposed shooters. They all made their way here, to this guy's house, followed a few minutes later by two Americans, a man and a woman. Couple moments after that, all hell breaks loose and we've got this dead guy, one veteran traumatised in his own home and the rest of the perps' vanished. Anonymous tip-off from a few minutes ago pointed the finger at the two Americans, said they were the shooters. We're chasing that up right now.'

Mackenzie looked down at the dead Oriental man laying in the hall of the home, and at once he knew that he wasn't looking at a Chinese man, but a Korean one. If Warner and Lopez did wander into something here, they may have had an element of surprise and been able to disarm or defeat the North Koreans for long enough to get Ernie away from them.

'Where is the home owner?' Mackenzie asked.

Amber led him to an old man who was sitting in a wheelchair being tended to by a paramedic, whose efforts were clearly considered an affront.

'I'm fine,' the old man uttered. 'Stop fussin' over me, I've been through much worse!'

Mackenzie approached and took a knee alongside the old guy. The man, whose name Mackenzie knew to be Henry Coleman, stared back at him and somehow there was a recognition of some sort, that of a kindred spirit.

'Henry,' Mackenzie said carefully, 'these assholes just tried to kill your friend. You got any idea who they were?'

'North Korean,' Henry spat in reply, 'Commies one and all. What do you know about my friend?'

'That he's in big trouble, and I need to find him before the North Koreans do. You got any idea where he went?'

'Nah,' Henry shook his head, 'he took off over the fence, and I ain't quite the man I used to be so I couldn't follow. The two Americans did though. They were different, y'know? Good folk.'

Mackenzie nodded. His job had just got a lot tougher.

'They're doing what they believe is the right thing, protecting Ernie,' Mackenzie said, deliberately using Ernie's name to win Henry's trust. 'Trouble is, they've only got half the picture and it's gonna run them into even bigger trouble. I need to find them.'

Henry shook his head. "I don't know where they'll go, really I don't. Ernie's been dead and gone fifty years and now he's walking around here alive and well. I don't get it.'

Mackenzie glanced over his shoulder and saw Amber Forsyth watching him, her expression neutral but alarm bells probably ringing in her ears.

'Like I said,' Mackenzie said to her, 'identity theft.'

'Pah!' Henry shot back at him. 'My ass! That was Ernie, plain and simple. He knew our bunk aboard *Bairoko* and the names of our crew. Even knew who my girl was at the time. That was Ernie!'

'The criminals are very sophisticated these days,' Mackenzie said quickly as he stood and led Amber away from Henry. 'We need to find the Americans as quickly as we can. I believe that they're part of the fraud conspiracy. Their names are Ethan Warner and Nicola Lopez.'

Amber memorized the names.

'What was old Henry there talking about? It could be important to the case.'

'The fraudsters target the elderly and infirm,' Mackenzie explained. 'Probably posed as an old shipmate down on his luck to borrow money or something.'

'A fraudster wouldn't know the details that Henry said he did.'

'Focus on the Americans,' Mackenzie insisted, 'find them, we find everyone.'

'Detective?' A uniformed officer hurried up to Amber's side. 'Ernie Walker's been spotted; do you want us to move in?'

Mackenzie replied before Amber could. 'No, encircle the area but don't apprehend him. I want to be there.'

***

XXVII

Jae leaned forward in his seat as the car drove south toward Norfolk, and listened to the broadcasts coming from police units around the area.

Jae had made a call twenty minutes earlier from a call box outside a mall to report the sighting of two Americans shooting at foreign men on Dupre in Oceanview. They had then got into the car and driven away, blending in with the traffic but staying in the general area, hoping to either catch sight of their quarry or have the police guide them in.

'Possible suspect sighting on West and 9th, all units position but do not approach the subject – repeat, do not approach them, stand-off.'

The police receiver unit was not the best and the transmission was scratchy, but Jae had listened enough to be sure that they were talking about Ernie Walker.

'It's got to be him,' Jae said as he glanced at the car's GPS screen. 'How far are we?'

The passenger tapped the screen and located the intersection at West and 9th, just four blocks north of their position.

'We can be there in two minutes.'

Jae nodded as the driver turned and began heading north, not driving too fast so that they attracted unwanted attention, but at the same time cursing softly as other drivers dawdled in their path.

Jae kept watch out of the rear windows. They had all changed into jeans, T-shirts, sneakers and hooded tops, hoping to better blend in with the pedestrians all around them. He knew that the police would have numerous uniformed and plain-clothes police already surging through the area, so if they could find Walker their best bet would be to snatch him and run before splitting up, hoping to divide the law enforcement assets arrayed against them. Either way, thanks to the two Americans who had scuppered their plans, the chances of them being able to grab Ernie Walker without getting into a firefight with either law enforcement or the two interlopers looked less likely by the minute.

'It's just up ahead,' the driver said.

Jae looked through the windshield of the car and saw an intersection ahead of them, traffic slowing for a red light. The driver slowed, and Jae was about to put up his hoodie when he hesitated. The Americans would be looking for three Oriental males in suits. If he put up his hoodie on this fine spring morning and was spotted, he would immediately look suspicious. If, instead, he just walked about like a regular guy, he might not draw as much attention.

'Keep your hoods down,' he said to the two men in the front. 'I'll call you if I see him.'

As if in reply, the radio crackled again.

'Unit four-seven, suspect matching description in sight, beige slacks and blue shirt, on 9th. Holding back.'

Jae didn't wait any longer. As their car slowed to a halt in the traffic, he opened his door and stepped out smoothly onto the sidewalk, closed the door behind him and started walking with his hands in his pockets and his head held high as though he had not a care in the world.

The bright sunshine illuminated 9th below the shadows of trees just coming into blossom as Jae crossed the street and turned to walk its length, his eyes scanning left and right for any sign of Walker. The despatcher had described him as wearing beige slacks, a blue shirt and white or gray shoes. Jae passed students and business people hurrying about their business as he searched for some sign of the man, hoping against hope that he would spot him first and grab him before the police could pick him up.

*

General Mackenzie spotted the street as Amber Forsyth aimed for a gap in traffic gridlocked in front of red lights on West.

'I'm out here,' he informed her. 'I'll head west down 9th.'

'Hey, you don't get to just wander down....'

Mackenzie got out of the vehicle before it even stopped moving, hit the sidewalk and closed the door as he hurried to the intersection and turned west, weaving this way and that between the bustling crowds. At six two, Mackenzie was taller than most and despite not wearing his uniform the crowds parted naturally before him as he hurried along, scanning the faces around him for some sign of Walker.

Right now, all he had imprinted on his mind was a fifty-year-old photograph of Walker, taken aboard *USS Bairoko* a few days before the Castle Bravo test. He knew that Ernie appeared to be an old man now, that somehow his passage forward in time had caused his body to age just the same as if he'd lived an entirely normal life. Neither he nor Kyle Trent had any idea how that was possible, and it would make positive identification of Ernie tougher than ever. Most everybody involved in the search had assumed that they were looking for a man in his early thirties.

Mackenzie was half way down 9th when he spotted an old man walking ahead of him on the opposite side of the street. Mackenzie saw the color of the man's shirt and slacks, and instantly he focused in on him as he sought a way across the street.

The vehicles were queuing both ways as Mackenzie moved between them, and as he did so he spotted an Asian man mirroring his actions. Short, stocky, wearing a hooded top and walking with his hands in his pockets as though he might be concealing something. It took only a moment's observation for Mackenzie to be sure that the man in the hoodie was heading directly toward Ernie Walker.

'All units, be advised, possible armed combatants in the area,' Mackenzie whispered into his microphone.

As he did so, the man in the hoodie spotted him. There was a brief moment when American CIA agent and North Korean assassin stared at each other for just a moment too long for it to be a coincidence, and then the man in the hoodie whipped his hands out of his pockets and Mackenzie saw the pistol in the man's hands, black and wicked as the barrel whipped up to point directly at him.

'Gun!'

Mackenzie hurled himself into cover behind an SUV as two shots rang out loud and clear over the sound of vehicle engines. A rush of screams of terror joined the cacophony as motorists realized they were being fired upon and were trapped in their vehicles.

Mackenzie pulled his own firearm from his shoulder holster and jumped back up, aiming for the man in the hoodie. He spotted him dash across the street and collide with the old man, and Mackenzie cursed as he realized that he couldn't shoot without perhaps injuring Ernie Walker.

Another car screeched into view, this time coming from the other direction on the far side of the lights. The car braked and swung broadside onto the intersection, its doors flying open as two more Asian men leaped out and opened fire on Mackenzie's position.

The general ducked down once more, flinching as he heard bullets zinging off metalwork or thudding into it all around him. The sound of screaming sirens echoed across the city as the police and armed units converged on the intersection, and Mackenzie knew that backup was now only seconds away.

He leaped from his position of cover and fired twice, both times at the man in the front of the vehicle. The first shot missed, shattering the passenger window alongside him, but the second caught the man in the side and he span away and collapsed onto the ground even as the vehicle in which he'd arrived accelerated away.

Mackenzie saw the man in the hoodie in the rear seat, and nearby the old man lying on the sidewalk, unmoving. Mackenzie dashed down the street to where the fallen North Korean was stretching to reach his firearm, and Mackenzie stamped down on his wrist before he could reach the weapon as he aimed his pistol down at the man's head.

'Don't move, or it'll be the last thing you'll ever do.'

Police cars screeched around a far corner and accelerated toward Mackenzie as the general looked across to the sidewalk. The old man was sitting up now, blood trickling from his nose, but even from twenty feet away Mackenzie could see that it wasn't Ernest Walker. The old man was wearing the same clothes, but it wasn't the man they were looking for.

The coincidence was too great to ignore.

'Warner,' Mackenzie uttered as he holstered his weapon.

Detective Amber Forsyth rushed to his side, her own weapon in her hand as police officers cuffed the North Korean. She looked up at him and then down at the man at their feet.

'What do you want doing with him?' she asked.

Mackenzie grit his teeth, anger coursing through his veins.

'You don't want to know. I need this event explained away; drug wars, robbery gone wrong, anything you like. This guy comes with us.'

XXVIII

University of Virginia, Charlottesville

'I'm not sure I like this idea.'

Ernie Walker sat in the rear of the car and peered out of the windscreen at the university in front of them. Ethan had driven for two hours straight to get them there after their escape from Norfolk, and was eager to stretch his legs in the warm afternoon sunshine.

'Trust me, this is the best way to get to the bottom of why the government and the North Koreans are so keen to get their hands on you.'

The air was warm as Ethan got out, and saw Rhys Garrett hurrying out to meet them.

'You made it,' he said, evidently relieved. 'I heard on the news there was a shoot-out in Norfolk.'

'Yeah,' Lopez replied with a vague shrug as she gestured to Ethan. 'Just another trail of destruction behind Captain America here.'

'We ran into some unexpected opposition,' Ethan explained. 'You know that the North Koreans are in the game?'

Rhys appeared genuinely surprised as he shook his head. 'How the hell would they know anything about all of this? They hardly ever cross their own borders.'

'They're here,' Lopez confirmed. 'They've already killed two CIA operatives and I don't think they're big fans of us now.'

'Great,' Rhys uttered, and then he hesitated as he saw Ernie get out of the vehicle.

There was a sense of reverence from Rhys, Ethan getting the impression that Rhys knew precisely who the man was despite them not yet having been introduced.

'Rhys,' Lopez said, 'this is Ernie Walker.'

Ernie peered at Rhys with interest but said nothing as the billionaire moved around the car to stand before the seaman.

'Is it true?' he asked. 'Did you really come here from 1954?'

Ernie seemed hesitant, but he nodded. 'Sure, it is. Now all I want to do is get the hell back there, where I belong.'

Rhys nodded, and the pair shook hands. 'I don't know how to do that,' he admitted. 'But we're trying to figure it out. I have something to show you all.'

Rhys led them inside the university. He could see Ernie looking around and taking it all in as they walked to a consultancy room that was dominated by what looked like some kind of MRI scanner, but one where the subject was able to sit upright rather than lying down.

Beside the machine a doctor was waiting for them whom Ethan recognised immediately.

Richard Boltman waited until Rhys had closed the door behind them, and then he looked at Ernie.

'You must be Ernest Walker,' he said with a smile. 'You don't know it, but you're already something of a star around here.'

'So I've noticed,' Ernie replied. 'What's that thing?'

Ernie gestured to the big scanner.

'This is an MRI scanner,' Dr Boltman explained. 'Magnetic Resonance Imaging. It can scan your brain from one end to the other, even its inside, without anything ever touching you.'

Ernie's eyes narrowed. 'Like an X-Ray, right?'

'Yes,' Boltman replied. 'It's a little noisier than an X-Ray machine but the effect is somewhat the same.'

'Why do you want to scan Ernie's brain?' Lopez asked, somewhat protectively. 'The guy's been through enough.'

It was Rhys that answered as Doctor Boltman placed Ernie in the MRI seat and activated the machine, which hummed and rattled quite loudly for such a modern piece of equipment.

'Doctor Boltman has done some work on prior cases where he noticed something unusual about people who claim to have psychic powers of one kind or another. Most such people can rightly be dismissed as hoaxers or delusional, but a small number of them seem to have something going on that modern science cannot explain.'

'Such as?' Ethan asked. 'And what's that go to do with Ernie?'

'Everything, as it turns out,' Boltman said, retaking center stage. 'You see, I think I know why it is that the government are so interested in apprehending Ernie. I don't think that it's all about interrogating him or questioning him on what happened, because I think it's fair to say that none of us yet really know how it happened. But we can infer certain things, and I believe that it ties in with events of a few days ago in North Korea.'

Now the doctor had Ethan's full attention.

'The North Koreans have been chasing Ernie since he got here, and we can't figure out how they would even begin to know about what happened in 1954.'

'That's because what happened at Bikini Atoll in 1954 was something that the North Koreans, among other nations, were watching very closely. The detonation of the Castle Bravo test was powerful enough that measurements of the event were recorded all around the world, and that meant that some nations may have also worked out since what happened to Ernie, and were just waiting for him to show up.'

Lopez frowned. 'You mean that they knew he'd been pushed forward in time?'

'We think so,' Garrett confirmed. 'In the fifty years since the nuclear test science has come a long way, and they would have studied the Castle Bravo test intensely because of the unexpectedly high yield that led to Ernie's disappearance. If they have any understanding at all of what happens to time in the presence of events like nuclear detonations and intense electromagnetic fields, then they may have recognized the conditions that occurred around the bow of *USS Bairoko* and put two and two together.'

'Again,' Lopez demanded, 'how does this tie in with Ernie?'

Doctor Boltman gestured to a map on the wall of the human brain, one that was colored in different areas depending on what those area's responsibilities were.

'A study in Brazil of people who claimed to be mediums sought to understand what happened inside the brains of people who claimed to be speaking to the dead, through the process of "channeling" written communications from "the other side" while in a trance-like state. They were not looking for evidence of the supernatural. Rather, they sought to explain rationally what they assumed must be a sort of delusion, a belief that people were speaking to the dead when instead they were channeling their own subconscious, for instance. What they found instead was extremely disturbing.'

Boltman tapped his own head with a biro pen.

'The subjects, all either experienced or novice mediums, were injected with a radioactive tracer to monitor brain activity during normal writing, and also the practice of psychography, writing in a trance while their hands are being supposedly controlled by the spirit they're in contact with. They were scanned using a single-photon-emission computed tomography machine, SPECT for short, to identify which areas of the brain were active during supposedly psychic and non-psychic activity. The experienced psychographers showed lower levels of activity in the left hippocampus of the limbic system, right superior temporal gyrus, and the frontal lobe regions of the brain during psychography, compared to their normal writing. This means that the mediums were experiencing reduced focus, lessened self-awareness and fuzzy consciousness during psychography.'

'Okay, so?' Lopez asked.

'Well, for the less experienced mediums, exactly the opposite was observed - increased levels of activity in the same frontal areas during psychography compared to normal writing, and the difference was significant compared to the experienced mediums. But the interesting part was that the writing samples produced were analyzed and it was found that the complexity scores for the psychograph content were higher than those for the control writing across the board. In particular, the more experienced mediums showed higher complexity scores, which typically would require more activity in the frontal and temporal lobes-- precisely the opposite of what was observed.'

'Which means?' Ethan asked, still not really understanding the point.

'Which means that the more experienced and more deeply entranced the subjects, the more accurate their channelled writing became, when all our understanding of the human brain suggests they should have been able to do little more than sit there. It's the opposite of what should have happened, and that suggests that…'

'Somebody else really is controlling their hand when they're writing in a trance,' Lopez said, understanding the issue. 'And the deeper they're in the trance, the better their connection to the supposed spirit world.'

'Precisely,' Boltman confirmed, and then he looked at Ernie. 'It's my suspicion that Ernie did not end up fifty years in the future because he just happened to be hit by a bolt of nuclear energy. I think that he ended up here because his brain was attuned in just the right way for the energy to do what was required.'

Ethan frowned.

'I don't get how that works.'

Doctor Boltman smiled.

'That's because we think of our brains as objects which look out into the universe and make rational sense of what we're seeing. My research shows that the opposite is true: our brains are not the controlling factor in what we see as reality. In my opinion, the brain is more like an antenna, picking up signals from the outside, and that means that if it's tuned correctly, the human brain is capable of detecting things that we would normally refer to as paranormal or supernatural.'

***

XXIX

Ethan still wasn't sure that he was following quite what the doctor was trying to tell him.

'The brain is an antenna?'

'Yes, in a manner of speaking,' Boltman replied. 'It makes sense when you think about it. Everything we see in the world around us comes through the retina of our eye, information that is absorbed by our brains, translated, assembled into something that we can understand. Our eyes actually see the world outside inverted – it's our brain that flips that image and allows us to see the world as it truly is.'

'But doesn't that mean that the brain is the repository of ourselves, contradicting what you're claiming?' Lopez asked.

'In ordinary circumstances, yes,' Boltman agreed, 'during everyday life our brain controls our responses and what we see, guides us in our daily routines, remembers things and so on. But, when you look at it, the brain is easily tripped up, deceived, sees things that are not there and misses other things that are. It is an imperfect device, even in our daily lives. Studies have shown that the human brain is more accurately described as a receiver of information that assembles that information into something that makes sense to it, to us. That doesn't mean that what we see is what truly is. Take the spectrum of light, for instance. We only see in what we call optical light, which accounts for a tiny fraction of the electromagnetic spectrum. The vast majority of what's visible in the universe is in fact invisible to us, or at least our eyes and therefore our brain. Modern cameras can see this hidden world, but we cannot. My point is, perhaps some of the supposedly supernatural phenomena that some people claim to see are in fact people whose brains are attuned slightly differently to ours, that they can sometimes see or sense what we cannot.'

Ethan thought about that for a moment.

'Maybe the government doesn't want Ernie for himself, but for his mind.'

Boltman nodded, and Ethan thought back to what the doctor had described during their previous meeting, places around the world where strange time-slips had occurred on regular occasions, too many to simply be the figment of people's imaginations. These events were occurring in many places and often enough that something had to be driving them.

'If Ernie has something unique in him that could help the government understand how he got here,' Lopez said, 'and they could then manipulate that...'

Boltman clicked the thumb and finger of one hand.

'Precisely,' he said. 'To understand the fundamental path of time and its relation to the human experience, to connect the two and allow us to travel through time, would change just about every aspect of the human story in a flash, and I think that I know how they intend to do it.'

'You *know* how they do it?' Lopez uttered.

'Well, I *think* that I know how they intend to do it,' Boltman said, 'so there's a difference, but in principal I think I understand why they want to talk to Ernie so badly. Ah, he's finished.'

The MRI scanner stopped humming, and Doctor Boltman helped Ernie out.

'How was it?' Lopez asked. 'Did the earth move for you?'

'I feel like I've been in a tumble drier,' Ernie complained. 'Was it worth it?'

Doctor Boltman hurried to a screen, and using a remote he pulled up several images of Ernie's brain. Despite himself, Ernie was fascinated both with the images and the fact that they were in full, vibrant color on huge flat screens.

'Gee whiz guys, this is incredible. Is that my brain?'

'Every atom of it,' Boltman confirmed, and as he scrolled through various slices of the image that the MRI had built, so he stopped and pointed at the image.

'And there we go,' he said as he gestured to an area of Ernie's brain that showed activity in the hippocampus. 'Ernest shows the same pattern of activity in that region of the brain that appears in the scans of Brazilian mediums and other psychic people around the world. Ernie has something that the government wants but cannot manufacture for itself.'

Ethan shook his head.

'It's like Project Stargate all over again.'

'Project what?' Ernie asked.

'Project Stargate,' Boltman replied for Ethan, 'a covert CIA program that ran during the 1970s and 1980s. American intelligence agencies discovered that the Soviets were investigating paranormal phenomena, with an aim of using it to gain an advantage in the Cold War, so they began their own programs into mind control, remote viewing and other esoteric skills to counter the Soviet threat.'

'Did it work?' Ernie asked.

'In a fashion,' Boltman said. 'The program was mostly closed down because the intelligence gathered was difficult to interpret. That said, the skills displayed by those recruited to the program was undeniable. Remote viewers identified rings around the planet Neptune long before NASA probes were able to photograph them, and others identified military structures behind the Iron Curtain that were later confirmed by spy planes and satellites. The only reason Stargate was not continued was because the viewers could see things clearly, but lacked the skills to properly identify what they were seeing. Much money was spent chasing up suspected Soviet nuclear arms facilities, for instance, only to discover that they were in fact ordinary power stations or similar. Regular spy photography from aircraft or satellites was eventually deemed more reliable, but the skills of the viewers was proven several times during the course of the program.'

Ernie blinked as he looked at the screen. 'And I have that ability?'

'I don't know,' Boltman replied, 'but what we do know is that the bolt of errant energy that hit *USS Bairoko* should have blasted half the ship's crew into the future, yet only you are here. That, to me, means that there's something particularly special about you, and I'm certain that your brain is wired differently to most people. That would tie in with my research into quantum fields, whereby the universe is what it is only because we are here to observe it.'

'What now?' Lopez uttered.

Doctor Boltman leaned against a desk and folded his arms as he replied.

'The simple fact is that experiments over the last fifty years have confirmed that electrons react only when they're being observed. Quantum mechanics states that particles like electrons can also behave as waves: electrons behave as waves when unobserved, but when they are observed they immediately act as particles. This means that the mere act of a scientist observing an experiment has an effect on the results of that experiment.'

'I think my head's about to explode,' Ernie moaned.

'In simpler terms,' Boltman said, 'the fundamental particles that make up our universe respond to us observing them. If our sense of self, who we are and what controls us resides in the brain, then the universe responds to the human mind.'

Ethan felt as though he was surfing the outer fringes of what his own labored brain could manage to understand, but he felt as though he saw a glimmer of where the doctor was going.

'Ernie had some control over his travel through time?'

Boltman smiled. 'Nice try, but not quite. It's my estimation that Ernie did not travel through time at all.'

'What?' Ernie snapped. 'Damn it, doctor, I'm right *here*.'

'Yes, you are,' Boltman agreed. 'You are here, *yourself*, your sense of who you are. I don't believe that it is possible for a human body to travel physically through time, either forwards or backwards, but I also don't believe that physical time travel is necessary. What if it's only our minds, our sense of self, our souls if you will, that are required?'

There was a long moment of silence.

'Okay, time out,' Lopez said, waving her arms. 'Unless you're about to roll some joints and start strumming a guitar, this is gettin' too weird.'

Boltman smiled. 'It *is* weird, but it explains a lot about what we're witnessing here, about what lots of people witness when they experience time slips of one kind or another. Look, it's a long shot I know, but we have to find some kind of mechanism to explain how some people see the past and others like Ernie end up in the future. Just those two events on their own are weird enough.'

'Sure they are,' Ethan agreed, 'why make it harder? Occam's Razor and all that.

'But Occam's principle applies well here,' Boltman argued. 'The simplest answer is often the most correct and should not be contaminated with other, larger mysteries. Look at time: it's governed by how much space there is, and how long light takes to travel across that space, which gives us a definition of time. We see the sun as it was eight minutes ago, the nearest star as it was over four years ago, the nearest galaxy as it was two million years ago. We see the past all around us. What most folks don't think about is that an intelligent civilization ten light years from here sees the Earth as it was ten years ago. They're seeing our past as though it was now, thus to them our past is the present, still on-going through their eyes. It is thus logical to assume that the past, being in principal still visible from some quarters of the universe, still exists.'

There was another long silence.

'*Soooo...?*' Lopez peered at Boltman.

'So, if one had the kind of mind that Ernie and psychics have, and they were surrounded by the right kind and amount of energy, then in principle it is possible that their mind could bridge the gap between past and present. They could leap not through time itself, but from their own presence in one frame of time to their own presence in another. It's not the body that travels through time, but the mind.'

***

XXX

'That doesn't make sense,' Lopez said as she thought about what Boltman had said. 'Ernie's right here in body *and* mind.'

The doctor nodded in agreement, but his expression was one of a man disturbed by what he was seeing.

'Yes, and that's the upsetting part about all of this.'

'Speak for yourself,' Ernie said.

Boltman sighed.

'What we really don't understand here is the nature of existence, the fabric of reality. That some people, sometimes, seem able to see glimpses of the past is a known fact, something that we can rely on. It's vanishingly rare, but it does happen. So, logically, some semblance of time travel by humans is possible. The extent and limitations of how that travel can be conducted is what we don't know, a frontier of science that is as nebulous as the clouds of gas between stars. Ernie is indeed here in body as well as mind, so does that mean he intercepted his own consciousness in the future? We just don't know.'

'Can't be that,' Ethan said. 'Ernie showed up at the same spot he disappeared from, fifty or so years later.'

'Ah,' Boltman interjected, 'but what determined his location? The future, as far as we know, is something that is fluid, forever changing, something that cannot be pinned down. Could it be that, accepting that the universe responds to our observing it, once Ernie was struck by that energy bolt, his future position was only then secured by the fact that he witnessed the bolt in the first place?'

'I need a lie down,' Lopez mumbled.

Ernie Walker rubbed his temples. 'Guys, this is giving me a real headache here. Can I get back again to my own time? And if so, how the hell can I make it happen?'

Ethan felt somewhat ashamed. They had been talking about Ernie's predicament as though discussing a lab-rat's, while he was standing right among them. Doctor Boltman removed his spectacles and cleaned them on his lab coat as he replied.

'In principal, the fact that you got here at all suggests that, yes, there should be a means to return you back to the time from which you came. However, your journey here was facilitated by one of the largest nuclear weapon detonations in human history, which isn't something you can pick up at Walmart.'

'Nuclear testing was banned in the 1980s,' Lopez said. 'And the world is orbited by satellites that look out for missile launches and detonations. Even if one were to occur, all that would happen is that the world would be brought to the brink of nuclear annihilation, which ranks real high on the list of Bad Outcomes for Everybody.'

'So, I'm stuck here then,' Ernie said, deflated.

Doctor Boltman nodded.

'There is no known mechanism on earth that I know of that would be able to generate the energies needed to replicate the events of the Castle Bravo test shot, and even if there were, and even if the nice people that ran the thing were to lend us the keys, there's no guarantee that it would work. Who knows what could happen? What if you were sent another fifty years into the future? Another hundred?'

Ernie seemed undeterred.

'It doesn't matter, I'd rather try than not try.'

'There's nowhere you can go,' Ethan said. 'We just don't have those sorts of explosions anymore.'

'Well, *we* don't,' Boltman said, 'but there are a few places where the energies are high enough that it might perhaps affect Ernie in the way that the Castle Bravo event did.'

'Where?' Ernie asked.

'The CERN labs in Geneva, the Large Hadron Collider,' Boltman replied. 'They accelerate particles there close to the speed of light and collide them together to see what fundamental particles pop out. Sometimes, when the energies are high enough, the collider creates miniature black holes. They're too small to last long, but their event horizons might be enough to affect an individual.'

'What's an event horizon?' Ernie asked.

Boltman smiled.

'The strangest place in the universe, is what it is,' he replied. 'The Event Horizon is the point around a black hole where gravity has become so intense that time effectively stands still. Beyond it, even light cannot escape. An observer on the edge of the Event Horizon would theoretically see the life of the universe pass by in an instant, while the observer outside would never see an object actually fall into the black hole. Of course, light is bent so completely that close to the black hole, that in truth the observer falling in would only ever see the back of their own head, and only then for a fraction of a second as their entire body was heated to millions of degrees and torn apart at the molecular level as…'

'Another high-roller on the Bad for Everybody list,' Lopez cut the doctor off before he hit a roll of his own. 'Look, we get the idea. Somehow, however mad it may seem, people can move through time. About the only thing we don't have is evidence of anybody being able to *control* that travel, other than what we call UFOs. They're supposedly flitting back and forth all the damned time, so how do we get one of them to show us how to get Ernie here back to 1954?'

Boltman's shoulders sank and he shook his head.

'I'm sorry, but I really don't have an answer for that, and I doubt you'll find an expert anywhere in the world who has the faintest idea how you would achieve it.'

Ethan shook his head.

'I know somebody who might know what to do, but we're gonna have a hard time finding him.'

'Who?' Ernie asked.

'He's talking about Kyle Trent,' Lopez explained. 'We think that Kyle works for the government now, and he's probably on the same team that's trying to hunt you down.'

Ernie leaned against a wall and rubbed his temples. 'Look, this is all happening way too fast for me and, to be real honest, I don't give a damn about electrons or event horizons or anything else. If there's a way that I can get back to my own time, I'm going to take it. If you want me to testify on the record that what happened to you, and to me, is a real thing, I don't have a problem with that. I'll do it. But in return, if you say this Trent person might know a way, then I want to meet him, and the North Koreans can go to hell.'

With that, Ernie walked out of the office and headed back in the general direction of their vehicle.

Lopez looked at Ethan and smiled. 'I like this guy.'

Boltman seemed less convinced.

'Having the CIA wandering around looking for you isn't something you want to happen every day,' he warned. 'They have a nasty habit of operating above and outside of the law.'

'We know,' Ethan replied, and then by way of an explanation added: 'Plenty of experience.'

'Let's go,' Lopez said. 'It's either Mackenzie or the Koreans, and I think I know who I want to take my chances with.'

Ethan turned to Rhys Garrett. 'We'll head back to Norfolk, quietly, and make contact with Mackenzie's team one way or the other. Stay sharp for us, we might need to get out of dodge real fast if the Koreans find us.'

'I'll have my jet on stand-by,' Rhys promised. 'Just say the word.'

***

XXXI

'How the hell did they know about Ernie Walker?'

Mackenzie stormed up and down inside a CIA safe house in Norfolk, their first point of egress after the chaotic shoot out. Fury seared and scalded his veins as he tried to figure out who the hell their attackers were and how they knew anything at all about Ernie Walker.

'We're searching the databases now sir,' an aide assured him as she typed feverishly into a computer terminal. 'We've accessed local law enforcement databases and are running searches, but all of the combatants were wearing hoods: that will make identification almost impossible unless we have some other way of imaging them.'

Mackenzie cursed. He knew that he'd looked the killer of CIA agents right in the eye before he'd escaped, and yet he also knew that any description of the man would be useless, as it was so tough to accurately describe an Oriental or Asian person and have them look different to another of their race.

'Check every CCTV system that's online,' he ordered. 'I want blanket coverage of every possible egress route and I want law enforcement monitored every minute of the day. If these people emerge again, I want them in our custody before their damned feet hit the sidewalk.'

'Yes sir!'

Mackenzie strode with purpose outside into the garden of the safe house, knowing that he could not take his anger out on his staff and knowing likewise that his best course of action was to allow them to do their jobs without having to look over their shoulders at him.

The sunshine was warm, the sky bright and blue, but he could not shake the cloud of misery that haunted him now. Two men dead, his people almost exposed to half the damned city, foreign agents on the run and all of it involving his supposedly covert team. What annoyed him most of all was that Warner and Lopez were, as ever, at the heart of the chaos. Now, he had several potential enemies in play and he couldn't tell which one of them had Ernie Walker with them, or if Ernie himself had simply escaped and, understandably, fled for his life.

'Sir?'

Wearily, Mackenzie turned and saw an aide waving to him. 'What is it?'

'It's command, sir.'

Mackenzie felt his guts flip as he considered the mess that was being created here in Norfolk, and how he was going to explain why they didn't have Ernie Walker in military custody yet.

He braced himself and then walked back inside the house and up the stairs to a secure communications suite that occupied one of the master bedrooms. Sound proofed on all sides, once he closed the door behind him it was just him and a row of four widescreen televisions mounted on the walls, each with a number beneath it. Filling each was an image of a senior SOG officer's face.

'General,' the oldest of them began, 'we just got news of what happened in Norfolk. Is your team safe?'

Mackenzie felt a rush of gratitude and relief as he realized that even at those echelons of power, there was still concern for the ordinary field agent and the dangers they faced.

'We lost two,' he replied briskly. 'We have learned that there are foreign agents on the ground, possibly North Korean, and they're not so keen on asking questions first.'

The officers before him nodded, deep in their own thoughts about what that meant for the project.

'General,' Mackenzie's superior went on, 'we can't risk exposure like this, but I do understand that this turn of events was unexpected. We can confirm that the North Koreans are involved.'

Mackenzie's heart flipped a beat and his fists clenched. 'Have you identified their agents?'

'No,' came the reply, 'but the National Security Agency has intercepted communications suggesting that Pyongyang is in contact with a small cell operating on America's east coast. Everything we have says they're in Norfolk.'

Mackenzie closed his eyes for a moment, barely able to supress his rage.

'How? How could they have known about any of this?'

'That's what we want you to find out,' the superior said. 'We understand that you have a captive, somebody from the Koreans?'

'Yes,' Mackenzie replied. 'He was injured during the confrontation. My team managed to get him away from local law enforcement before the media arrived.'

'Good. You have authority to use all necessary means to extract identifications for all the North Korean players. Pyongyang will of course deny all knowledge of their presence here, and likely suggest that they are tourists and demand their return. The fact that nobody leaves North Korea without permission, on threat of death, betrays that lie, but diplomacy being what it is we won't be able to hold them for long unless you can prove that they were behind the murder of our agents.'

'Don't worry,' Mackenzie replied in a tight voice, 'I'll make damned sure that they're put on the hook for it.'

The superior nodded. 'And ensure that anybody else involved in the chaos down there is likewise suitably punished by the law. I don't want any loose ends after this has all blown over.'

'No sir.'

'How long before you have Walker in your custody?'

Mackenzie knew better than to lie to such men, for they had no qualms about replacing him with another should he fail to perform his duties to their satisfaction.

'Unknown. We have the area surrounded and it's air tight, so they cannot leave, but that area is large and we have few resources. Law enforcement is on our side, but it'll be tough to label Ernie a fugitive and then snatch him away from the police should they locate and arrest him. Too many questions will be asked.'

'Then what do you propose, general, to both bring these problems to a close and suitably cover our tracks?'

Mackenzie thought for a moment.

'Witnesses described the men as Chinese, so we can cover that as having them portrayed as immigrant gangsters, looking to rob the home of an elderly veteran. Our agents can't be named, obviously, so I will endeavour to keep their murders out of the media eye. The detective leading the investigation is on our side, and understands there is a need for discretion.'

That got a nod of appreciation from all four men.

'And the two Americans, Warner and Lopez, who again seem to be caught up in all of this?' the officer demanded.

'They're in this because we put them in it,' Mackenzie said. 'They're patriots for sure, but they're also angry and looking for answers. How the hell they got wind of what happened to Ernie Walker so quickly I don't know, but they're citizens and we can't just put them in jail or otherwise stone wall them. They won't give up.'

That didn't get a nod.

'Deal with them, one way or the other,' the officer insisted. 'We can't afford any more public exposure to the operation. The facility you asked to be constructed at Kwajalein Island is almost ready for the first test, but until we have Ernie Walker here, we can't go ahead. I don't think I need to remind you that the North Koreans conducted their first tests some time ago?'

'No, sir,' Mackenzie replied. 'Ernie can't run forever, and I'm assuming that the fact the North Koreans are here at all suggests that their own test has failed. They must need someone like Ernie just as much as we do.'

'Agreed,' came the response from Number Three. 'The Koreans will attempt to reacquire Walker before he can leave Virginia, but they must also have only a small team in play. Obtain the identities of their team, and ensure that they cannot move freely anywhere in the continental United States, likewise for Warner and Lopez. Force their hand, and get Walker in custody. We will fly him out to the island as soon as you are ready.'

With that, all four screens blinked out and left Mackenzie alone in the silent room. He took a brief moment to compose himself, to set firmly in his mind his intentions, and then he turned and opened the door. He walked out of the room and down the corridor to another, this one also soundproofed. He opened the door, walked in and closed it behind him.

This room contained a single chair, upon which was sitting the North Korean agent they had captured. The man was utterly still, as though he was some uncannily accurate waxwork. His smooth oriental skin furthered the illusion, and at first glance it seemed to Mackenzie that the man was in some kind of induced trance, oblivious to the room around him.

To either side of the captive stood a member of Mackenzie's security team. Both men were former Special Forces, both conditioned to the harsh world of covert operations.

'Full authority,' was all that Mackenzie had to say to them.

The two men moved instantly.

The first walked to the captive and grabbed a handful of his hair. He yanked it back so that the North Korean was pinned awkwardly in place.

The second man lifted a tiny syringe that contained a dribble of clear fluid, and without hesitation he injected it into the captive's neck.

Mackenzie knew what the fluid was. He had seen it used before, and seen grown men weep within seconds of its application. The syringe contained the concentrated venom of the South American bullet ant, the insect with the world's most agonising bite.

The syringe emptied into the man's neck, and for a moment there was no reaction. Then, slowly, the captive's eyes widened and sweat began to bead on his forehead. His body began to shake and shudder, his teeth gritted, and then, just as he opened his mouth to scream, the first of the real venom started to hit his bloodstream and he let out a horrifying shriek of unimaginable agony that caused Mackenzie's ears to ring.

The operative holding the Korean's hair kept his head tilted back as he held him in place and lifted a second syringe.

'This will make it all go away,' he said, letting their captive see the syringe with a blue fluid within it. 'Start talking. Where are you from?'

The Korean squeezed his eyes shut, hyperventilating and writhing in his seat, and then he collapsed into horrendous shrieks of raw pain as Mackenzie waited for the captive's resolve to break.

***

XXXII

Jae-Hyuk Pak crouched in the darkness and waited, silent as a panther and just as determined.

There was no time to lose now, and despite his focus on the task at hand, forever in the back of his mind was an image of his wife and children back in Pyongyang, wondering, waiting, facing an abysmal doom should he fail to achieve his task.

The loss of Tian was a terrible blow to Jae, their driver captured by the Americans. The fact that he had still been alive was an even greater loss, for Jae knew that the Americans would by now be taking him to pieces in some CIA black prison somewhere.

The Geneva Convention supposedly applied to prisoners of war, but Jae knew that it was a token gesture, a guide, not a set of rules. His men had executed two CIA agents one day previously, so by now the Americans' blood would be up and they would physically shatter Tian in order to learn what they could about the North Korean team. Tian was a patriot, a man who knew that his best bet in life was to serve their Dear Leader with absolute conviction, in order to shorten the odds that he would be sent to the *gulags* with his family for some indiscretion or other, whether real or imagined. But nobody could resist pain, no matter what the ridiculous *Hollywood* movies portrayed: it simply was not in the human psyche to be able to resist the agony of electrical shocks or having a limb sawn off. Tian would fold, and if he was smart, he would fold quickly and ensure that he could someday make it back home to Pyongyang, if he still had a home to go to by then.

Jae had been forced to contact Pyongyang via agents in Manila after the deception in Norfolk, in order to report their progress and ask for more resources. The loss of Tian had been followed with intelligence data, which Jae had picked through with a fine-tooth comb in order to figure out where to take his team next in the search for Ernest Walker.

About all they had was a silver sedan seen leaving the area of the shoot-out just before it occurred. The CCTV image of the vehicle, and of Ernie Walker alongside it, was blurry and indistinct but it was clear enough for Jae to be sure that it was their man standing there, and with him were the two Americans, the woman's long dark hair easily identifiable.

Jae's contacts back in Pyonyang had hacked their way into the American traffic network system and been able to follow the sedan all the way to a university in Charlottesville. Jae had almost leaped in pursuit, only to find that the vehicle had then been seen returning toward Norfolk. Jae had no idea why the occupants of the vehicle would return, and had immediately wondered whether it was some kind of ruse once more, to deceive Jae and his team into following another false lead. Then he considered the fact that the two Americans had fought to evade the CIA also, and wondered whether they had suffered a change of heart. The hackers had also revealed the location of the man with whom Jae had exchanged shots in Norfolk, tracking his vehicles to a non-descript property in the south of the city.

To that end, Jae had decided to turn the tables on his nemesis, the American CIA. Despite his limited numbers, Jae had split his team into two: Jae's team would go after Ernest Walker, while the other would move to silence Tian and remove the CIA units from play, cleaning up any loose ends along the way.

The hacking team had tracked the American's vehicle back to a motel just south of Norfolk, while Jae and his men had moved west to intercept it.

Jae's team now crouched amid bushes opposite the run-down motel on the edge of town as he waited for what he hoped would be his chance to grab their quarry and run. Time was of the essence, because there was no doubt that the CIA would be tracking the same data and would be here within minutes, and Jae had to get Ernie out of whichever room he was hiding in and away into the night before he and his team were overwhelmed.

'Go, now.'

Jae directed his five accomplices, each to a wing of the motel as he hurried across the parking lot and approached the motel reception. He pushed his way through the entrance into a small room that was tidy but run-down, the carpet thin and the paint on the walls faded with age.

Behind a counter sat an overweight woman with spectacles, reading a trash magazine as she stuffed a donut into her mouth.

'Fifty bucks a night, pal,' she snapped without looking at him.

Jae walked up to the counter and smiled. 'I'm looking for somebody.'

'Ain't we all, honey?' the woman replied, still without making eye contact. 'Fifty bucks.'

Jae's smile tightened. 'It's important.'

'So is my livelihood, fifty bu…'

The woman's words dried up as Jae pushed his pistol against her podgy temple, the smile long gone.

'For the sake of your livelihood, you should help me, don't you think?'

The woman nodded, donut crumbs spilling from her quivering lips. 'Three people travelling together, one American man, one Latino woman, one older man. Where are they?'

The woman managed to whisper her response.

'Room 401,' she uttered.

Jae nodded slowly, then looked the woman's bloated frame up and down. 'You need to eat less,' he whispered. 'Allow me to assist.'

*

'We can't just head right back there!'

Lopez stared at Ernie as though he had lost his mind, which in some respects Ethan supposed that he had.

'Why the hell not? It's the CIA that want me, right, so why waste time here?' Ernie asked.

'We told you, we need to take this slow and do it right! We can't just wander about and hope that the CIA teams spot us first.'

'It's my life, and I want it back,' Ernie snapped. 'That's not going to happen rotting away here in this two-bit godamned motel. I told you to take me to the CIA right away.'

'We can't rush in,' Lopez explained for what felt like the fiftieth time. 'The North Koreans are watching us too, remember? What if they get here first?'

'Maybe they've got a way of getting me home, for all their faults?'

'They've got a way of getting you into an early grave,' Ethan shot back. 'You really think they'd have your best interests at heart? If Doctor Boltman is right, and there's something up there in your head that makes you capable of travelling through time, the Koreans will probably try to make their lives easier by just cutting it off and taking it home with them.'

'So, the CIA is the best bet,' Ernie replied as he stormed out of the room, 'because so far you two haven't got me any closer to home than I managed myself.'

Ethan sighed and glanced at Lopez, gestured for her to join him as Ernie sat down and watched the small television mounted on the wall facing the bed.

'He's losing it,' Lopez whispered.

'Can you blame him?'

Lopez shook her head. 'Gotta be tough on the guy, but he's right, we can't help him. The only people with the technology he needs to have even the slightest chance of getting home are the very people we can't trust.'

Ethan nodded. He'd been wracking his brains to try to find a way to get Kyle Trent out of the CIA's sphere of influence for long enough to solicit his help, but the kid was wrapped up tight within the security apparatus of the agency and there was little that Ethan could do to reach him. As far as he could make out on the Internet, Kyle's entire existence had been wiped from the face of the Earth: no Social Security number, no high school record, no driver's license, nothing. Yet he was the one guy on the inside who might have some sympathy for their plight, and that of Ernie.

'They've buried Kyle inside the agency,' Lopez said, guessing Ethan's train of thought. 'About the only way to get to him would be for us to literally hand ourselves over and hope for the best. For all we know he's working underground in Area 51 or something.'

Ethan was about to reply when he heard a faint popping sound coming from outside: two of them, distant thump-thumps that were barely audible and yet in an instant he felt the fine hairs on the backs of his arms rise up as he recognized the sounds for what they were.

'Too late,' he said. 'They're here.'

Lopez whirled away and killed the lights as Ethan dashed back into the bedroom and switched off the television.

'Hey, I was watching that!' Ernie complained, and then disappeared from sight as Ethan switched off the main light.

'Stay down,' Ethan snapped. 'The North Koreans are here.'

The only light coming through the threadbare curtains was from a streetlight outside over the parking lot, but it was enough for Ethan to see Ernie's face crease with concern as he shuffled to the far side of the bed and ducked down behind it.

Lopez came out of the bathroom and shook her head.

'No way out the back. It won't take them long to find us, and we're not going to have time to try your little wall trick.'

Ethan and Lopez had once escaped together from being cornered in a motel room just like this by kicking through the thin walls and slipping into an adjoining room, pulling a cabinet over the hole behind them to conceal what they had done. Here, there was no time: Ethan suspected the receptionist had just been killed and now the Koreans were coming for their room.

'We're gonna have to do something real fast if they come through that door,' she added.

*

Jae strode across the parking lot and spotted room *401* from thirty yards out. There was no light on inside the room but he knew that the Americans and Walker must be inside. Jae saw his team moving with him, staying near their assigned blocks but shadowing his every move as he closed in on room *401*. As he did so, they moved away from their blocks to concentrate their presence and their firepower on the room Jae was approaching.

Jae kept his pistol holstered as he approached the door, keeping to one side of it so that anybody who might take a pot-shot through the door when he knocked would miss. He stepped up onto the veranda, hugged the wall to one side of the door and then knocked twice, briskly.

'Mister Walker, would you step outside please?'

Jae listened, but nobody responded from inside.

'This is your last chance, come out now with your hands up and your back to the door!'

Jae waited, the long silence drawing out. He looked up at his men and ordered them with a wave to join him, and without any further hesitation he turned, pulled out his pistol, and with all of his strength he aimed a kick at the door.

The thin door shuddered beneath the blow but it did not give. Jae tried again, and then stepped aside as one of his men slipped neatly into line and planted two hard kicks just below the door handle before making way for another agent.

The third man's final kick shattered the wood around the door, and the fourth man in line ran at the door and slammed his shoulder into it. With a crack the door flew open amid a shower of wood chip splinters as Jae and his team charged into the room and hit the lights.

The room was empty, the bed made and nothing in the room disturbed.

Jae gestured with a nod to the bathroom door, which was shut. One of his men hurried over and tried it, but it was locked.

'Break it down, fast!'

The agents began hammering at the door with kicks, each shifting aside as the next man attacked. Wood splintered and shattered as the panels collapsed beneath the blows, and finally the entire top half of the door collapsed and fell away into the bathroom as Jae rushed up and shoved his pistol through the doorway.

The bathroom was as empty as the bedroom.

'That's not possible, we know they were in here!'

The sound of a car starting up in the lot outside alerted Jae and he ran through the motel room and outside in time to see a silver sedan pull out of the lot and accelerate away.

'After them, now!'

***

XXXIII

'You're such a smart ass.'

Ethan said nothing in reply to Lopez as he turned the sedan and accelerated into the night, hoping against hope that he could give the Koreans the slip.

The oldest tricks often work the best, Doug Jarvis, his former mentor, had once told him. Ethan and Lopez had hired two rooms; Ethan had paid for *401*, and Lopez had arrived minutes later and bought *307*. *401* was across the lot, while *307* was much nearer the entrance and its proximity to reception was what had allowed Ethan to hear the gunshots. It had been a gamble, but it had worked: the Koreans had hurried past room 307 on their way to *401*. The locked bathroom door had kept them occupied as Ethan, Lopez and Ernie had fled *401* for their vehicle.

Ethan knew that the CIA would be on top of them within minutes and, incredibly, the Koreans were already here and in pursuit.

'They're onto us,' Lopez said as she checked their mirror and saw two vehicles pull out of the motel lot and accelerate hard in pursuit.

'This is where the fun begins,' Ethan grinned without humor as he pushed the accelerator to the floor.

The sedan surged, and Ernie Walker lowered himself into his seat as they roared along the highway, headed south out of town.

Behind them, he could see the two pursuing vehicles closing steadily in on them. The Koreans were probably using hire vehicles on false credentials, and would have been sure to hire the kinds of vehicles capable of pursuits should they be needed. Ethan knew that he wouldn't be able to outrun them for long, but there was more than one way to bring the Koreans to a halt.

'Hang on,' he said to Lopez and Ernie.

At the first intersection he reached, Ethan purposefully ran a red light and swung hard left, the sedan screeching across the asphalt as two other vehicles swerved to avoid him, their horns blaring in the night.

Behind them, the two Korean vehicles turned in pursuit, a man hanging out of a passenger window and taking aim with a pistol. Ethan ducked as he heard the shot, which went well wide of their sedan, and glimpsed in his mirror people ducking and dashing into the cover of parked vehicles and storefronts as the gunman shot by.

'Are you nuts?' Lopez snapped. 'That's going to bring the law right down on us!'

Ethan gritted his teeth as he focused on driving as fast as he dared.

'And on them, and that's the last thing they want!'

Ethan kept the throttle to the floor as he aimed for another intersection that would allow them to turn left again, this time headed back toward Norfolk and the busiest parts of the city.

'I always wanted to be on T.V,' Ethan said. 'Let's see who we can get to follow us all.'

The sedan screeched around the intersection, Ethan again running a red, and this time the two Koreans behind him closed up, one running over a grass verge in order to cut the corner off the turn.

In the distance, across the far side of the intersection, Ethan saw a set of blues flash into life as a police cruiser launched from where it had been parked outside a *Dunkin' Donuts* store.

'Here we go,' Ethan said.

The vehicles behind were closing in fast, their headlights illuminating the sedan's interior as Ethan drove flat-out down the two-lane highway and swerved past a truck's glowing red tail lights. The big rig rumbled past as Ethan pulled in again, streaking through the night and hoping that the police cruiser would start focusing on the Koreans and not the sedan.

'They're right on us!' Lopez snapped.

The Koreans swerved in front of the truck and then advanced until all Ethan could see in his rear-view mirror were two huge rectangular headlights blazing with a fierce white light: big SUVs, wide and long wheelbases, tough but cumbersome.

'More police up front!' Lopez warned.

Ethan looked up and saw in the distance two more sets of flashing hazard lights rushing toward them on the opposite side of the highway.

He glanced in his mirror and saw that the cruiser behind them was hidden by the big-rig's bulk.

'Hang on!'

Ethan jerked the wheel to the right and swerved out into the other lane, then slammed the brakes on hard. The sedan screeched along the asphalt as the two SUVs lurched past them and overshot.

Ethan turned hard left and mounted the grass divider, slammed on the gas and the sedan hit the opposite lane, Ethan accelerating south as the roaring big-rig lumbered past.

Lopez glanced over her shoulder and saw the two Korean vehicles struggling to turn to follow as Ethan accelerated away. The big rig flashed past the two floundering SUVs and the cruiser spotted them and immediately locked up the brakes as Ethan flashed past on the far side of the highway. Ethan risked a glance across and he could see that the police officer at the wheel was looking not at him but at the two black SUVs.

'Okay,' Ethan said with grim satisfaction as he gripped the wheel. 'Let's see what happens now.'

*

'We've got an identification.'

General Mackenzie sat downstairs in the safehouse, trying not to hear the terrible noises that he'd been forced to endure for almost half an hour in the interrogation room, the echoes from which bounced back and forth through the lonely vaults of his mind. That one man could resist almost unbearable agony for so long had surprised not just Mackenzie but both of his interrogators, and he had almost called off the interrogation for fear that the victim would suffer a heart attack and die, before finally the Korean had broken down and begged for surcease from his suffering.

Mackenzie's security team had administered the antidote to the bullet ant venom, after which the North Korean had sobbed uncontrollably for several minutes. Mackenzie had been eager to learn more about the North Korean's cell, but instead he had learned quickly that their victim's family was being held in Pyongyang and would almost certainly perish if he did not successfully complete his mission. The shame in realizing just how low the North Korean leadership would sink to achieve its aims was what forced Mackenzie to leave the room, to be alone with his thoughts.

Now, the chief interrogator stood alongside him.

'What did he say?' Mackenzie asked.

'He was part of an eight-man team, dispatched with official sanction by Kim Jong-Un himself. One of the team is now deceased, as we know, and all of the men are under strict protocols while outside of the country. It seems that the regime has all of their families held hostage, to ensure their loyalty.'

Mackenzie nodded. The lengths to which the North Korean leadership would go reminded him of the Nazis of World War Two, or the Soviet leadership during the Cold War.

'How did they know about Walker?' he asked.

'He doesn't know, and we believe he's telling the truth. The only one he says knows everything is called Jae-Hyuk Pak, a senior officer from the North Korean People's Army. He's somebody we already know about.'

The officer handed Mackenzie a slim file, and he opened it to reveal an image of a North Korean soldier, about the same age as Mackenzie. A stern, uncompromising gaze glared back out of the shot, depicting Jae in full uniform with images of the Korean flag and Kim Jong-Un behind him.

'Intelligence reports sent from Langley and the NSA place this guy in the same spot at the same time as the electromagnetic emissions we detected in North Korea,' the officer said. 'If so, they might know about Ernie Walker because they already knew what to look for. The North Koreans might also be researching some form of time displacement.'

Mackenzie nodded, alarmed and surprised that the North Koreans were so advanced in this kind of research. He would not have anticipated the country's willingness to dabble in what was still considered in many circles to be an esoteric, almost unspeakably supernatural arena of research.

Perhaps the Soviet experiments into the paranormal during the Cold War had extended their influence further east than anybody had realized.

'This is the smoking gun,' he said. 'As soon as we find Jae and his team, we apprehend them with all necessary force. Holding them here as North Korean spies will give us a major coup against any actions or claims by the regime there.'

'We've got them!'

Kyle Trent appeared at the doorway and waved for Mackenzie to join him in the operations room.

General Mackenzie stood up and walked across to an operative's work station, saw an image on a screen where a stream of text was filtering past. He could not read it fast enough to keep up, but he could see at once that the police were involved in a pursuit with three vehicles, two of them black SUVs, the third a silver sedan.

'It's occurring just south of here,' Kyle Trent confirmed. 'Either the Koreans have him and Warner is in pursuit, or it's the other way around.'

Mackenzie knew who was in the silver sedan.

'Warner wouldn't use a black SUV, too conspicuous. The Koreans are after them, which means Walker is with Warner. If the local police units get involved this is going to be a bloodbath and we can't afford to lose Walker. Get us down there, right now.'

***

XXXIV

'They're onto us!'

Jae swivelled in his seat to see a police cruiser mount the grass and swerve into pursuit behind them. He cursed under his breath as he looked ahead and saw the sedan cruising along, trying to look like any other vehicle on the road while drawing attention to Jae's men.

'Walker must be with them,' he snapped. 'Catch them at any cost. Ram them off the road if you have to. I will take care of the police.'

The driver accelerated, the interior of the vehicle now flickering in the glow of the flashing police hazard lights as they closed in on the pursuit from behind. Jae knew that they would have little time here to extract Walker and make it to safety, and with the police on the scene the CIA would not be far behind.

He slipped his pistol from its holster and prepared for what he knew was going to be a major confrontation.

'Get ready,' he ordered his companions, 'we won't be getting out of this without a fight. Where are we?'

A glance at the car's GPS screen revealed the forests of Chesapeake.

'Highway 168, near the Northwest River.'

Jae nodded.

'Cut them off at the river, we can use it as a secondary escape plan if we can't lose the law enforcement vehicles.'

The driver accelerated hard as the vehicles approached the river, signs for deep water flashing as they reflected the headlights and the flickering blue and white hazard lights of the pursuing patrol vehicles.

Jae looked over his shoulder and saw one of the police vehicles moving up alongside them. He shuffled across to the passenger side, his pistol held out of sight. The police officer in the front seat of his vehicle had lowered his window and was gesticulating to the driver to pull over.

Jae lowered his own window. The police officer looked back at him, and Jae pointed his pistol out of the window. The police vehicle's brakes slammed on, and Jae glimpsed clouds of smoke from its tires as he fired.

The bullet hit the officer square between the eyes and the car jerked hard to the right and spun out behind them, the second pursuit vehicle plowing into it with a deafening crash as it flipped end over end and smashed down on its roof onto the darkened highway.

*

'Things just got ugly!' Lopez snapped.

'I saw it,' Ethan replied, hanging on grimly to the wheel as he saw the pursuit vehicles spin out behind them amid clouds of shattered glass and smoke.

The two SUVs accelerated, moving into a side-by-side position behind him to block any chance of Ethan braking and forcing them into an overshoot again.

'We're running out of options,' Lopez said as she watched the vehicles in her mirror. 'Any other bright ideas?'

'Nothing just yet,' Ethan snapped back. 'Fancy contributing anything?'

'Sure.'

Lopez reached down and yanked the handbrake fully on. Ethan almost shouted in alarm as the sedan slid to an abrupt halt in front of the two SUVs, leaving them with no room to brake and absolutely nowhere to go. Lopez released the handbrake an instant before the two vehicles smashed into their trunk.

The SUVs plowed into the back of the sedan with a deafening crash that shattered the rear window and showered Ernie with glass. Ethan felt the sedan jerk forward as the two larger vehicles both spun out to either side of them, and he slammed the sedan's throttle down and spun the vehicle around, once again mounting the reservation and pulling away in the opposite direction. He could hear the sedan's rear wheels grinding against the bodywork with an awful rending of metal and rubber.

'We're not going to last long now,' he pointed out.

'A bit longer than we would have done before,' Lopez said defensively. 'Police will be all over the area within minutes, we don't have to last forever.'

Ethan glanced in his mirror and saw the two SUV's behind them. Once was stuck in position, the impact presumably having damaged its steering in some way, and he could just make out men running from it into the other vehicle, which then swung around to pursue them once more.

'One down,' Ethan said with a smile.

A gunshot snatched the smile from his face as it zipped past them, and Ernie wailed from the rear seat.

'Jesus, I'd have been safer in godamned World War Two!'

Ethan didn't reply as he saw on the horizon multiple flashing hazard lights as law enforcement descended upon the area *en masse*. He looked in the rear-view mirror and saw the SUV start to hang back, and then it turned around and fled in the opposite direction.

The battered sedan crawled its way south until the police vehicles swarmed around it, and as Ethan pulled into the side of the road, he heard a helicopter thunder overhead as police leaped out of their vehicles, their weapons pointed at the sedan.

Ethan put both his hands out of his window, as did Lopez, and as the police approached, he feigned a good impression of a terrified citizen.

'They're headed north,' he called, 'black SUVs, they're insane, rammed us off the road!'

'Get out of the car! Keep your hands in the air and your back turned to us!'

Ethan complied, exiting the vehicle and allowing himself to be handcuffed along with Lopez. Face down on the ground and surrounded by officers, he couldn't see the sedan.

'Our passenger, he's elderly,' Ethan said, 'and pretty shaken up by it all. Go easy on him.'

The police said nothing as they swarmed over the vehicle nearby, and Ethan heard other vehicles showing up around the highway, blocking the vehicles in. Moments later, he heard boots stomping as the police helped him to his feet.

An officer walked back from the sedan and spoke to his superior.

'Car's clean, no alcohol or drugs found. A truck driver witness confirms their story, the SUVs were shooting at the sedan and tried to ram them off the road.'

Ethan turned and saw men all around the sedan, but suddenly he realized that he could see nothing of Ernie.

'Where's Ernie?' he asked the officers.

'Who?'

'Our passenger,' Lopez said. 'He was in back.'

The officer who had joined them frowned and shook his head. 'Car was empty when we checked it, there's nobody in there.'

Ethan and Lopez exchanged a glance, and then Ethan spotted a vehicle that started its engine and quietly slipped away, even as other vehicles were arriving. He could see a female detective with long auburn hair driving it, a woman who looked vaguely familiar, and in the rear seat he could just make out Ernie Walker, sitting low in order to conceal his presence.

Ethan moved to say something, but Lopez nudged him with her elbow and offered a fractional shake of her head, then nodded to a large vehicle that had pulled up nearby.

Ethan turned and recognized Mackenzie the moment he saw him. The general spotted them and walked with two security guys alongside him. Neither appeared armed, but Ethan didn't doubt that they were carrying.

Mackenzie moved to stand before them, glanced at their cuffed wrists and smiled.

'Good to see you both staying out of trouble.'

'The only reason we're in trouble is because of you,' Lopez snapped.

'I left you alone,' Mackenzie pointed out. 'You should have left well alone yourselves.'

'You left us to die, is what you did,' Lopez pointed out tartly.

Mackenzie gestured to the cuffs, and moments later they were both freed from their bonds by the police.

'Ernie?' Ethan asked.

'Is fine,' Mackenzie replied. 'You should have brought him to us right away, and avoided all of this.' The general gestured to the carnage all around them.

'You took time from us,' Lopez pointed out.

'I did no such thing,' Mackenzie replied, interested now as he looked at them. 'Is that why you're here? I thought that you wanted revenge?'

Ethan peered at the general. 'If you didn't know anything about our lost time, then you *did* leave us to die in the desert.'

Mackenzie watched Ethan for a long moment before he replied.

'You were dying,' he said. 'Both of you. There was nothing that I could have done to save you, which is why it's all the more remarkable that you're here now. What happened?'

Ethan could not believe what he was hearing. He wasn't sure if Mackenzie was playing dumb or in earnest, but he could not think of a single reason why the general would deny having saved their lives – it wasn't exactly something that helped his cause.

'You actually don't know?' Lopez uttered.

Mackenzie appeared both interested and confused. 'Should I have?'

Lopez lost it. She lunged at Mackenzie and would have made it if Ethan were not in the way. He stepped in and caught her fist in mid-flight, looked down at her.

'No, wait,' he said.

'This son of a bitch used us and left us to die!' she growled at him. 'What's there to wait for? Let me at him!' She glared past Ethan at the general. 'You want to travel through time, asshole? Five minutes and I'll have kicked your sorry ass into next week!'

Mackenzie's two security men moved forward, and Ethan turned and shook his head at them.

'Trust me, don't mess with her.' He looked at the general. 'There was a bright light over us, and then we were driving down a road, the same one we'd taken three days before when we first arrived in Nevada.'

Mackenzie looked back and forth between Ethan and Lopez as though he was seeing them for the first time.

'You were subjected to a time-slip?'

'Figures,' Ethan shrugged. 'Don't ask how, that's what we've been trying to figure out. Our work led us to Ernie Walker, who showed up here in Virginia.'

Mackenzie stared into the middle distance for a long moment, as though somehow having thought of something that had never crossed his mind before, a revelation that made him suddenly and unexpectedly smile.

'What?' Lopez snorted. 'Somethin' about us nearly dying funny to you?'

Mackenzie shook his head in wonder.

'No, not at all,' he replied, and then seemed to snap back to the present. He looked directly at her. 'Nicola, Ethan, I'm glad you're both alive. You've got it all wrong here. I can't talk about what I know, I had to leave you in that desert.'

'Had to,' Ethan echoed. 'Tough life, general.'

'It's not like that.'

'You wanna tell us what it *is* like?' Lopez challenged.

Mackenzie was about to reply, when his guards' radios both crackled with transmissions. Ethan could hear the reports loud and clear.

'We've got a problem here, we've lost Pioneer.'

Ethan saw a look of panic cross the general's face. 'You've *lost* him?'

'Police are at the safehouse sir,' came the reply. *'Four foreign men broke in and abducted him. Reports say they were Asian, maybe North Korean.'*

Ethan watched the general closely. For a moment he seemed lost, stunned by the news, but then Ethan saw his resolve harden as he made whatever decision it was that would take his mission forward.

'Who's Pioneer?' Ethan asked.

Mackenzie almost replied, but then he caught himself and shook his head.

'It's not your problem,' he said. 'Both of you, you have to stay away from this. You don't understand what's at stake here.'

'The Koreans,' Lopez said, 'they're killing anyone they take. Pioneer's a dead man.'

Ethan saw Mackenzie's face crumble briefly, and somehow, he suddenly knew who *Pioneer* was, the code-name clear in its description of the man's abilities.

'It's Kyle, isn't it,' Ethan said. 'The Koreans split their forces: some went after Ernie; the rest went after your team. They've got Kyle.'

Mackenzie's jaw hardened.

'Stay out of it, both of you,' he ordered them.

Mackenzie and his two guards hurried back to their truck, and moments later the vehicle pulled out from the side of the road and accelerated away into the darkness toward Norfolk.

Ethan and Lopez exchanged a glance, but they did not have to say a word, for they both knew what the other was thinking.

'Folks,' a police officer asked, 'can we give you a ride anywhere?'

Ethan nodded.

'Norfolk,' he said. 'As fast as you can.'

***

XXXV

Kyle Trent knew that he was going to die.

He could see nothing, his eyes veiled by a blindfold tied so tight he could feel his blood pumping through the constricted arteries on his temples. His wrists were bound behind his back, his ankles likewise bound and pulled up to connect to the bonds around his wrists. Utterly defenceless, he was laid on the back seat of a vehicle that was driving through the night to where he knew not.

Kyle had known, had been warned, that his work was potentially hazardous. Still, given all the security around him and at Groom Lake he had never really believed that he would be targeted by foreign nations. Now, he knew otherwise. The men had been foreign, maybe Chinese or North Korean, highly aggressive, well-armed. The safe house had fallen within seconds of their entry, two armed CIA agents despatched with ease and Kyle apprehended within seconds as he tried to flee through a backroom window. Two blows with the butt of their pistols and he was on his knees, blood pouring from the side of his head.

The vehicle slowed, heightening Kyle's fear as he knew that whatever fate awaited him was now close. He thought of his mother, back in Nevada, protected by the CIA. Would she be abandoned if Kyle died, no longer of interest to the government now that their star hacker was out of play? Tears welled in the corner of his eyes, and then the car stopped and he was hauled from the rear of the car and dropped with a thump onto cold, hard asphalt.

The blindfold was ripped from his eyes and he looked around to see that he was in the middle of a disused warehouse of some kind, no light coming in but from the faint glow of streetlights through grubby windows.

Kyle's bonds were cut, and he was unceremoniously dragged to his feet. His captors were all North Korean, and he hated them all on instinct. One of them, shorter and stockier than the rest, reached up and removed Kyle's gag. He tossed it onto the floor and watched Kyle in silence for a moment before speaking.

'They train you, don't they, for moments like this?'

Self-preservation exercises, they called them, Kyle recalled. Resistance to interrogation. All that he'd been taught came flooding back to him. Don't be a hero. Don't fight back. Reveal as much of the truth as possible but hold back all that you can for as long as you can.

He nodded, once.

'You won't need any of that,' the stocky man said. 'My name is Jae, and I have only an hour or two to extract from you all the information that I need to complete my mission. I understand that you won't want to tell me anything about what you do for the CIA, and I know also that to get you to tell me anything will require the application of pain.'

Kyle swallowed but said nothing. Jae smiled.

'I can see from the look on your face that you're afraid, and I can tell from your body language that you're not a field agent, not the kind of person we normally come up against. There is no sense in trying to be brave, it's not what you're here to do. You're here to delay, to hold out for as long as you can before telling us what we need to know.'

Kyle nodded again, slowly.

'I am here to tell you that, back home, all of our families are being held hostage. My wife and children will be sent to concentration camps if I am unsuccessful. They will die there, starving, cold and alone. Do you understand what I am willing to do in order to ensure that I am successful?'

Kyle's legs began to quiver beneath him. He nodded.

'Good,' Jae said. 'I am going to ask you once only. I need to know why it is that Ernie Walker was able to travel *forwards* in time.'

Kyle's eyes widened and panic ripped through his nervous system.

'We don't know,' he replied. 'That's what we're working on right now, why we went looking for him.'

Jae smiled, almost sympathetically. 'That's a good answer, but we know it's not true. There must be something about Walker that makes him different, and you know what that something is.'

'I don't!' Kyle bleated. 'I'm the tech guy, not the biologist! We know we're missing something but we don't understand what it is!'

Jae peered at Kyle for a long moment, as though momentarily uncertain of whether he was telling the truth or not. Then, he stood back and smiled.

'Tell as much of the truth as possible, without giving too much away,' he said, as though quoting the CIA handbook on how to deal with interrogations. 'Last chance, Kyle: what's special about Walker?'

'I promise you I don't know,' Kyle replied. 'They're taking him away now to find out! That's what the whole search was for and…'

Jae was no longer listening. He gestured to his men and suddenly Kyle was surrounded and gripped by powerful, uncompromising hands.

'I'm telling you the truth!' Kyle shouted. 'We don't know what Ernie did to travel through time at all, forwards or backwards! We know the blast was something to do with it but it doesn't work on its own, there's something else at play but we couldn't tell what until we had Ernie Walker in custody.'

Jae did not respond. Kyle was dragged back to the vehicle and pinned in place, his ankles and wrists spread out as the bonds that had once pinned them together were now used to tie his ankles to the SUV's front fender and his wrists to the wing mirrors.

The men stood back as Jae walked back towards Kyle, a six-inch blade in his hand that glittered in the dim light filtering through the filthy windows.

'I'm not lying!' Kyle shrieked.

Jae smiled at him, his eyes black. 'Perhaps not, but I wish to send a message to anybody else that gets in our way.'

'Please, no!' Kyle screamed, tears spilling down his face.

Jae leaned in, and pressed the blade to Kyle's sternum before pushing down hard.

*

It wasn't hard to find the safe house, and the police officers dropped Ethan and Lopez off near the end of the street.

Police were everywhere, ambulances outside and detectives working the case taking notes from witnesses who heard gunshots and dialled 911. Ethan could see numerous bodies being wheeled out on gurneys from the house, and he could hear the detectives speaking to media teams from where he and Lopez loitered among homeowners from elsewhere on the street.

'... *looks like some kind of drug dispute or a deal gone wrong...*'

'... *two victims, both known to local law enforcement as drug dealers...*'

'... *foreign gangs may be involved, perhaps Triads or similar...*'

Ethan and Lopez slipped away from the throng.

'Easy cover up,' Lopez said, 'sounds like nobody actually saw the shooters.'

'Yeah. Even if they did, it's dark and they moved fast,' Ethan replied. 'They're not going to find it hard to cover up that this was a CIA safe house. Cops will be looking for a non-descript black SUV on a dark night in a city where there are probably ten thousand such vehicles.'

Lopez looked up and down the street.

'Where would we go if we were foreign agents seeking data, if we were in a hurry and with law enforcement on our tails, with an abducted government employee to hide?'

Ethan thought for a moment.

'We'd stay to back roads, avoiding CCTV coverage wherever we could. Wouldn't go far, the more we travel the more likely we are to be seen and identified. We'd head someplace dark, no coverage, because we need to interrogate Kyle real fast and find out what's happening to Ernie Walker.'

'We'd be up against time,' Lopez agreed. 'Mackenzie and his people will get ahead of our research if we don't find them. So, we need to do this quick and dirty, the old way, thumbscrews and needles.'

'An old, run down place nearby, quickest we can get to, easiest place to hide bodies,' Ethan added. 'The other team can't have been far ahead of us after the bust on the highway, they'll have only arrived here recently.'

Lopez had her cell phone in her hand, and a moment later she showed it to Ethan.

'Industrial buildings off Lake Edwards, high crime area, a few abandoned warehouses, that kinda thing.'

'It's all we've got,' Ethan agreed. 'C'mon, we're on foot.'

They set off at a jog toward Lake Edwards, which was barely five hundred yards from the CIA safe house. Ethan knew that they had no idea how many enemies they would be facing should their hunch be correct, only that they would be armed and would not hesitate to kill both Ethan and Nicola if they were caught.

As soon as they were out of sight of the police, they hit their stride, running the entire distance to the industrial park, which consisted of nothing more than a series of run-down lock-ups and low warehouses, some of which were occupied by businesses and some of which had been sealed up, old signs over their roller doors, weathered by the passing of years.

Ethan jogged with Lopez to the entrance and at once they could see that the double gates had been forced. The gates were closed, but the padlock was severed, probably by a vehicle simply driving through them. The

North Koreans had been sufficiently thorough to push the gates closed behind them to conceal the damage.

They slipped through the gates and hurried along, heading for the rear of the buildings, out of sight of the main road. As they rounded the corner, they saw a single shutter door that was open, off the ground by maybe eight inches.

Ethan slowed, creeping forwards with Lopez alongside him as he crouched down, and through the partially open shutter he could hear a voice that he recognized instantly.

'I'm telling you the truth! We don't know what Ernie did to travel through time at all, forwards or backwards!'

Ethan gently laid down and rolled under the gap beneath the shutter doors, Lopez following. They could see the rear of the SUV parked inside the building, and could hear the voices, but the occupants of the building were all out of sight, standing around the hood of the SUV.

Ethan crept up to the rear of the SUV with Lopez, and they looked at each other. They both knew that this was a hell of a long shot, but they could hear Kyle's increasingly terrified screams and they knew that he only had moments to live.

'I'm not lying! Please, no!'

Ethan took a deep breath and then launched himself out from behind the SUV and rushed straight at the North Korean standing over Kyle with a large knife in his hand. He could see five more North Koreans behind the knifeman, each as surprised as the other.

The Korean looked up in surprise even as the other men reached for their weapons. Ethan swung a wild punch that landed on the knifeman's face with a loud crack and sent him spinning into his companions.

Ethan reached for the nearest gunman's wrist and grabbed it with both hands as he pivoted on one heel, yanked his arm down with all his might as he jerked his right knee up beneath the man's elbow. The limb snapped at the joint and the man screamed as Ethan ripped the pistol from his grasp and fired three shots in the general direction of the scattering North Koreans.

All of the men dove for cover as Ethan fired repeatedly at them, then backed away for the door of the SUV as he heard Lopez start the engine. Ethan leaped into the passenger seat, still firing as Lopez shoved the vehicle into reverse and hit the gas.

The SUV lurched backwards, Kyle screaming on the hood as Ethan fired two more shots right past him and then ducked inside and slammed his door shut. The SUV smashed through the shutter doors, the thin metal tearing from its mounts to spin over the hood and clatter to the floor of the warehouse. Lopez hauled the wheel to one side and the SUV's tires screeched as it swung around, Lopez slamming the vehicle into drive and gunning the engine.

The SUV roared out of sight as the Koreans opened fire, bullets clipping the bodywork, and then they were away. Lopez hit the main road and swerved hard right, driving away from the warehouses with Kyle still strapped to the hood.

'Jesus Christ!' Kyle yelled from in front of them, his hair flying in the wind. 'Jesus, oh Jesus, oh…'

Lopez drove two blocks down, then turned hard right and pulled into the sidewalk as Ethan leaped out and quickly unstrapped Kyle from the hood. The kid slid from the vehicle, his knees shaking too much to hold his weight as he slumped onto the asphalt.

Lopez leaped out and rushed to his side, threw her arms around him.

'You're okay, Kyle,' she said quickly, smothering him as though he were her own child. 'You're okay.'

Ethan watched them for a long time, Kyle gradually regaining control of himself as he huddled in an almost foetal position, Lopez holding for as long as was necessary.

'We need to move,' Ethan said. 'They'll be looking for us.'

Lopez looked down at Kyle. 'Do you know where Mackenzie is taking Ernie?'

Kyle, his voice so soft they could barely hear it, whispered his response with a nod.

'An atoll in the South Pacific. They need him for the machine to work.'

Ethan and Lopez replied to him in unison.

'What *machine*?'

***

XXXVI

Bucholz Army Airfield,

Kwajalein Atoll, South Pacific

General Scott Mackenzie peered out of the window of the huge C-5 Galaxy transport airplane as it lined up for landing at an airbase perched on the south eastern corner of an idyllic atoll. The sun was just rising in the east, searing light streaming across the deep blue Pacific, the shallow waters of the atoll glittering like burnished bronze.

Kwajalein was a Japanese-built airfield that had been occupied by American forces during World War Two, and had remained in the hands of the Army ever since. Its position almost mid-Atlantic made it the perfect stop-off for refuelling airplanes both civil and military, although no civilian was ever allowed to step off the airplane. Its remote location also made it the perfect place to test weapons and systems far from the prying eyes of the mainstream media. Mackenzie knew that the Marshall Islands were paid a handsome annual stipend by the United States Government, which both served to support them and also ensured their silence when it came to operations at the airbase to their south. The populations of the islands had been forced to endure relocations after the nuclear tests at nearby Bikini Atoll, and as such their subsistence lifestyle had been disrupted sufficiently that they now relied upon that stipend, for there were no longer the resources to support the population crammed into the town four miles north of the airbase.

Despite the size of the airbase, it was not the focus of Mackenzie's attention. As the Galaxy came in to land, its wings buffeting on the dawn breeze and the air roaring past its flaps and undercarriage outside, the general looked down and saw the small island of Ennylabegan as it passed by a few miles to the north of their port wing. Unpopulated, pristine, with only a few small buildings and a tiny dock, the island was the location of one of the most secretive projects in the history of the United States' Black Budget, and the reason that Ernie Walker was here.

'Feels strange to see it again,' Ernie said from a nearby seat, where he had been reading a massive amount of material about human history since 1954 that Mackenzie had supplied him with.

Mackenzie nodded, wondering at just how the old man must feel right now.

'Not much has changed,' he said. 'The nuclear tests meant that most of the atolls remain unpopulated even after half a century. They're about as pristine as any islands you'll find anywhere on earth.'

'Just the way it should be,' Ernie replied. 'Shame it took a thermonuclear blast to get people to leave nature well alone.'

Mackenzie sat back in his seat, his stomach tight. He'd never been a great flier, and the buoyant thermals coming up off the warm Pacific below the airplane were doing nothing to allay the nausea growing within him.

'Why have you brought me back here?' Ernie asked. 'You and your men have said nothing to me the whole damned time and dragged me half way around the world. I've got a right to know. I'm an American citizen.'

'If you'd stayed where you were at Majuro, we wouldn't have had to drag you back,' Mackenzie pointed out.

'I thought that you wanted me dead.'

'Why the hell would we do that?' Mackenzie asked, but then he remembered the photographs of the injured seamen aboard *USS Bairoko* that he'd seen, and the cover ups that had followed. 'We don't work like that anymore.'

Ernie peered at him. 'Ethan and Nicola reckoned otherwise.'

'They would say that, because wherever they go, they leave a trail of carnage behind them. They couldn't buy milk without getting into a fight with somebody.'

'They worked hard to protect me.'

'They worked hard to keep you from being properly protected.'

'They lost time too, and they said that you left them for dead.'

Mackenzie couldn't really argue with that. He had no idea why it was that Ethan and Nicola thought that they'd lost time, or why they'd believed that he had somehow been the cause. In truth, he liked the pair a lot, but he knew that his mission overrode every human instinct that he had. His urge for compassion, his desire for justice, both absolutely had to be buried somewhere where they would not bother him, because without doing so he knew that he could not have found Ernie and brought him back here.

'What happened to that kid who was always with you?' Ernie asked. 'Kyle, wasn't it?'

Ernie had him cornered, and as the Galaxy' wheels thumped down onto the asphalt and the knot of anxiety in his guts loosened, he decided that honesty, now, was the best policy.

'He was taken by the North Koreans,' Mackenzie said, 'and yes, I left him there. I did leave Ethan and Nicola to die, although I honestly believed that they were already lost, which it turns out was probably the right call. I could not have saved their lives even if I'd called in the Marines, the Navy and the Air Force all together. I have a job to do, and it's damned hard enough as it is without being called out on the sacrifices that everyone, including myself, has had to make in order to complete this mission.'

Ernie nodded slowly, his old eyes never leaving Mackenzie's.

'Selling your soul, huh?' he said finally. 'How does it feel to be a machine, a cog in your government's network, knowing that you must have become the same thing to them that you see Ethan and Nicola and Kyle to be: *expendable*.'

Mackenzie said nothing, because he knew that there was nothing that he could say. Ernie had him boxed into a corner, but rather than deliver the fatal blow Ernie backed off.

'Again, why did you hunt me down?'

Mackenzie gratefully took the out Ernie was offering him, watching as the Galaxy taxied off the runway toward low-slung maintenance buildings on the edge of the aprons, surrounded by gently swaying palm trees.

'It's all to do with something in your mind,' he replied. 'There's something about you that allowed you to not just survive the Castle Bravo blast, but also end up thrown forwards in time.'

Ernie nodded.

'I already know that. I didn't travel through time, right? My mind did.'

'So Kyle believed,' the general agreed. 'He felt that it was possible to travel physically into the past, but only the essence of our minds or something about the soul or whatever could move *forwards* in time. Seems as though the metaphysical is capable of things that our physical bodies cannot achieve.'

'So, what does that have to do with coming here?'

Mackenzie knew that what he was about to say was so highly classified that he could be Court Martialled for it, but Ernie had been through hell and he felt the old guy had earned the truth for his troubles. Anyway, Mackenzie didn't like being called an "expendable asset" and liked to think that he'd kept his morals, what was left of them, anyway.

'The Montauk Project is alive and well,' he replied. 'We never stopped researching and recently we were able to construct a device that may be able to allow limited travel through time. The physics said it should work, but it didn't. It took us a while to figure out why.'

'The person is a part of the machine,' Ernie guessed.

Mackenzie nodded.

'Kyle explained it to me many times but I never understood it,' he said. 'The fact that the fundamental particles of the universe only act the way that they do when they're being observed, otherwise they do something else; the fact that everything we see around us is effectively an illusion, that solid matter is not solid, that atoms are mostly empty space, that energy and mass and time are all the same thing. The whole circus always went right over my head and I'm pretty sure the suits at the Pentagon felt the same way. But Kyle was able to prove it, when you popped up fifty years after the Castle Bravo test. An observer has to be a part of the machine otherwise it simply does nothing, doesn't react no matter how much energy is pumped into it.'

Ernie sat for a moment, thinking. 'So, how does it work?'

'You're asking me?'

'Ain't nobody else,' Ernie pointed out, 'so you're the closest to an expert I've got, and you want me to walk into whatever contraption it is that you've got down there.'

Mackenzie sighed. The Galaxy came to a stop and the engines shut down as they got out of their seats and walked to the airplane's cavernous rear hold, where an enormous ramp was lowering onto the apron as the rear of the airplane opened up.

'Bottom line,' the general said, 'is that an enormously powerful electromagnetic field is generated within a confined space, the energy contained within a sphere that is around the subject but does not touch them physically. Somehow, and we don't know how, this field can interact with our awareness, or sense of self, and can link with that same sense of self in other time periods.'

Ernie thought about that for a moment as they walked down the rear ramp of the airplane, the stale odors of metal and grease replaced with an ocean breeze coming from thousands of miles of unpopulated Pacific in every direction.

'So, you fire up a giant dynamo and somehow that zaps me into the future, or the past?'

'More or less,' Mackenzie agreed. 'The device is not even that complicated, but the energy fields that it interacts with are immense and we don't have even a basic understanding of how they do what they do, only that they *can*. Kyle managed to figure out that the field on its own can still affect time, causing slips in that time, but that people cannot travel through them. They can be seen, and people from the time that's being seen can also see the viewer, but neither can cross through permanently. However, place a person within that field, contain it with enough force, and the supposed barrier between past and present breaks down and an individual can remain within the other frame of time when the energy field dissipates.'

The sun was rising over the eastern ocean, casting brilliant light across the silent airfield as Ernie came to a halt and squinted at the sun, shielding his eyes with one hand that trembled with age.

'That sun is a gigantic ball of electromagnetic fields,' he pointed out. 'How come time isn't dilated there?'

'It is,' Mackenzie replied, 'Einstein found that out a century ago. Stars imaged close to the sun's horizon don't appear where they should, because the sun bends their light due to its gravity. The gravitational bending of light is the warping of space-time, so time is dilated all the time when an object gets closer to the sun. Same thing happens here on earth, believe it or not: the earth's gravity affects time for us on the ground slightly more than orbiting GPS satellites. If the satellites weren't programmed to account for that time dilation, then GPS would be wildly inaccurate.'

Ernie lowered his hand and turned to the general.

'Can you really send me home?' he asked.

Mackenzie shrugged.

'We're hoping so, Ernie. We don't just want you so we can test our machine and get the data we need. If we can send you home too, that's what we want to do.'

'And you said that we can travel back into the past physically, but only our souls can travel forwards. So, does that mean I end up back in 1954 as an old man?'

Mackenzie didn't know. Kyle would have known, or at the least have had a decent idea of what would happen, but Kyle was gone now and there was nothing the general could do about it. Fact was, Ernie could end up an old man in 1954 and be dead by the turn of that decade, and that was something that Mackenzie's superiors both knew and secretly hoped for. With Ernie long dead, his "loose end" would be tied up long before it ever actually occurred, and nobody would believe his story way back in '54.

'I don't know, but we have a lot of people working here who do. We leave for the island within the hour, they'll explain everything as soon as we get there. Right now, you have some more reading to do. There's a great deal of knowledge that I want you to take back to 1954 for us.'

***

XXXVII

Ethan sat in the rear seat of the Gulfstream jet as it cruised 35,000ft above the west coast of the United States, the coast of California drifting by in serene silence beneath a scattering of cumulus cloud.

The sun was rising behind them, just casting its dawn light across the deserts of the sunshine state. Ethan found himself mesmerized by the creeping dawn as they raced it across the surface of the earth. Once, the Anglo-French supersonic airliner Concorde had raced daily from London to New York, flying at twice the speed of sound, and arrived in New York just before it had departed from London. So fast was the airplane, outpacing a rifle bullet in its cruise, that it could leave the dawn behind.

The difference in time was an illusion, of course, and only really corresponded with the Concorde's fearsome dash across the earth's surface as the planet rotated, but the supposed loss of time was real enough to anybody fortunate enough to have experienced it. So, Ethan assumed, was the crippling jet-lag for anybody enduring the return journey.

'We land at Majuro in four hours,' Garrett said as he made his way back through the jet from the cockpit.

Ethan nodded. He knew that he should probably get his head down, Kyle and Lopez both sleeping on fold-out beds further down the jet's fuselage, but the passage of time and what it meant for everyone was haunting him.

'You think that they can really do what Kyle says?' Ethan asked as Garrett sat down in one of the plush leather swivel-chairs that occupied this section of the jet. 'Send somebody back in time, after they've seen the future here?'

Garrett opened a bottle of liquor and poured two tumblers, the dawn sunlight glowing through the drinks in fascinating patterns, sunlight through amber that was laced with gold.

'Who the hell knows, but you and Nicola have been through enough things to know by now that nothing seems impossible these days. If Ernie gets back to his own time, he's going to know everything that's coming, presuming he's had time to learn.'

'He knows about the Internet, and other things besides,' Ethan said. 'He's only got to know about what Amazon is, or Intel, Microsoft, anything like that, and invest at the right time and he'll be a billionaire.'

Garrett handed Ethan a tumbler and raised an eyebrow.

'I'd better watch out then, there could be competition on the horizon.'

Garrett sat down, took a sip of his drink and looked down at the earth far below.

'What do you think they're up to out there?' he asked. 'Some kind of experiment?'

Ethan shook his head, as much in the dark as Garrett was.

'Who the hell knows, apart from Kyle, and he's out cold right now. The Koreans damned near sliced him open.'

'If it weren't for you two, he'd be dead,' Garrett agreed, then he seemed to think about something for a moment. 'Look, I get why you went after the kid, but why are you chasing this Mackenzie guy so hard? What's the pot of gold at the end of this rainbow that you're so determined to find?'

Ethan felt momentarily stumped. Truth was, he and Nicola had merely set out to discover how and why they'd lost three days of their lives, how they'd found themselves back before their previous escapade had even begun. They had naturally assumed that Mackenzie and his team were somehow behind it, that they had twisted history to prevent Ethan and Nicola from ever finding out what had happened at Area 51 or to Kyle, but now it seemed that the general was as much in the dark as Ethan. But if not Mackenzie, then who? Had they just somehow got incredibly lucky?

'I don't know,' Ethan replied finally. 'I don't know about half of what goes on behind the government's closed doors, and maybe that's for the best, but I guess we just don't like being kept in the dark.'

Garrett smiled, glanced down at his drink for a moment. 'They say that ignorance can be bliss.'

Ethan didn't smile back.

'Ignorance was what kept mankind in the Dark Ages for a thousand years, back when the churches banned learning for all but their own hierarchy, to hold power over ordinary people. We were lucky to escape from it, the Enlightenment called so for a reason. I can't just sit back knowing that somebody willingly messed with my life and pretend that nothing's happened.'

'I know,' Garrett replied, 'what I don't know is that if Mackenzie was nothing to do with this, then who the hell messed with you guys?'

Ethan was about to answer that he didn't have a clue, when Kyle answered for him.

'They did.'

The kid was up, a blanket wrapped around his shoulders as he slumped down alongside them in one of the big leather armchairs. Ethan realized that Kyle wasn't really a kid anymore anyway, a young man now who looked as though he'd had the weight of the world on his shoulders.

'You doin' okay?' Ethan asked.

'Never better,' Kyle replied, and nodded to the drink. 'You got any more of that going on?'

Garrett poured Kyle a tumbler, and Kyle surprised them both by downing it in one and sinking back in his seat for a moment with his eyes closed.

'Mother, but everything seems a little better after a shot.'

Garrett refilled Kyle's tumbler, and Ethan was pleased to see that Kyle didn't down the second shot. He'd just needed the hit to clear his mind.

'Who are *they*?'

Kyle took a deep breath and spoke clearly, his strength and confidence returning by the minute.

'A year ago, General Mackenzie offered me a job at Groom Lake,' he said. 'My skills in hacking were of use to them and they liked what I'd done, so I figured it was better than serving ten to fifteen for threatening the CIA. Turns out I couldn't have been more wrong.'

Using his *Disclosure Protocol* algorithm, Kyle had sent crystal clear images of UFOs to the agency, demanding they fully disclose what they knew about the phenomena, or else he would go public with the images. Kyle's actions had unfortunately attracted the attention of Russian sleeper agents in the USA, and all hell had broken loose as the opposing sides attempted to track Kyle down. Then, as now, Ethan and Lopez had found themselves in the middle of the entire storm, part of the biggest covert manhunt in the history of the United States.

'What did you see there?' Garrett asked. 'Groom Lake is the official name for Area 51 isn't it?'

'Sure is,' Kyle replied, almost bitterly. 'They took me to a bunker, and inside was an elevator shaft that takes you down into the base. Most of it's below the desert, the runways and surface buildings just a cover. Down low is where the action's at. Mackenzie took me to a room, put me inside, and then left. What happened next gives me nightmares even now.'

Ethan watched Kyle as he spoke, the computer hacker's eyes dark despite the dawn light streaming through the airplane's windows.

'I didn't know it at the time, but the room was designed to magnify electromagnetic energy, to condense and amplify it. They put me in the middle and zapped it with huge amounts of power, and as a result, I saw into the future.'

Garrett almost dropped his drink. 'Are you kidding me?'

'No sir,' Kyle replied. 'It wasn't for long, because it takes so much energy, and it made me feel real sick for a while afterward too, but I saw a few moments of the future as it unfolded on that very spot. I don't know how far in the future I was seeing, nobody does. All I know is that I saw them, and they saw me.'

'*Them*?' Ethan asked.

'Them,' Kyle replied. 'The beings that inhabit the UFOs that we see in our skies. I know who they are.'

It seemed as though the air in the airplane's fuselage had been sucked from it. Ethan could see that Lopez was also awake, listening, hanging on Kyle's every word as he spoke softly in the dawn light, in an aluminium tube zipping along at four hundred knots, seven miles above the earth.

'They're us,' Kyle said. 'They're not all from other worlds at all. UFOs are things from a future that we can barely understand. They're not travelling across galaxies, they're travelling through time.'

***

XXXVIII

Nobody spoke for quite some time, the only sound the distant roar of the engines outside. Ethan sat in a bubble of his own thoughts, wondering at how he'd never thought of the possible origins of UFOs as human before. Spacecraft made of metals and elements that were recognizable to humans, beings that had two arms and two legs, a head, a physicality that closely resembled human form.

Lopez finally broke the silence. 'Geez, that's gonna take some getting used to.'

'So, aliens, the Grays, they're us?' Garrett asked.

Kyle nodded.

'Us at some point in the future. We don't know how far. Biologists have worked on the problem for the government for some time. It's not my area of expertise, but most reports suggest that it would take upwards of a quarter of a million years for our bodies to naturally change that much, to become something resembling a Gray.'

Ethan leaned back in his seat. 'That's long enough to develop technologies that we can't even imagine right now.'

'More than enough,' Garrett agreed. 'A hundred years ago we'd only just started using electricity, and the first airplanes had only just got off the ground. Look at us now. We have satellites leaving the Solar System, air travel, the Internet, man's been to the moon and space probes to every planet, all in a single century. A quarter of a million years might be more than enough to conquer time travel, especially if we're already working on it now.'

'What else did you learn?' Lopez asked, moving to sit next to Kyle and borrowing a sip of his drink. 'Just testin' it for ya.'

Kyle smiled faintly at her before he replied.

'They've been coming here for millennia,' he said. 'Ancient Egyptian records detail what appear to be UFO sightings, and medieval and Renaissance paintings from around the world have clear depictions of metallic flying discs in them. Modern art scholars ignore them, won't talk about them, but they can't deface the paintings as they're often worth millions so the UFOs on them are plain for anyone to see. They're not even disguised or anything, they're really obviously UFOs. What we don't yet know is why they're coming back here.'

'Same reason we would if we could,' Lopez guessed. 'Everyone would like to *see* the past, but nobody wants to stay there.'

'That's one possibility,' Kyle said, 'but there have been so many cases where interaction between them and us has taken place on a scale that is almost terrifying. It's often said that travelling to the past is fraught with danger, because messing with history could change everything so much that there would be no future for the traveller to return to, the so-called grandfather paradox: if I go back in time and murder my father before I'm born, then I cease to exist.'

'Heard of that one,' Garrett said, 'and somebody else pointed out that if there are infinite universes, then there could be infinite outcomes and so the paradox is solved.'

'Occam's Razor,' Kyle reminded him, 'don't answer one mystery with another. We don't know what's possible, and the teams at Groom Lake are grappling with these things all the time. All we know is that we're a part of what's happening, that we humans are somehow part of the fabric of time and space, more so than just in terms of our flesh and blood. There is something about us, something about all life really, that binds us to our universe in ways we have for millennia suspected are there, but have never been able to quantify. Ghosts, phantoms, UFOs, aliens, second-sight, remote viewing, psychokinetic phenomena, all of them are called "supernatural" and yet the conclusions we've drawn at Groom Lake suggest that all of these things are just different natural aspects of the same threads that bind everything together. We don't know what to call them yet, and we don't know what they are, but Ernie Walker's unexpected leap through time is one of them, and that's why the team were so determined to track him down. Mackenzie and I both felt that understanding Ernie might unlock the clues we need to progress our research, because we were going nowhere fast.'

Ethan got where he was coming from.

'So, Ernie is part of that thread somehow?'

'Yes,' Kyle replied. 'Ernie, and people like him, have a little something extra, that hint of being psychic or whatever. Such people are mocked, and most are nothing but charlatans and cold-readers, but just a tiny few are genuine and more prone to these kinds of experiences than most all other people. They're literally special, but finding a genuine one among all the others is like finding a needle in a haystack.'

Lopez shrugged.

'Finding a needle in a haystack isn't all that hard if you happen to sit on it. There must be lots of skilled psychics or whatever that they could have used, but I guess they're too damned lazy to look. So, you're saying that my great-great-great-great-grandchildren are gray-skinned aliens zipping around somewhere over Mexico, scaring the locals?'

Kyle smiled again. 'More or less.'

'Cool,' was Lopez's typically laconic reply.

'Ernie Walker is the perfect example,' Kyle said. 'He couldn't have faked it, is fifty years out of his own time, there were witnesses to his sudden arrival and an orbiting satellite detected the energy burst that brought him here. Ernie was ground-zero for proof that not only can people move through time, under the right circumstances, but that also their own persona, their own self, was something to do with how they could achieve what most people rightly assume is impossible. The team felt that everybody has the capability for this, but that in most people it's somehow dormant: only a few are different.'

Ethan figured that someone like Ernie, a bona fide time traveller, would indeed be gold dust to Mackenzie, and for that matter, the North Koreans too.

'If Pyongyang was researching something similar, or maybe watching what Mackenzie's team were doing, then that may be how they got wind of Ernie and what he meant to the project,' Ethan said.

'Pyongyang have been building their own time-dilation device,' Kyle explained. 'They're operating it under the guise of their nuclear test program, which is a bit ironic when you think about it. We detected energy emissions similar to those seen around Ernie's arrival in the South Pacific, and we figured they were at about the same place that we were but were having the same difficulties making their machine work. Ernie shows up, and boom, North Korea are all over the Pacific and Norfolk trying to chase him down before we could get to him.'

'What does this device do?' Lopez asked. 'I mean, we saw another time-dilation device once and it was all kinds of complex, but there were no humans as part of it.'

'The Tokomak Device, built by the late Joaquin Abell,' Kyle confirmed, apparently already knowing about the construction of an underwater facility off the coast of Florida where, once, the billionaire Abell had been able to contain miniature black holes within an intense magnetic field, and place cameras watching news feeds close to their event horizons. So close, that time dilated. Gradually, the cameras had seen news reports from ever further into the future, allowing Abell to capitalize upon the knowledge.

'He used black holes, right?' Ethan said.

'Yeah, a clever but difficult process,' Kyle replied. 'It didn't work out, as you both know, but this process is different. The gravitational field of even a large object like the sun does indeed dilate time, but only by a fraction. By studying locations around the world where time slips were considered common or often reported, as well as similar events around UFO sightings that we were able to make, we figured out that it was much more efficient to replicate the electromagnetic fields around a black hole rather than the black hole itself: it's a means to an end. The fields seem to be what is doing most of the work when it comes to bending time for an observer, because they interact directly with that observer. A black hole is different, and actually bends time and space around it so tightly so that light, and therefore time, cannot escape. Similar, but subtly different processes.'

'And they're gonna put Ernie inside one of these things?' Lopez asked, somewhat horrified.

'They will,' Kyle said. 'Ernie probably wants to go home. He was twenty-three when he got zapped fifty years into the future. Now he's an old man and his life is over before it even began. If Mackenzie follows protocol, he'll try to help Ernie back home, but he'll also have him memorize just about as much stuff about the future as his brain can hold.'

'Why not just give him a laptop to take with him?' Garrett asked.

'Because a laptop is a physical thing and it won't travel back in time with him,' Kyle explained. 'Remember, it's not his physical body that's heading back, it's his soul, for want of a better word for it. Ernie's essence is what will make the journey. Of course, we don't know if his memory will remain intact: for all we know people are zipping back and forth through time every day and just don't know it. The whole thing is a frontier of science that is beyond anything we imagined possible.'

Ethan was starting to see why the North Koreans were so interested in the project, and in Ernie.

'The North Koreans failed to stop Ernie falling into enemy hands,' he said. 'They'll almost certainly attempt to grab him again, or at the least destroy whatever Mackenzie's people are working on.'

'We should call them,' Lopez said, 'let them know.'

'Already tried,' Garrett said. 'The island's on lockdown and the civilians in Ebeye are unable to contact anybody on the base. Looks like Mackenzie and his team have taken over and they're making sure nobody else gets to see what they're up to. Chances are, they don't know that the North Koreans are heading their way.'

Kyle shook his head.

'There were only a few of them, and Mackenzie's got half an army out here.'

Ethan felt an uncomfortable knot form in his stomach as he thought about that for a moment.

'North Korea is utterly outclassed by the west on every front, but the ability to alter history could change all of that. They could make themselves the first country to develop atomic weapons, the first to invent the Internet, win the space race, you name it. I don't think that Pyongyang would hesitate to send forces out to the Marshall Islands if they thought that they could grab technology as powerful as this device that Mackenzie wants to test.'

'You think that they'd risk all-out war?' Lopez asked.

Ethan didn't know, but he did know that right now they were the only people who knew what was happening on both sides of the covert conflict.

'We've got to beat them to it.'

***

XXXIX

Ennylabegan Island,

Kwajalein Atoll

The Pacific sunshine was warm on Ernie Walker's back as he rode in the small tug that was taking them from the main island to this smaller, satellite paradise. If he closed his eyes, he could almost be back on USS *Bairoko*, the scents of the ocean and the steel decks, but there was no smoke from the boilers, no odors of engine oil, grease or aviation fuel. Here, far from any human habitation, the air was as clean and pure as it had ever been, and ships seemed far more clinical now than they had been in his day.

His day, so long ago but to him literally just last week.

Ernie watched as the island drew closer, and with it perhaps his chances of seeing his family again. They seemed so far away, someplace else where he could never hope to reach them. It had been tough in the Navy, being at sea for months at a time, but that was nothing compared to the yawning abyss of decades of lost time. Ernie's body felt weaker by the minute but also more remote, as though somehow it did not belong to him, that he was an imposter here.

'You okay?'

General Mackenzie was watching him closely, and Ernie thought for a moment that he glimpsed a flicker of genuine concern in the younger man's eyes.

'I'm fine,' he said, then glanced at the armed guards watching over them both from the rear of the tug. 'Expecting company, or do you think I'm going to leap overboard and swim for it?'

'They're not for us,' Mackenzie assured him, 'they're island security. Trust me, you're the only civilian in history who's getting to see this.'

Ernie nodded. 'I'll be happy if this history never happens again.'

The general didn't reply. Ernie wanted to say something to him, about how all of this felt wrong, about how he could feel his sense of self slipping away from him. On the journey over, Ernie had been forced to read and memorize vast quantities of material; military campaigns, foreign political histories, industrial and commercial growth, big corporations and their assets and business plans. He was no fool: he knew that he was being armed with information that could be used against American foes should he make it back to his own time intact.

The problem for Ernie was that he could feel his mind slipping away from him. Sometimes he would be standing there and realize that he could not recall the past few minutes. At other times, he realized that he could not recall his own name, or that of his wife and children's names, or where he lived. There was something about his being here that just wasn't *right*.

Ernie was not a religious man. Although his family went to church every Sunday when he was on shore leave, and although they all considered themselves Christians, like most kids he'd hated Sunday School and never really believed all the stories their local pastor had shoved down their throats. Still, like most all folks he had the suspicion that life was about more than just, well, *life*. Stories of life after death, ghosts, strange happenings and such like had enthralled his childhood self just as much as the next kid, and they all had known that behind the spooky stories was some nebulous thread of truth, something beyond the human experience that he could never quite put his finger on. Strange, that he and so many others would secretly reject Biblical myths, but accept those that their own instincts suggested *might* be true.

The burden became too much, and as the tug approached the island's south coast and a small jetty, he turned to the general.

'Scott, there's something that you should know, in case this doesn't work out.'

Mackenzie looked down at him, waiting patiently.

'I've been getting this feeling,' Ernie said carefully, 'that I'm not supposed to be here.'

'That's understandable,' the general replied, 'leaping forward in time is something that would shake anybody up.'

'That's not what I mean,' Ernie tried again. 'I mean that, somehow, there's some *other* reason that I shouldn't be here.'

If the general was concerned about what Ernie was saying, he didn't show it.

'It's just nerves,' he promised. 'We'll have you back in your own time before you know it.'

Ernie said nothing, but he hoped that the general was right.

The tug slowed and pulled in alongside the jetty, soldiers leaping out with practiced efficiency to moor the tug as Ernie followed Mackenzie out. Soldiers quickly formed a phalanx around them as they marched off the jetty and toward a narrow path between dense ranks of palms swaying in the ever-present ocean wind. He could see a landing pad to his right, a fearsome-looking helicopter sitting on it, all straight-angled lines and what looked like machine guns and rocket launchers hanging from its sides.

'What the hell have you got out here, anyway?' Ernie asked. 'There's a civilian population only twenty miles south of here.'

'They don't bother us,' Mackenzie explained, 'they're reliant upon US financial support to live here. Without us, they're off the islands as they can't subsist.'

'Lovely,' Ernie mumbled back, 'I'm sure they thank Congress every day.'

'They know the score,' Mackenzie said. 'Out here it's much easier to maintain cover on covert operations than in Nevada or Utah. People just don't come out here much, but we allow tourism to exist under carefully controlled conditions to help conceal what's really happening on these atolls. The government has had a presence here ever since the tests of the 1950s, and it's not all about fuel stops over on the main island.'

The soldiers led them through the jungle of palms for a short distance, maybe three or four hundred meters, and they emerged into a clearing in the trees where Ernie could see a simple block house, a sort of radar dish and a lot of camera tripods and other equipment scattered about. He stopped, staring around him.

'Where is it?'

'Where's what?'

'This great device of yours?'

Mackenzie stamped one boot on the ground.

'It's underneath us,' he explained. 'But what actually happens is right here. The device generates the energy field, which encircles the center of this clearing. I know you were probably expecting more, but the reality is that you only have to be within the energy field, not strapped to some vast and impressive construction right out of *Stargate* or something.'

'What's Stargate?'

'Never mind,' Mackenzie said. 'Look, you need to speak to a few of the people here. They're going to help you get some idea of what will happen, and what we hope will happen afterward. I'm going to check on security.'

With that, the general walked away as two men approached Ernie, each flanked by an armed soldier. Ernie could never tell whether the soldiers were there to protect the workers, or to ensure that he did as he was told. Probably both, he figured.

'Mister Walker,' one of the technicians gasped, 'it's an honor to meet you, sir. Thank you for your service.'

Ernie blinked, bemused by the kid's deference. 'General says you're gonna explain this whole show to me.'

'I sure hope so, sir,' the kid replied. 'Come with me, please, and we'll get you ready.'

*

'Talk to me.'

The bunker was small, located on the island's north shore, but small was strong and it had been constructed decades before to withstand the force of a nuclear blast. General Mackenzie stood behind two technicians who were working the island's high-security communications suite.

'Nothing from the North Koreans,' came the response. 'They're radio silent, which is a concern in itself. It's possible the cell got off the US mainland, in which case they could be anywhere.'

'And talking to anybody,' Mackenzie noted. 'What about the local islands? Any of our spotters notice anything there?'

'Nothing reported yet,' came the response, the technician listening to multiple radio frequencies while also watching CCTV feeds from nearby Majuro.

'Okay,' Mackenzie replied. 'Contact me instantly if anybody shows up that we don't want to see here.'

'Yes sir!'

Mackenzie walked out of the bunker and looked up at the perfect blue Pacific sky. He had no doubt in his mind that the North Koreans and perhaps even the Russians would do something to either steal or destroy Project Montauk. There was simply too much to gain in controlling the technology that could alter the past, and yet he could not see how they could reach the islands undetected. Right now, the United States Navy's USS *Dwight. D. Eisenhower* carrier battle-group was stationed a hundred nautical miles off the atoll's north-west shores, FA-18E *Hornets* flying combat air patrols and Grumman E2C *Hawkeye* reconnaissance airplanes bathing the area in radar energy. A fly could not slip through the net without somebody in the fleet knowing about it. Yet, despite all of that, Mackenzie knew that he was missing something.

'Where are you?' he asked out loud, wondering whether he would see Ethan Warner and Nicola Lopez suddenly appear on the island's beaches.

For their sake and safety, he hoped they did not.

***

XL

DPRK *Gaecheogja,*

Marshall Islands

Jae-Hyuk Pak stood within the hot, cramped interior of the submarine's hull and tried not to sweat too heavily as he watched the crew guide the vessel through the darkened depths of the ocean. The dimly-lit submarine glowed an unhealthy shade of red, as though the crew were demons laboring in a Hadean dungeon, surrounded by the thick odor of closely-packed humanity, steel and plastic.

'How long?' he demanded of the captain.

The submarine's commander did not look away from his periscope as he replied, his voice distracted by whatever he was watching.

'As long as it takes.'

Jae was not used to being dismissed so easily, but the crews of submarines answered to nobody. He knew that these were hard men, operating in vessels that were dilapidated, former Soviet ships and submarines that often failed while on active service. Jae knew of at least one submarine that had sunk in the past few years, its hull collapsing while on manoeuvres with the loss of all souls. They faced death every day even when not at war, so to them, Jae and his men were a mere irritation in their daily duties.

The submarine was the latest in the North Korean's inventory of some sixty diesel-electric submarines, most of them *Romeo*-class former Soviet vessels. Classified as *Gorae*-class, after the North Korean word for "whale", the submarines displaced two thousand tons submerged, and held a crew of over fifty. Armed with *Pukkuksong* 1 "Polaris" ballistic missiles, she was built to provide a second-strike capability in the event of a nuclear exchange with the United States.

Although the pride of the DPRK Navy, Jae knew that she was impotent against the overpowering might of the US and South Korean air and sea forces. The DPRK was so utterly inferior to the enemy that the only way to strike back was to go underwater, and even then, they were hopelessly outclassed by the enemy's submarine and naval forces. Still, the submarine was now operating close to the Marshall Islands and had yet to be detected.

'We are now forty miles north of the target,' the captain said softly, by instinctive reflex whispering to minimize their acoustic signature. 'Soon, you and your men will be able to travel alone.'

Jae nodded, grateful for the update.

'My men and I shall prepare for this, our *greatest* day.'

The *Gaecheogja* was leading a tiny force east across the Pacific, after being re-tasked from the Japan theatre of operations after Jae had reported in to Pyongyang on a secure network. He and his men had been forced to flee the United States under pre-prepared documents, and had headed immediately across the Pacific to the Solomon Islands, and from there had linked up with DPRK Naval forces operating in the South Pacific.

Jae was under no illusion that Pyonyang was not impressed with the way things had gone in Norfolk. That he had not yet been recalled suggested that they at least understood some of the difficulties he and his team were facing, but there was no going back now. If he did not recover the American, Ernie Walker, or at least perhaps the technology needed to improve the reliability of their own tests, then he knew that his life would be over along with that of his family.

He turned to look behind him in the cramped bridge of the submarine, and saw his men still waiting patiently for him. They had followed him without reserve, and they knew as he did that there was no going back if they failed. Death awaited them unless victory was achieved, just as it had awaited earlier overseas missions.

In 1996, a Sang-O SSC operated by the DPRK Reconnaissance Bureau was grounded on the shores of South Korea. South Korean troops chased down all of her crew but one: all had committed suicide or been murdered by their own superior officers to avoid capture. A similar Yugo-class midget submarine became snared in the nets of South Korean fishing boats in 1998, and was towed to a naval base. When opened, the five crew and four North Korean agents within were all dead: the agents had killed the crew, and then committed suicide. Not one man had wanted to return to

Pyongyang beneath a dismal cloud of failure, to serve out the rest of their lives alongside their family in the murderous *gulags*.

Jae knew that somewhere out there, in the depths around them, were four midget submarines, each carrying ten commandos. Dispatched from their hiding places and from spying missions around the Solomon Islands, they were now closely following the *Gaecheogja* as she closed in on the remote islands of the Marshall chain.

'How close can you get us to the island?' he asked the captain, well aware of the fear of being grounded.

The captain raised the periscope and thought for a moment.

'The Americans have a powerful net around the islands, we were lucky to sneak past the carrier group, but they're not so strong in defence close to shore. We should be able to surface under cover of darkness within a few miles of the islands. The midget submarines will then have to proceed alone to the target. We will not be able to support you once your cover is compromised.'

Jae nodded. Although the captain had not explicitly said so, he knew that the *Gaecheogja* would not be able to wait around long for them to return. In the event of an all-out firefight, American forces would eventually descend on the island *en masse* and there would be no escape for Jae. The DPRK submarines would slip away into the night and abandon them to their fate at the hands of the Americans or, more likely, themselves.

'Understood,' he replied without emotion. 'Once on station, hold for as long as you can. We will attempt to return, but if it is not safe to do so you should leave and maintain your cover. If there is no hope of us reaching you, we will withdraw in another direction in order to draw the Americans away.'

The captain stared at Jae for a moment, and a warm respect glowed in his eyes. Jae was willing to abandon his own escape in order to avoid scuppering the captain and crew's ability to leave undetected.

'May the people go with you,' he said, and extended his hand.

'And you,' Jae replied, shaking the captain's hand before he turned to his men.

They walked together from the bridge down a narrow corridor, the air stale and heavy. Jae hated submarines, and longed for the fresh air outside, even if it was laced with radiation from America's nuclear tests of decades before. Many of the waters they were sailing through were restricted areas, where human beings had not lived for decades.

They reached a small cabin where Jae had laid out a series of maps and satellite imagery on a table to brief his men. Each would lead the commandoes from the midget-submarines out to the island, each man ready to kill as many Americans as they could in their quest for Ernie Walker and whatever technology the Americans had at the site.

'We land here,' Jae pointed to a small enclosed man-made harbor on the island's south west corner. 'We can expect resistance from here, but there is nowhere else shallow enough for us to make our landing within reach of the shore. Speed, surprise and overpowering accuracy, not force, will allow us to prevail and gain the beach.'

Jae watched the eyes of his men. One could tell a lot about what soldiers thought of a plan by the way they either nodded in agreement or stood in silence and without motion: not wanting to disagree, fearing repercussions, but not agreeing with the plan. None of the men were moving.

'You disagree?' he asked.

'No, sir!'

Jae knew that this was not the time for threats or fear from their own side. 'There are no repercussions. If you have a stronger idea or tactic, share it now.'

For a moment none of them moved, but then one pointed to the satellite image that accompanied the maps.

'Look there, to the north east. The breakers would stop the submarines getting in close to most of the shore, but there's a narrow deep-water channel running in to the coast where the rollers aren't there. We could disembark from the submarines and swim ashore without alerting anybody to our presence, and we'll be closer to whatever they're hiding on the island. If we use the harbour, we're fighting from the moment we make landfall and have to cross the entire island doing so.'

Jae looked down at the satellite image and instantly realized that the agent was correct. The normally pale azure waters changed to a dark channel where the waters were calmer, enough so that divers could make their way into the shore without breaking the surface.

'Excellent,' Jae nodded. 'That's a much better way in, and it leaves the submarines undetected off shore, which gives us a greater chance of making it out of there.'

Jae felt the tension in the cabin subside, saw his men visibly relax as they realized that this operation was going to go a lot better than they had anticipated.

'Our objective is Ernie Walker,' Jae went on. 'He is the key, for reasons we don't yet fully understand. Without him, the Americans have nothing. We either abduct him, or we kill him if the abduction is no longer possible. As long as the Americans are denied Ernie Walker, we can be said to have achieved our mission. We move out in one hour.'

***

XLI

The *Atoll Angel* stank of grease, metal and old rope, an odor that was thankfully snatched away by the brisk ocean winds as her bow rose and plunged into the Pacific rollers.

Ethan stood at the bow and watched as the sun began to sink toward the western horizon, searing the sky gold behind torn banners of cloud that glowed orange against the evening sky. They had landed in Majuro several hours previously, and had quickly located Captain Trent's trawler. Short of a crew and severely upset, Trent had not hesitated to help them.

'Hell of a sight.'

Lopez moved to stand alongside him, balancing herself with natural grace against the pitch and roll of the trawler's deck. Out here, far from land, the sky and the ocean seemed vast and awe inspiring, leaving Ethan feeling utterly insignificant against even this tiny patch of nature.

'Probably what the Castle Bravo shot looked like just after it went off,' Ethan said, out of the blue.

'Nice,' Lopez replied. 'The same, but for the radiation and people burning to death and all that other inconvenient stuff.'

Ethan nodded, caught up in a strange melancholia. He didn't know why, but there was something about what they were doing that was haunting him, as though some unseen figure or force was watching over his shoulder, judging his actions.

'You feelin' it too?' Lopez asked.

Ethan was momentarily surprised as he looked at her. Lopez was not known for any supernatural beliefs, although after everything they'd seen in their work it wasn't as though she didn't know that there was more to everything around them than just what they could see with their eyes.

'Monkey on my back, but I can't see it,' Ethan said.

'Yeah, it's bugging me too,' Lopez admitted. 'It's like we're playing a game that already has an outcome, that we can't change anything. Or maybe that we shouldn't be changing anything.'

Thinking about time always messed with Ethan's head, just like most everybody else's. The idea that one could travel back in time and alter things was brain-bending, and the consequences so complex and yet misunderstood that he couldn't really bring himself to consider them.

'What we do here, what Ernie might do, has already affected us in the here and now,' he said finally. 'It messes with your mind.'

'And how,' Lopez said. 'We're not dead yet, so I'm guessing that whatever might happen isn't bad. Or maybe it hasn't happened yet and when it does, we'll just be somewhere else and not know a thing about it?'

Ethan didn't really have a response for that, but he could recall Boltman's opinion that people might be slipping back and forth through time, and not really know anything about it if the slips were just an hour here, an hour there, perhaps even seconds. There had been countless times he'd driven a car on a sort of mental autopilot, thinking about other things while traveling on a familiar road, his reflexes controlling the car. Minutes would pass by in seconds, time itself dilated by nothing more exotic than boredom. Likewise, short periods on guard duty as a Marine had seemed to take an age to pass by, time again warped by nothing more than the human mind.

'You folks sure you know what you're doin'?'

The *Atoll Angel's* skipper, Barnie Trent, strode up to the bow and lit a cigarette, the blue smoke whipped away on the wind as the ship busily chugged its way north.

'We know what we have to do,' Ethan replied. 'How we're gonna do it is another question. We appreciate the ride.'

Trent blew a cloud of smoke downwind.

'My frickin' pleasure,' he snapped back. 'Those North Koreans killed four of my best men in Manila, so anybody who can take the fight back to them is welcome aboard my boat. Hell, I'd come ashore with you if I had a suit.'

Ethan glanced back down the ship, where two locked metal cases held a collection of weapons and three diving suits provided by Garrett Industries. Ethan had decided that the time for going into dangerous situations unarmed was passed, after what had happened out in Nevada the previous year.

'The more the merrier,' he said, 'but for now just having someone outside who can pick us up...'

'What's left of us,' Lopez interjected.

'... will be more than enough. Don't bring the ship too close to the islands, just do what you do and wait for us to return. If we don't show up within forty-eight hours, we're either dead or on our way to a military black prison somewhere in the Balkans.'

Trent spat a globule of phlegm over the bulwarks, the spray from the ship's bows now glistening like diamond chips in the air.

'We know what we saw,' he said. 'Walker appeared in a flash of light. If we hadn't all seen it, I wouldn't have believed it. If you find yourself taken to places you shouldn't be goin' and you can get the word out, let me know. We'll find you.'

Ethan shook the captain's hand, as did Lopez.

'Be careful out there,' Trent said as he flicked the butt of his cigarette over the side in a casual display of contempt for nature. 'We'll make the islands within about an hour.'

Ethan watched him go, as Kyle joined them from their berth.

'You sure you're up for this?' Lopez asked him.

Kyle nodded. He'd gotten over his near-death experience at the hands of the North Koreans, his shock and horror turning slowly into rage and the desire for payback.

'He left me there,' Kyle replied. 'Mackenzie left me to die and you came for me. I don't work for that asshole anymore.'

'He could have you Court Martialled,' Ethan pointed out, 'send you into a Supermax for the rest of your life.'

'He thinks I'm dead,' Kyle replied. 'Let's keep it that way. I like to think it bothers him somehow.'

'Oh, it bothers him all right,' Lopez said. 'Mackenzie's become a part of the machine, lost his morals in pursuit of the mission, but they never really erase the man inside. I have the sense that somewhere deep within him, he's rotting, knows it, and can't do a thing to stop it.'

'Yes, he could,' Ethan said, 'but like so many of them he won't break ranks in order to do so. They all believe that the ends justify the means, even if it means sacrificing innocent lives to achieve their goals. We saw it all before with Majestic Twelve. They get a taste for power or knowledge and can't let it go.'

Kyle nodded.

'The installation is on an island to the north west of the military base on Meck Island. The exclusion zone means that the ship can't get within a few miles of the island, so we'll use the motorized underwater gliders to get there undetected. I know the security layout, I helped design it, so I know where to put us ashore and how to disable one or two security measures to let us slip through.'

'Then what?' Lopez asked, looking at Ethan. 'Mackenzie and his team aren't the enemy, but they'll shoot on sight if we're spotted.'

Ethan knew that she was right, that Mackenzie would not intervene if they were captured. He'd let them be shot right in front of him, in order to maintain security over Project Montauk.

'We record everything, covertly,' he said. 'We have a set of covert body cameras that we should keep switched on throughout the entire thing, to record everything we need to prove that this went down; that Ernie was here, that Mackenzie and his team were present. Then, we take it away with us and we reveal it to the world. If the North Koreans show up, then we can alert Mackenzie's security teams and slip away.'

Ethan cast his mind over the plan one more time. They would have to be close, very close, to the action to be able to record it in detail sufficient that nobody would be able to question its veracity. But, as long as they stayed low and in cover, Ethan figured that most all those present at the test would have their eyes on Ernie and whatever the test was going to do, rather than the jungles surrounding them.

He glanced at the sun, now just below a horizon seared with molten metal.

'It's time,' he said. 'We'd better get suited up.'

***

XLII

Ennylabegan Island

Ernie Walker sat alone in a tent that was illuminated by a single lamp and listened to the evening breeze rumbling the canvass around him. He could hear the preparations ongoing all around the island, but for a moment here and there he could believe that he was once again a young man, on shore leave, somewhere exotic.

The illusion was made all the greater by the fact that he was wearing his own uniform, scorch marks and all. It hung from his emaciated frame now, all the muscle and vigor of his youth long gone. He looked down at his bony hands, laced with purple veins, and was both appalled and saddened that he should have to suffer such an indignity. Not only that, but he had to visit the bathroom almost every hour, an embarrassing thing for a twenty-four-year old to have to do, no matter how damned old he might look to the other people on the island.

The tent flap was pulled aside, and General Mackenzie leaned in.

'You ready, sailor?'

Ernie nodded, tried to get up, but his weary legs failed him and he stumbled slightly. Mackenzie caught him quick as a flash, steadied him.

'Easy there,' the general said, 'I don't want you going and breaking a hip right before heading back.'

Ernie managed to stand up straight and walk out of the tent into the night, the air warm and the sky above sprinkled with countless stars glittering like jewels above the palms.

The clearing was now devoid of clutter, and where there had once been nothing but a stone block building there was now a large metal ring lying on the sand, huge cables running from it in various directions, some vanishing down into the ground. Soldiers guarded the metal ring, which was maybe ten feet in diameter and seemed to be made from aluminium.

'Do you remember everything that we asked of you?' Mackenzie asked him as they walked toward the metal ring.

'Sure,' Ernie lied, his mind full of stuff but not much of it what the general had asked him to focus on. 'I know what to do.'

Mackenzie said nothing more, and Ernie wondered whether the general believed him or not. Ernie had indeed read the books they had given him, hastily printed tomes filled with the history of life on Earth since 1954. Ernie was stunned at how fast mankind had developed, how staggering the technology of this modern age was, but was also appalled at how so many other countries still lived in what seemed like almost medieval conditions. One thing that had stood out for Ernie had been the Internet, and he had asked for a connection so that he could study further than the books allowed. There, he had made his plans, memorized what he needed to know, and now hoped to hell that his addled mind would be able to recall it all should he survive this trip into the unknown.

'The technicians have told you how this works,' Mackenzie said, 'but I'll run it through for you one more time. You'll stand inside the metal ring, and when everybody's ready the generators will start up and produce an electromagnetic field within the ring that's at least as powerful as that which was generated by the Castle Bravo shot back in '54. The difference here is that instead of it being dissipated all around, it'll be focused just on where you're standing using a ring of further electromagnets that are installed beneath ground.'

Ernie nodded, kind of understanding it but knowing that the technology was as beyond his grasp as that of the Castle Bravo weapon half a century before. If the general had told him the device was powered by jelly beans he'd have probably shrugged and accepted it.

'The theory is that when the field reaches a certain intensity, it will trigger the mechanism that allowed you to arrive here, and send you back from where you came.'

Ernie thought about that for a moment.

'How do you know it won't send me another fifty years into the future?'

Mackenzie smiled tightly.

'I don't,' he replied. 'But the guys here seem confident that they know what they're doing. I asked them the same question and they said that if you do show up fifty years in the future from now, at least this time there will be people there to help you, and they might have learned how to do a better job by then.'

Ernie didn't really know how to respond to that. 'Wonderful.'

'It's not all bad,' Mackenzie said. 'The team have studied energy fields at places around the world where people claim to have seen the past, and they have identified key aspects of those fields and their polarities that suggest a certain amount of energy, delivered in a certain way, should produce the desired effect. They even think that you'll be here on this island when this is all over, that you won't just pop up in the open ocean again like last time.'

'*Bad, should, think*,' Ernie echoed. 'The odds aren't great, are they?'

Mackenzie sighed. 'We've never done this before, so we don't know what will happen. But if you want any chance of getting back to your own time, this is pretty much the only one we have.'

Ernie nodded, stiffened his resolve, and walked with Mackenzie to the edge of the metal ring, which was entombed in pipes and wires and hummed softly as though alive.

The general turned to Ernie, and extended his hand.

'I know you've been through hell, and I know you think your government abandoned you, and that we're just using you to take information back into the past,' he said. 'It's all true, but it's all not true at the same time. I want you to get back home, Ernie. The people there won't know that you've been here, nobody will, and nobody will believe it until any predictions that you make start to come true. It's going to be up to you to decide what to do with your knowledge, should you make it back safely.'

Ernie had not thought of that: that despite all that they controlled, Mackenzie and the US Government were basically relying on him to do what they were asking: that once he went back in time, they would have no control or even knowledge of what had happened. Travelling forwards through time at least gave those in the future the possibility of a heads' up that somebody was coming. Head back into the past, and nobody would know a thing about it. Just like UFOs.

Ernie shook the general's hand as a sudden idea popped into his head.

'I'll be in touch, general,' he promised as he shook Mackenzie's hand.

With that, Ernie turned and stepped into the ring.

'We've got a contact.'

Ernie turned as a technician nearby called out the warning. Other soldiers turned also, and Ernie thought that they were going to initiate a fire fight with North Korean soldiers that might be storming the beaches somewhere nearby.

But instead, he saw technicians at computer monitors working furiously as others gathered around a series of tripods, each equipped with cameras on motors that automatically began swivelling toward something in the sky.

Ernie turned, and to his amazement he saw a brilliant orb against the velvety blackness of space, like nothing that he had ever seen before. It pulsed and fluoresced as though alive, as large as the full moon but far more powerful. The colors within seemed to flow like oil through water after recent rains, swirling and coiling around each other, and he was suddenly aware that the endless ocean wind had fallen away and the jungle around them was deathly quiet.

'What the hell is that?' Ernie asked, mesmerized by the sight.

'They're us,' Mackenzie said, and he looked at Ernie. 'I think they've come here to watch you.'

***

XLIII

Jae-Hyuk Pak pulled on his wetsuit, surrounded by his men who were likewise preparing to leave the submarine. The air was hot, humid, their discomfort made worse by the tight-fitting black suits that stuck to their skin like a slick blanket.

The submarine was now in shallow water, just off the shore of Ennylabegan Island, or so the captain had assured him. They had slipped past the American fleet hours previously, and then again through the detector fields that lay on the ocean floor around Meck Island and others, there to detect the passage of enemy vessels. The Americans possessed much technology, but ingenuity was not solely an American virtue: the submarine contained sensors that reflected and broke up the signals, making the submarine look far smaller than it was. Any radar signal detected made the submarine appear to be a small whale or perhaps a large dolphin, sufficient to render them of no apparent threat to the American islands.

Jae watched as seamen prepared to flood the airlock in which he stood. The airlock was only large enough for four men, so his team of sixteen would have to exit in two batches of four, eight in total from each of the two midget submarines moving in toward the islands from different directions.

As Jae pulled on the last of his equipment, he heard the soft hum of the electric motors die down as the submarine reached its designated location and slowed. The captain had set the sub's ballast so that it would not have to vent air at all while it remained near the islands, further concealing its presence from the Americans. That cautionary approach, and the vessel's draught, meant that the submarine also had to remain a little further out from the shore than Jae would have liked.

Jae pulled on his oxygen mask and checked that of the man next to him. Satisfied that his team was ready, he gave a thumbs-up to the sailor manning the lock, and the sailor saluted back before slamming the door shut. The locking mechanism spun tight, sealing them in. Moments later, the hiss of seawater filled the airlock at the same time as extractors drew out air through vents in the top of the airlock sides, allowing it to fill with seawater at natural pressure.

It took only a couple of minutes for the airlock to fill, Jae waiting until the flow of water had ceased before he reached up and opened the access door to the submarine's upper hull. An interior light within the airlock switched off automatically when he unlocked the door, and for a moment they were in complete and utter blackness. Then, the faint light of a moon filtering through the dark water spilled into the airlock, and Jae led them up and out.

The submarine was suspended perfectly in the water, twenty feet above the sea floor and some thirty below the surface of the ocean above. Jae looked up and could see the moonlight rippling and flickering above them as he turned for the shore and began swimming. His men followed, each with a holdall over their backs containing a variety of personal and section weapons with which to wreak havoc on the Americans. There was no chance of subtlety in this mission now, no hope of sneaking ashore and spiriting Ernest Walker away unnoticed. The island was too small and, once the Americans were alerted, it would be almost impossible for the submarine to make it away undetected. This was a mission to deny the enemy their advantage, using as much force as was humanly possible.

Jae swam silently through the blackness, watched as the sea floor came ever closer, the rollers above pulling him along more swiftly as the water became more shallow. He could see the narrow gulley that his team member had identified, a deeper section of seafloor that provided a natural entrance to the shoreline that led almost up to the jungle itself.

Jae was sure that the route into the shore would have been identified by the Americans, so his team were prepared. Each wore Infra-Red goggles that could see heat signatures in absolute darkness, allowing them to pick out troops concealed within vegetation on the island. Each man also carried gas-grenades and other silent weapons that could be used to silence and incapacitate an enemy long before they were alerted to Jae's presence.

Jae reached the point where the gulley's depths rose up to the shallow water of the beach, and slowly he crept on his belly out of the water, keeping his eyes peeled on the shore as around him more of his men slid out of the rolling water, silent and deadly, concealed by the darkness of the night around them. None of the men advanced onto the sandy beach, where their black suits would be easily visible against the pale sand. Each remained in the water, only the upper parts of their heads peeking out.

Jae instantly saw the tell-tale glow of two American soldiers concealed within vegetation perhaps ten yards from the treeline, one further back than the other in a position to cover his comrade should they come under fire. Where they had positioned themselves gave them perfect fields of fire no matter where Jae might attempt to break the surface and come ashore, and he knew that he and his team would be cut down in an instant.

Jae slowly reached down to his belt and unclipped a single gas grenade. The term grenade was somewhat misleading, as the device contained no explosives. It was designed to float, and had a small mechanical timer that he could set. With the wind blowing off the ocean from behind Jae, he could release the device and let it spew toxic gas right into the American position.

Jae set the timer to sixty seconds, then released the grenade. The device floated away from Jae, bobbing on the surface of the water as it was washed inland and rolled up onto the beach. He waited, watching the grenade. There was nothing to see when sixty seconds had passed, the grenade lying among reeds and other natural debris and looking completely innocuous, but the device would by now be spreading its silent and invisible death back into the jungle behind it. Jay watched through his IR goggles, saw the heat signatures of the two men begin to move as they were hit by the fast-acting agent. The chemical within caused two major responses in human victims: restriction of the throat and vocal chords, preventing a call for help, and the suppression of the brain's cerebral cortex, preventing movement.

Jae waited a few more seconds, saw both of the men struggling to get up as they tried to fight the effects of the gas, and in that instant, he launched himself up the beach with his men right behind him.

They ran the few paces across the open sand and plunged into the jungle, Jae ignoring the first flailing victim and heading for the second. The soldier was on his knees, his radio in one hand, his rifle in the other, trying hard to both call a warning and fire his trigger to alert other units.

Jae ploughed into him and knocked him onto his back, smashed the radio out of his hands as he yanked out a huge knife and drove it point-first straight through the man's throat and out through the back of his neck, severing his spinal column with one brutal blow.

The soldier's eyes flew wide even as his body went limp. Jae savagely snapped the knife left and right, severing the carotid artery as blood spilled in copious floods down the man's neck and his eyes emptied of consciousness. Behind him, Jae could hear the other man being overwhelmed and killed in silence.

They didn't wait to move the bodies. There was no time for covert action, for they could only hope to remain undetected for a few minutes before the inevitable firefight that awaited. Jae led his men in a low crouch through the jungle, following a faint path between the trees that led inexorably inland toward the center of the island.

The light was the first thing that Jae saw as he reached what looked like a clearing up ahead. It filtered down between the palms above his head, flickering and changing color in a kaleidoscopic display that was both natural and yet somehow alien and disturbing, not of this earth. Jae tried to keep his eyes on the path ahead, but he could not help himself but to glance at the mesmerising light as it hovered over the island. He didn't know if it was something that belonged to the Americans, maybe some kind of spy drone, and he wondered for a moment whether it could see him and his men creeping toward the clearing ahead. He slowed, watching it as he moved, but he could hear no alarms or cries of warning, nothing to suggest that the object, whatever it was, was reacting to their advance.

Ahead, he could see structures now, lights, and within the glow of those lights were soldiers standing with weapons at port arms, half of them looking inward at whatever was happening therein, the other half facing outward to watch for trespassers. Jae figured he could get to within maybe ten yards of the soldiers before he and his men would be seen. Right now, they were well concealed from view by the trees, through which even the best IR goggles could not see, but once they left the treeline they would stand out like beacons against the forest.

Jae crouched down. The other DPRK team would be making their way ashore from the far side of the island, and he could see no sign that they had been detected. Sixteen men in total, they were facing an American force of what looked like perhaps a hundred or more men, plus unknown others who were probably guarding other entrances to the island. The American fleet nearby would be able to bring in large numbers of American Marines at short notice, so this was going to have to be quick and dirty. Jae could see no sign of Ernie Walker, and although he was sure that he was somewhere in there with the Americans, he could see no way that they could reach him without being seen.

Jae turned his head slowly and saw his men behind him, all hiding within the foliage and behind tree trunks, all waiting in silence for him to decide how they were going to do this. Jae thought of his wife and children at home, and then he made his decision. He, along with his fellow soldiers, was being held hostage by a leader who did not care for them or their welfare, only that they completed their mission. Jae decided that he would not try to bring Ernie Walker back with them – why the hell should they risk so much under threat of losing their own lives and perhaps those of their families back home? No. Jae would return home having inflicted a terrible, bloody blow to the Americans in their Dear Leader's name, the best he could do under such tremendously difficult circumstances.

Jae reached down and pulled a grenade from his webbing, and with one gloved hand he slipped a finger through the pin, ready to pull it and toss the grenade into the watching Americans. *Take as many down as you can, all at once: shock and awe, as the Americans like to call it.*

Behind him, every man on his team mirrored his decision.

***

XLIV

The deep waters of the Pacific Ocean were just as dark as those of any other as Ethan led the way through the inky blackness, following a compass rose on his underwater jet-ski. The device pulled him effortlessly through the water, a small, blinking light giving Kyle and Lopez something to follow as they travelled north-west toward Ennylabegan Island.

Ethan knew that were they to be discovered, they would be shot on sight or at the very least treated as criminals and saboteurs. They had no business being here, other than the fact that Ethan was sure the North Koreans were going to attempt to attack the island and they had no way of warning General Mackenzie other than making their way here and raising the alarm.

Ethan had no idea what they were going to do, but he felt sure that despite the risks, this was the right course of action. What happened to Ernie could affect all of them, as he could change the past and the future for everyone. Ethan could not ignore the possibilities that presented, and as he thought about his own troubled past, he could not help but hope that Ernie would be able to help in some way, to change some of the troubles and heart aches that Ethan had suffered over the years.

The seabed passed by beneath the glowing headlight of the jet-ski, which was angled down both to prevent easy identification from the shore and also to illuminate obstacles as he negotiated his way between reefs toward the beach. He could see rollers churning twenty feet above him, glistening with diamond chips of light from the half-moon glowing in the sky above.

A faint movement far to his right caught his attention and he glanced across, peering into the endless blackness. There had been the briefest glimmer of light reflected off something out there, the rippling patterns of moonlight through water cast across the shape of something moving on a similar path to Ethan.

For a moment he wondered whether they were being shadowed by a whale or some other large aquatic creature, then he wondered whether his eyes had just been playing tricks on him, his mind trying to make sense of the shapeless darkness of the deep.

Then the light flickered again.

It was a faint shimmer, as clouds passing over the moon parted briefly and its light was cast into the depths in shimmering curtains and rays. The light hit something large and smooth, was curved around it, and Ethan noticed immediately that it was too uniform, too smooth to be anything other than a man-made object. He knew at once that he was looking at a submarine, black, cold, hovering stationary in the darkness. What he couldn't know was who the submarine belonged to. Its size, brief as the glimpse he had of it was, appeared to be much smaller than a United States nuclear submarine, which demoted it to some kind of covert intelligence version, a midget-submarine of the type often operated during World War Two by the Nazis and also later by the Soviet Union.

It was possible that, out here, the U.S. Navy was operating similar vessels but Ethan couldn't take that chance. If the North Koreans were here, then a midget submarine would probably be the only hope they would have of sneaking close to the island without being detected.

Ethan pushed on. Clouds of dislodged sand began to billow outwards as the rollers churned the seabed, so he slowed, preparing to shut down the jet-ski before he reached the shoreline. He didn't want any American soldiers on the beaches to see him, but equally he didn't want to tip his hand to any North Koreans making their way ashore: surprise would be their greatest asset, but now it would also be his.

Ethan killed the lights on the jet-ski before he surfaced and slid silently along with the rollers, searching the beach for any sign of troops. There would be Americans covering the jetty to the west of the island, and the beach would be either mined or equipped with pressure plates to alert the base to any trespassers.

To his right he spotted a break in the rollers, a narrow channel of water that travelled right up the beach and almost to the treeline. Ethan turned and made his way to the channel, following it up until the water was too shallow to travel any further. He let himself come to a stop on the sand and remained motionless, watching for any sign of troops waiting to put a slug in his head the moment he stood up.

The trees were almost motionless, but the sand in front of Ethan showed signs of recent movement. He could see boot prints, large, heavy, the sign of men moving out of the water. Myriad tiny pits in the sand betrayed where water had spilled from their wet-suits as they walked up the beach, or perhaps had run at a crouch into the cover of the foliage. That he could see no bodies suggested that this section of the beach was unprotected, for if the American forces stationed here had been out in force then it would by now have been littered with the bodies of the interlopers.

Ethan scrambled up the beach and into cover, ripping off his goggles and breathing apparatus as Lopez and Kyle followed him out of the water and dashed to crouch alongside him.

'That was too easy,' Lopez whispered. 'This whole place should be under observation.'

Ethan nodded as he hefted his jet ski to one side, concealing it with leaves and fallen palms.

'Did you see the submarine?'

'Sure,' Lopez replied, both of them talking in hushed whispers to avoid betraying their location. 'Figured it was ours.'

'Maybe,' Ethan replied. 'Maybe not.'

Kyle and Lopez concealed their jet-skis, and Ethan pulled from a waterproof holdall two assault rifles, one of which he handed to Lopez. Also, inside the holdall were three 9mm pistols, which again he shared out among the three of them. Kyle took one of the pistols and hefted it in his hand, clearly unfamiliar with its weight.

'For protection only,' Ethan warned him. 'If you need it, don't hesitate to use it, but try to stay out of the way if you can.'

Kyle thought about it a moment longer, and then held the pistol with a grim determination in his eye.

'The North Koreans were going to kill me,' he replied. 'If they try again, me hesitating isn't something you need to worry about.'

Ethan figured that Kyle would be able to look after himself on this jaunt. With that, he checked his rifle, then turned and peered into the jungle. As dark as any he'd ever seen, only limited moonlight was making it down to the ground, and the beach was utterly silent but for the gentle whisper of the rollers and the palms swaying in the ever-present ocean wind.

'You know where we're going?' Lopez asked.

Ethan was about to reply when he saw something appear in the night sky ahead of them. It looked like a ball of incandescent light that hovered in the night sky somewhere over the center of the island, high enough to cast a glow on the scattered clouds drifting through the night sky.

'That's not a coincidence, and it's not an aircraft flare,' Ethan said.

'It's one of them,' Kyle replied. 'I'd know them anywhere now. They're here to watch whatever's going to happen, which means Ernie and Mackenzie are here.'

Ethan set off immediately in the direction of the light, keeping low and following a faint trail through the undergrowth. Islands like this one were too small to harbor large animals, so the trail had to be man-made, perhaps back in the day when the island's small structures were built.

He'd only made twenty paces into the jungle when he saw something lying across the path. Ethan slowed, his rifle trained on the object, and as they closed in on it, he saw the form of a human body. Ethan hurried up to it, and in the faint moonlight he saw the corpse belonged to a male soldier, his uniform bearing no insignia, his throat cut from ear to ear, glistening with black blood.

'They're here,' Ethan said, referring to the North Koreans. 'Stay low, follow my lead. Our only chance now is to surprise them before they can slaughter the rest of Mackenzie's men.'

***

XLV

Ernie Walker moved to the centre of the metal ring as instructed by Mackenzie's technicians, who were monitoring instruments in droves at computer terminals to one side of the ring. Above him, he could see the glowing orb of light swirling and twisting with rivers of fire, like some bizarre magical omen from a fantasy novel. Another had appeared, slightly further away, watching it seemed as Ernie waited for the machine to start. Although the lights were too bright to see any detail, Ernie could just make out the shapes of disc-like craft behind the brilliant orbs.

Mackenzie and his men had backed away, and Ernie could see banks of television cameras all trained upon him as he stood, his back and legs aching now with fatigue. Truth be told, he just wanted the whole damned thing over with. If this contraption of theirs fried him he didn't much care, as long as he didn't have to deal with the crippling pain in his joints and the strange, frightening lapses in consciousness and awareness that plagued him.

The general watched from behind the cameras, directing his men as a group of technicians behind a thick, clear shield worked computer terminals. Ernie could sense in the air a sort of energy, benign, distant, like static electricity that tingled the skin on his forearms and his scalp. Now, he sensed that energy change.

Gradually, as he watched the men working before him, he felt himself being pressed in from all sides, as though he was underwater and yet able to breathe. He heard a rising humming noise, something reverberating deep within the ground beneath him, and he figured that the engineers had started the machine and whatever was about to happen was going to happen to him, right here, right now. Suddenly he was afraid, not of death but of the unknown, the fact that he hadn't known how he'd got here and now he didn't know where he was going. A rapid series of cataclysmic thoughts ran through his mind; images of arriving in a desolate future after mankind had annihilated himself through nuclear wars; of arriving in the medieval past with no way of *ever* returning again; finding himself floating in space because of some unpredicted error in timing or placing or…

Ernie's nerve wavered, the last thing that he would have expected to happen, now that he at least had the chance of returning home. He put one foot forward and began walking out of the ring.

Intense pressure pushed him back and he felt immense energy flow around him like water. He shuddered, repelled by the experience, and suddenly was overcome with a terrible sense of melancholy, like something was seriously wrong with everything they were doing. The emotion overwhelmed him, a terrifying black wave of depression that he had truly crossed a line, that he was guilty of something so terrible that now the universe was coming to wreak its revenge, the reaper at the window.

Ernie called out, reached out for help, saw the hairs on his arms rising up as the humming became ever louder around him, so much so that it became a physical thing, holding him in place so that he could not even place his fingers in his ears. Tears of misery streamed down his face as he saw the technicians stand back from their terminals, watching with interest as all around Ernie a huge ball of pulsing blue light materialized from out of thin air.

Ernie's eyeballs began to vibrate within their sockets, causing him great pain, but now he could not move a muscle, frozen where he stood to endure this horrible ordeal with his eyes open no matter what he saw. The jungle around the site flickered in and out of view, darkness replaced by even greater, deeper darkness, and endless depth that sent waves of vertigo flooding through his nervous system.

And then he saw them.

The jungle seemed to explode in slow motion with balls of flame and fire as figures rushed out, their rifles blazing.

*

Ethan followed the trail through the darkened jungle, and as he moved so the whisper of the wind through the palms above them faded away and a deathly silence descended over the island. Ethan was not prone to detecting subtle shifts in atmosphere, but this one was so prominent that he stopped in his tracks, overcome with the sensation that he was walking through a sort of physical field of energy.

'The hell's that?' Lopez whispered from behind him.

Ethan didn't know, but now he could sense a humming energy from somewhere in front of them that was growing with every passing second. It was accompanied by a glowing orb of blue light that flared outward, reaching into the jungle in blue-white shafts. Ethan averted his eyes from the light to protect his night vision and headed left, cutting away off the faint path and moving toward the light from one side. As he did so, he saw the men before him, tucked into the undergrowth and waiting to launch their attack.

He could only see four of them, but he knew that there must be more hiding elsewhere, for it would be suicide to attack such a large American force with so few soldiers. Ethan quickly signalled to Lopez, pointing first to his eyes, then signalling four fingers and pointing ahead.

Lopez nodded as they crept forwards, and Kyle hurried alongside Ethan and tapped his shoulder.

'They're running the machine up too fast,' he said, 'I can tell by the sound. If they get this wrong, they'll fry Ernie like an egg.'

Ethan nodded.

'Lopez and I will take care of the North Koreans. You head for Ernie and either get him out or get him home, okay?'

Kyle nodded, and without hesitation he set off through the jungle to get himself into position. Ethan grinned; despite the danger that they were all in, he found himself impressed at how Kyle was stepping up without any prompting. If he and Lopez ever needed a protégée, Kyle was swiftly shaping up to be that person.

'What do we do about these guys?' Lopez asked in a whisper, although now the humming was becoming loud enough that Ethan knew nobody else could hear them.

'They'll strike now,' he said. 'There's nothing we can do but flank them and hope we can cut them down when they break cover, before they can cause too much damage.'

'Great,' she replied. 'I'll take the right.'

Ethan moved to the left and hurried through the darkness, knowing that the North Koreans must strike within a few seconds, using the growing noise from the American encampment to disguise their attack. Sure enough, even as he moved to the south of their position and checked his rifle one last time, he saw them move.

There were eight in all, each crouched in the foliage as they swung their arms up. Ethan saw eight grenades launch out of the jungle on high trajectories, arcing over the heads of the guards encircling the site, aimed to land in silence between those looking outward and those looking in toward Ernie Walker.

Ethan knew that he could not stop the carnage that was about to occur, for it was too late. All he could do was shout a warning to anybody who could hear.

'Grenade!'

His voice sounded meek compared to the deep throbbing resonance coming from the device in the American camp, but he saw several of the American troops glance in his direction. Ethan stood up, made himself seen and pointed to the North Korean position.

It seemed as though time had slowed to a crawl. He saw the Americans turn to face him, rifles coming up, not understanding that he was not the threat and that he was trying to warn them. Ethan kept pointing, one hand holding his rifle. He saw confusion on the faces of the soldiers as they realized that he was trying to indicate something, but their training dictated that they confront the immediate threat first and they began to turn toward him.

Moments later, the grenades detonated.

Ethan flinched and ducked down as the eight grenades burst like new born stars in the night, eight rapid explosions that shattered the air and sent shockwaves through Ethan's body that hurt his very bones. The blasts and shrapnel tore through the American soldiers, cut them down with a scythe of fire along with ranks of unarmed technicians and scientists behind them.

Ethan rolled flat on the floor as the cloud of lethal shrapnel flew over his head, and as the North Koreans launched themselves from cover with their rifles blazing so he opened fire from the prone position.

His first bullet cut one of the North Koreans down in mid-stride, the second tore through another man's belly but he kept on running. Ethan did not try to stay on the same target, firing at each man with rapid, single-shot bursts. He saw others of the North Korean team cut down from the far side as Lopez opened fire, catching the attackers in a crossfire that dropped five of them before they'd crossed the open ground between the jungle and Ernie Walker.

The Americans were in disarray, and Ethan could hear gunfire from the far side of the encampment as what must have been a second team of attackers launched a similar strike on the far side of the base. Bullets zipped this way and that as the infernal humming noise from the device at the center of it all reached a new intensity.

Ethan leaped to his feet and ran at the remaining North Koreans as they crouched down behind computer terminals and storage boxes, preparing to fight their way through the remaining American soldiers to reach Ernie Walker. In their haste the North Koreans had not noticed either Ethan or Lopez flanking them, and now they both moved through the shadows toward the remaining three enemy.

Lopez got there first, rushing up behind one of the North Koreans and firing as she ran. The bullets from her rifle snapped the man's head sideways and he slumped onto his knees, his chin on his chest as she turned for the soldier in the middle.

Ethan rushed in from the far side, fired a single shot that caught his target behind the ear and shattered the back of the North Korean's skull, spilling blood and brain matter down his back as he toppled sideways onto the sand. Ethan turned his attention to the remaining man, and in an instant the North Korean leaped up and swung the butt of his rifle at Ethan's head.

Ethan saw the North Korean's face and instantly he recognized the man from Norfolk, Virginia. Short, stocky, with a hard face and black eyes that radiated contempt for all around him.

Ethan ducked the blow and came up with his own rifle flipping to try to hit the North Korean's chin, but the soldier was too fast and ready for the counter-attack. He jerked back out of range and side kicked Ethan in the belly.

Ethan doubled over as the wind rushed from his lungs, and felt the barrel of a rifle pressed against his head.

'Time for you to leave, American, permanently.'

Ethan peered up at the North Korean, in time to see Lopez press the barrel of her own rifle against his head.

'Rain check on that, asshole?'

Ethan swung his own rifle up and around, bashing the North Korean's weapon to one side as he jammed the barrel up under the soldier's chin.

'Welcome to America,' he smiled.

He was about to push the North Korean into sight of the American soldiers when the shooting stopped. There was a long silence, and then suddenly four North Korean soldiers rushed into view, their weapons pointed at Ethan and Nicola.

Ethan looked up and saw Kyle on his knees, a pistol to the back of his head.

The North Korean before Ethan smiled and reached up, slowly taking Ethan's rifle and turning it against him. The man turned and looked over his shoulder at his companions, many of whom were injured and bloody, and he smiled at them.

'The area is secure?'

'It is done, Jae,' came the reply in surprisingly good English. 'They are overpowered.'

'Jam their signals, make sure the American fleet doesn't know what's happening.'

'Already done,' came the reply, the DPRK soldier apparently as surprised as Ethan at the speed and success of their attack. 'They don't know a thing.'

***

XLVI

Ethan could see the surprise in Jae's expression as they were led out into the encampment. The North Korean's attack had been brutally swift and extremely effective. Almost half the American soldiers had been brought down by the grenade attacks, along with most of the technicians, and now the other half were on their knees with their hands behind their heads, utterly overwhelmed by the small team of North Korean soldiers.

Ethan, Lopez and Kyle were shoved into position at the head of the captured force, and Ethan could see General Mackenzie on his knees with his men, his shoulder a bloody mess where a bullet had caught him. His face was twisted with pain, his skin sheened with sweat and he was breathing heavily.

Jae shoved Ethan to his knees and then turned his attention to Ernie Walker.

The old man was inside the sphere of energy, and it was instantly clear to Ethan that he was suffering. His body trembled and quivered, his eyes were open but unseeing, trapped in some indescribable netherworld within a seething altar of energy.

Jae put his rifle to Kyle's head. 'What is happening to him?'

Kyle looked up at Jae.

'The energy is not yet enough to make the process work. He needs more power, which he would have got if you and your goons hadn't interfered.'

Jae smiled without warmth, then crouched down in front of Kyle.

'You know what will happen, if we don't come to an agreement,' he said as he slipped his huge knife out from a sheath at his waist. 'We have unfinished business, you and I.'

Kyle leaned back, and promptly spat in Jae's face.

The North Korean's eyes widened, and Ethan saw the other North Korean soldiers stand back, their eyes fixed on their leader. Jae wiped the spittle from his cheek, his black eyes fixed on Kyle, and then he turned and stabbed the knife straight out to the side.

The blade sank into Lopez's chest with a rasping sound. Ethan cried out and jumped to his feet, only to be pinned in place by four North Korean guns. Kyle's features twisted in horror as Jae leaned in close.

'You will die here this night,' Jae growled. 'So will your friend, if you don't do precisely what I say. Switch off the machine, pull him out of there, and then I will take his place. You will send me back to last month, where I will be able to complete this mission without flaw or the loss of my men. If you try anything to stop me, my men will kill each of your countrymen in front of you, then take you back to Pyongyang and slice you apart, piece by piece, for the next ten years.'

Kyle glared at the North Korean for a moment, but then he nodded once. Jae stood up, and pushed Kyle toward the various computer terminals surrounding the metal ring and the orb of light. Kyle stood in front of a terminal for a moment, then he began arranging a series of controls and the hum from the metal ring subsided, the glow of light fading away.

Ethan watched as Ernie slowly sank to his knees, his shoulders slumped and his head sinking until his chin touched his chest. The old man was utterly exhausted by his ordeal, and as he slowly looked up Ethan could see the pain on his features as he realized that he had gone nowhere. Slowly, Ernie focused on Jae, and Ethan saw the contempt radiate from the old man's face as he recognized his nemesis.

'You,' he hissed.

Jae strode toward Ernie as Kyle waited and watched. Ernie somehow managed to get to his feet, his legs trembling and his shoulders shaking as the North Korean pointed his rifle at him.

'Get out.'

'Go to hell.'

'Last chance, old man, or I'll blow you out of my way.'

Ernie smiled. 'What, and take my young life?' Ernie looked up at Kyle, and the smile turned calm and quiet. 'Killing me now would make no difference at all, would it?'

Ethan saw Kyle's eyes widen, and one hand moved to the terminal controls.

Jae shrugged and lifted his rifle. 'Suit yourself, old man.'

Jae fired.

The shot hit Ernie Walker in the centre of his chest and propelled the old man back into the center of the ring. Kyle slammed the controls wide open and the huge oval of blue-white light flared into life again. Jae was hurled back by the force of the energy field as Kyle yelled out.

'Get down!'

Ethan hurled himself flat on the ground as from within the earth beneath them soared a horrendous sound, that of generators running to breaking point as Kyle activated the device. The blue-white light became overpowering and Ethan felt heat searing his skin, his entire body vibrating as the ground trembled, and then there was a blinding white flash. He glimpsed a brief image of himself running from within the jungles, saw the firefight and the Korean victory, saw the lights in the sky hovering over the entire exchange, and then everything fell into darkness and silence.

Ethan opened his eyes and turned to Lopez. She was slumped on her side, the knife handle poking from between her ribs. Ethan turned and saw the North Korean agents still standing over them, Jae getting to his feet, Mackenzie still injured and cradling his bloodied arm.

Ethan looked for Ernie Walker, but he was nowhere to be seen.

Jae stood up, stared at the empty ring, then whirled to his men, his face twisted with hatred and rage.

'Kill them all! *Kill every last one of them!*'

The North Korean soldiers turned their weapons to point at their captives, and Ethan saw Jae rush at Kyle with his knife held aloft, racing to plunge the weapon into Kyle and cut him apart while he still lived. The blade flashed toward Kyle, and then Jae's head snapped back as a single gunshot hit him square in the face and hurled him onto the sand.

'Down on the ground, hands behind your backs, now!'

Ethan saw United States Marines pour onto the encampment from every direction as overhead four Black Hawk helicopters thundered through the night sky, two of them lighting up the area with brilliant white shafts of light that turned night into day. To his amazement he saw another entire platoon of Marines storming the west side of the compound as from the south an armored assault vehicle growled into view, machine guns trained on the North Koreans as they threw down their arms and got to their knees as instructed.

Ethan turned to Lopez, who was breathing softly, but her eyes were open and she looked at him amid the chaos and noise and managed a weak smile.

'I've got this terrible itch in my chest.'

'Medic!' Ethan yelled above the thundering helicopters and yelling Marines.

A Marine medic sprinted across to them and was working on Lopez within seconds, preparing her for medevac as Kyle stood and watched, a forlorn expression on his face. Ethan stood up and pressed one hand down on his shoulder.

'She once got shot four times and came through,' he assured Kyle. 'This won't keep her down for long.' Kyle nodded, and Ethan squeezed his shoulder. 'You did good.'

Kyle didn't look convinced. 'We lost Ernie. He got shot.'

Ethan looked again at the now empty ring of metal, and then he glanced up into the night sky. Apart from the helicopters there was nothing to be seen but stars and clouds, the strange orbs of light gone.

'We don't know that yet,' Ethan said.

Ethan turned to where General Mackenzie was being treated for his shoulder injury, and walked across to him. Mackenzie looked up, his features apologetic.

'You guys came in at the right time,' he said. 'If you hadn't flanked the attackers on the east side…'

'We did what we had to do, because some idiot in charge here keeps trying to put us out of the loop.'

Mackenzie nodded, but didn't say anything. Ethan figured that he knew he'd screwed up, official protocol and all, when he should have pooled his resources and brought in anybody who knew anything about what had happened.

'The tighter you try to secure this operation and others like it, the more they'll slip through your fingers. We already saw that with Majestic Twelve. Why is it you guys can't learn from the mistakes of your predecessors?'

Mackenzie shrugged.

'It's not the point,' he said. 'You can't be allowed to learn of what's happening here, of what we've discovered. It's just too dangerous.'

'So dangerous that it should be in the hands of people who get outwitted by sixteen North Korean agents?' Ethan asked. 'You said it yourself, if we hadn't been here and intercepted their attack, you'd all be dead. When are you gonna start waking up to yourself and admit that this isn't your field of expertise? You're a soldier, a man used to commanding platoons and battalions, not dealing with subterfuge and covert operations. And as for what you're up to behind the scenes, I'm pretty sure we've got a good idea.'

Mackenzie sighed but said nothing as the medic finished working on a field dressing for his shoulder. The general got to his feet as Ethan took a look around.

'You're just lucky your Marines turned up here when they did. If you hadn't put the call out for them, we'd have been dead by now too.'

'I didn't call them,' Mackenzie said. 'The North Koreans sabotaged our radios.'

Ethan peered at the general. 'Then how did they know we needed support?'

Mackenzie smiled, the first Ethan had seen for a long time, and suddenly it dawned on Ethan.

'You thinking what I'm thinking?'

'I have work to do,' Mackenzie said. 'I hope that I can take it that you and Lopez will be gone when I get back, so that I don't have to fill out any more paperwork with your godamned names on?'

Ethan nodded.

'Figures. We weren't here, nothin' ever happened…,'

'…I didn't see you. Who the hell are you? What are you doing on this island?' Mackenzie finished the sentence for him.

With that, General Mackenzie turned and marched off into the frenzy around them as fresh technicians were hurried into the encampment to begin the task of analysing the data they had recovered from Ernie's presence within the device.

Ethan saw Lopez being stretchered off toward a waiting helicopter that was hovering with expert precision near the edge of the encampment, its rotor blades battering the palms around it.

'Sir, this way sir!'

A Marine took Ethan's arm without force and guided him toward another waiting helicopter. Ethan looked for Kyle, but the kid had already been snatched by Mackenzie's men, and Ethan figured that the general would have some serious explaining to do when it came time to debrief his team.

Ethan climbed into the helicopter, exhausted now, and cast one last glance back at the metal ring where Ernie had vanished, wondered where on earth, or *when* on earth, Ernie had gone to.

***

XLVII

Guana Island,

British Virgin Islands

There were many places on Earth that most people never got to see. Some were in remote and inhospitable areas, deep within deserts or mountain ranges, buried within jungles or perched on high plateaus far from civilization. Some, however, were within plain sight, yet few could tread there.

Guana Island was one such place, set in the heart of the Virgin Islands. Although it possessed a small tourist resort, high in the hills stood a mansion that no ordinary civilian could visit. White-walled and easy to see, yet impossible to reach unless one used the main access road, which was blocked by gates close to the mansion, but far enough away that one could not observe the building with ease.

Rhys Garrett had never been to the mansion before. Despite being a billionaire, there were men and women in the world whose power dwarfed even his, who could command the loyalty of Prime Ministers and Presidents, of entire countries. It was people like that who had murdered his father decades before, and he had committed his life to hunting them down alongside Ethan and Nicola, so to be invited here to this mysterious place which everybody knew about, and yet nobody knew anything about, was both an honor and a discomfort. The invite itself had come out of the blue, addressed to him personally, hand-written but unsigned. Rhys was spending most of his time worrying about what had happened to Ethan and Nicola, who had been dark since departing Majuro some days before. Rhys had heard from local fishermen that there had been some kind of blast in the night somewhere north of Meck Island, and had been due to travel there to find out what had happened when the mysterious invite had waylaid him.

His driver pulled up beside huge entrance gates, and as instructed Rhys got out of the vehicle and allowed it to turn around and drive away. His staff were not permitted in here. Nobody but he could walk through those gates.

As if on cue, and in absolute silence, the gates slowly opened, and for a moment he had the impression he was walking into the movie *Jurassic Park*. As he passed through, the gates closed behind him and he walked alone up the path between swaying palms.

The sky was overcast gray, the air humid and heavy as Rhys walked up to the mansion. Its white walls towered over the hillside, an open-air swimming pool overlooking the hills and the vast ocean beyond. The windows were made from smoked glass, reflecting the view and concealing the home within. Rhys figured the place to contain at least twenty bedrooms, and he could see a glossy black Mercedes parked behind wrought iron gates on the far side of the property.

As he approached the main doors, they opened automatically. Rhys walked inside into an elaborate foyer, a grand staircase rising up before him, chandeliers hanging from the ceilings, the air fresh and cool. The doors closed behind him, automatically, and the silence within the home was almost unnerving. Most such abodes would have had staff to maintain them, but here everything was automated to a degree that one person could live here alone for an indefinite amount of time.

Rhys saw that to his left a door was open, that led into a room where a further set of doors opened out onto a balcony. Seeing no other obvious route, he walked through what emerged to be a drawing room and study, the walls lined with books, and out onto a beautiful balcony overlooking the rest of the island to the north-west.

There, sitting on the balcony, dressed in a white cotton suit and wearing a simple thatch hat, was Ernie Walker. Rhys hesitated for a moment, unsure of what to say or do, but then he saw Ernie stand up, a smile on his face and genuine warmth on his features.

'Mister Garrett,' he welcomed him, 'it's been a *very* long time.'

Rhys shook the hand that was offered, Ernie gesturing to a seat alongside him, a glass of fresh juice with ice awaiting.

'Ernie?' Rhys said finally, 'aren't you supposed to be on Meck Island?'

Ernie smiled as they sat down, took a sip of his own drink before replying.

'I was, Rhys,' he replied, 'and Ethan and Nicola were there too, with the young man, Kyle. There was an attack by North Korean forces who were attempting a last-ditch abduction or murder of myself and anybody else in the area. Thanks to your friends, I made it out.'

Rhys looked around him at the mansion. 'Do you know who lives here?'

Ernie chuckled. 'Yes, yes I do. It's *my* home, Rhys. When I said that I made it out, I made it out of now and back to 1954. In fact, I did a little better than that.'

Rhys Garrett was immediately full of questions.

'How so? The machine worked? You actually went back in time again? How did it work? Were there any side-effects? How did you feel when you got back there and...?'

Ernie raised a hand to forestall Rhys.

'There is much that I have to tell you,' he said. 'It's why I invited you here, now, before Mackenzie and his teams arrive. They will know by now that it worked, that I made it back home, largely because my timeline will have been altered a great deal. I no longer vanish from *USS Bairoko* in 1954, because I'm not aboard her.'

Rhys felt like he was going to explode, so desperate was he for answers.

'Tell me, everything,' he pleaded.

Ernie took another sip of his drink.

'I was shot in the chest by the North Korean, but Kyle hit the controls of the device and boom! Back I go. I woke up lying on my back on the island, and for a moment I thought that somehow it had all failed. But when I got up, there was no gunshot wound and the facility that Mackenzie and his team built wasn't there. All that was there were a few stone buildings, nothing like the way it is now. Best of all, I was a young man again.'

Ernie took a breath, his old lungs weary now.

'I managed to get off the island, found transport home. Turns out that I'd shown up in 1951, a year before I'd joined the Navy.'

Rhys could scarcely believe it.

'My god, it worked, but you showed up a little earlier than planned? How did that work?'

'It's complicated,' Ernie admitted, 'but this time around I knew a sight more than I did before. I got home; my wife was frantic because I'd been missing for two weeks. I told her that it was okay, I'd just needed to go away for a while, but now everything was fine. She didn't really get it back then, and I knew that I couldn't tell her everything until I'd proven it, so I got to work right away.'

'You handed the data you had to the American government?' Rhys asked.

'The hell I did,' Ernie shot back. 'What the hell do you think a McCarthy government would have done with all of that? We'd have been in a nuclear war in no time! No, I kept it to myself and I started work on something else entirely.'

Ernie set his glass down, took a breath.

'General Mackenzie had me memorize an awful lot of political and industrial knowledge of history, but I also was given access to the Internet. I did a little research of my own and came up with a game plan. To put it simply, I invested in companies that invented technologies that became world-changing, starting from 1951. If it was due to become successful, I bought shares in it. By 1960, I'd made my first billion dollars.'

Rhys rolled his eyes. 'If only it had been that easy for me. What happened after that?'

'I invested all the time, winning every time of course, but I kept myself out of sight, used agencies, everything done by phone and mail back then. The government doesn't like insider trading, but because I had absolutely no connection to any of the companies I was investing in, they had no grounds to charge me. I was able to just carry on without interference, and was considered to be one of the luckiest traders alive. When I built up enough financial power, I started a corporate group alongside President Eisenhower. The group was supposed to become a sort of "control" group, a cabal of powerful men who would provide a rein on the military-industrial network to deny the government the chance to operate in complete secrecy. Unfortunately, it did not work as planned and the twelve men became as corrupt as any others in power.' Ernie sighed. 'The cabal was called Majestic Twelve.'

Rhys sat in silence, his blood suddenly running cold through his veins. Majestic Twelve, or MJ-12, the very people that he had pursued all of his adult life, the people who Ethan and Lopez had fought for years, all of whom had finally wound up dead on a remote island similar to the one on which they now sat.

'*You* founded MJ-12?' Rhys uttered, appalled.

Ernie nodded.

'It's not something that I am proud of,' he said. 'It was begun with the best intentions, but before I knew it, they were all drunk on power and President Eisenhower refused to support or endorse them any further. He even gave out a presidential address at the end of his tenure, warning of the power of the military-industrial complex. I also walked away, hoping to find some way of undoing the horror that I had created. But it was too late, and it was only when Ethan and Nicola became involved that I was able to assist from behind the scenes.'

Rhys could not believe what he was hearing.

'They murdered my father,' he whispered. 'You knew that. We told you that. They murdered thousands of others. You could have stopped them and you did *nothing*?'

Ernie shook his head.

'That's not true. It's what I brought you here to tell you. There's something about what the government is doing that it doesn't understand yet, and it could ruin everything for our entire species if they don't learn to leave it well alone. This is about more than you, or me, your father or anybody else.'

Rhys fought the urge to pick Ernie up and toss him over the edge of the balcony.

'You're the cause of everything we've fought against for years!'

'I'm the reason much of it didn't go as well for MJ-12 as they would have hoped! They sought me for years, but never found me. I truly believed that Ethan and Nicola would track me down, but then I realised that they never really could, for they would have no knowledge of me until now. The timeline had changed, but there was no point of reference to me for them to follow, nothing for anybody to understand, and it's that which I need to tell you about Rhys: we *can't* change history.'

Rhys stared at Ernie for a moment.

'You already have.'

'No,' Ernie said, 'this is the biggest thing I've learned since I reappeared in 1951: time for me changed, but time itself always corrects its course. There is no escaping destiny: it's a real thing, Rhys. Our course is set.'

'I don't believe that.'

'Nor did I,' Ernie replied. 'Nor did I want to, but it is so. Rhys, I will soon die. I will be shot in the chest. It *will* happen, because now is the moment when everybody who knows what happened on that island will know to search for me in history. They won't find me in the Navy, but it is inevitable that they will track me down here, and it is equally inevitable that I will die.'

Rhys didn't understand. 'How do you know? You can't know the future…'

Ernie smiled, a strange, haunted little smile.

'The past, the present, the future; they are all one, Rhys. Time is something that we perceive as a species, as a form of life, but to the inert universe of atoms and particles time has no meaning. Time means nothing to an atom of hydrogen for it cannot perceive anything, it is not alive. Only forms of life with sufficient intelligence can perceive the passing of time, and in doing so become a part of it.'

Rhys didn't quite get it.

'The answers are not out there,' Ernie tried again as he pointed to the sky, then he turned his finger to point at his own head. 'They're in here.

We can send probes into the cosmos, photograph nebulae and black holes, use math to unveil the secrets of quantum science, but those techniques allow us only to be *observers* of our universe. Everybody knows that there's something more to our lives than just our bodies and our brains. Every ER nurse who's seen people die, day in, day out, knows and occasionally sees evidence of the soul leaving the body. One nurse in the UK wrote the very first scientifically accepted paper documenting that very same phenomena. This is not fringe science, Rhys. It's not paranormal. It's what we and every other living thing represent: the keys to the universe itself.'

For a moment, Rhys didn't know what to say.

'That's what they're covering up?' he finally uttered. 'The kind of thing that a local palm reader would say they already know about?'

Ernie's enthusiasm waned and he shook his head.

'No,' he replied. 'That's not what they're covering up.' He sighed, and looked out over the ocean and the skies. 'It's amazing, isn't it? Everything so perfect for us, for life? Some say it would have to look this way, because if it didn't, we wouldn't be here to enjoy it. Others, scientists, have developed a different viewpoint and it's so disturbing that they keep it to themselves. General Mackenzie and his team are closing in on that truth, probably suspect it already, and when they finally crack it then our future will be set in place, we will fulfil our own destiny.'

Rhys leaned closer to the old man. 'What destiny?'

Ernie leaned back in his chair. 'I brought you here to carry on my work, Rhys. You're a man of ample means, with no weakness for corruption or greed – you have more than you'll ever need, and thus covet nothing. Your father was murdered by the kind of people I set out to stop, and you, along with Ethan and Lopez, are doing a better job of it than I ever did. So, what I'm about to tell you will change your life forever. If you want in, I'll tell you. If you want to walk away, I wouldn't blame you. It's your choice.'

Rhys didn't hesitate.

'I didn't come all this way to leave empty-handed, Ernie,' he said. 'This has been my life's work, not a passing hobby. What are they after, Mackenzie and his people?'

Ernie nodded, satisfied.

'The mathematicians, the theoretical physicists, and the mediums and the psychics of this world are heading for a collision course. Einstein's theories and those of quantum physics are both accurate and yet have never gelled, and to combine them in some way is to create something known as the Theory of Everything. It is the goal of every scientist in the field, to surpass Einstein's work with something that will unify the physics of the very large, Relativity, with that of the very small, Quantum. As it turns out, the answers are not found on a page, although the clues are.'

Ernie leaned closer to Rhys, as though even out here there might be people trying to listen.

'It's already appearing in science papers around the world, hinted at, never spoken overtly but outlined everywhere. The universe itself is not a natural act.'

Rhys felt the skin on his spine crawl. 'What does that mean?'

'The numbers,' Ernie replied. 'The symmetry of the universe around us, the way in which it reacts to our observations but remains inert without us. Life affects our surrounding universe in ways we do not yet fully understand, but Mackenzie and his team are reaching a point where they finally figure out that our universe was manufactured.'

Time seemed to stand still around them, the lonely hillside devoid of other people, no boats visible in the harbor.

'Manufactured? You mean like the film, *The Matrix*?'

Ernie nodded, his eyes haunted.

'It's not science fiction,' he replied. 'Every bit of advanced mathematics applied to our universe is suggesting that it's holographic in nature, a fallacy, an incredibly elaborate illusion. Everything we're discovering about the universe says that it exists only in *one* moment of time. Everything that's happened, everything that will ever happen, looped over upon itself to the extent that it is possible to move through space-time, just as we see UFOs doing all the time. At some point, our species becomes capable of it, and Mackenzie and his people want access to that capability before anybody else. They want to find out what our universe really is. They want to find out who built it.'

Ernie leaned even closer, his old voice barely a whisper that seemed to drift toward Rhys like the distant whisper of the rollers far below them.

'They're quite literally looking for God.'

***

ABOUT THE AUTHOR

Dean Crawford is the author of over twenty novels, including the internationally published series of thrillers featuring *Ethan Warner*, a former United States Marine now employed by a government agency tasked with investigating unusual scientific phenomena. The novels have been *Sunday Times* paperback best-sellers and have gained the interest of major Hollywood production studios. He is also the enthusiastic author of many independently published novels.